PRAISE FOR MATTHEW FARRELL

"A young crime writer with real talent is a joy to discover, and Matthew Farrell proves he's the real deal in his terrific debut, *What Have You Done*. He explores the dark side of family bonds in this raw, gripping page-turner, with suspense from start to finish. You won't be able to put it down."

—Lisa Scottoline, *New York Times* bestselling author

"A must-read thriller! Intense, suspenseful, and fast-paced—I was on the edge of my seat."

—Robert Dugoni, *New York Times* bestselling author

"One hell of a debut thriller. With breakneck pacing and a twisting plot, What Have You Done will keep you guessing until its stunning end."

—Eric Rickstad, *New York Times* bestselling author

"A must-read thriller! *What Have You Done* is a rollercoaster of a novel that grabs hold and refuses to let go. Fans of Meg Gardiner and Mark Edwards will find lots to love in this debut. I can't wait to read what Matt cooks up next."

—Tony Healey, author of the Harper and Lane series

WHAT HAVE YOU DONE

WHAT HAVE YOU DONE

MATTHEW FARRELL

THOMAS & MERCER

Published by Thomas & Mercer, Seattle
www.apub.com

Amazon, the Amazon logo, and Thomas & Mercer are trademarks of Amazon.com, Inc., or its affiliates.

ISBN-13: 9781503902404 (hardcover)
ISBN-10: 1503902404 (hardcover)
ISBN-13: 9781503900646 (paperback)
ISBN-10: 1503900649 (paperback)

Cover design by PEPE *nymi*

Printed in the United States of America

First edition

For Cathy—
we did it, babe.

1

The first things Liam noticed were the mattresses lined up on the living room floor. The furniture had been pushed to the walls on the outer perimeter of the room, leaving the mattresses placed strangely in the center, where the couch and coffee table should have been. There were three of them, side by side, no covers or sheets, just a single bouquet of paper flowers their mother had learned to make at a craft party her friend Patty had hosted when she was pregnant with her second bundle of joy. One bouquet for each mattress. Their bright colors painted a dreadful picture against the otherwise dark surroundings. The shades had been drawn. The house was silent. Liam's stomach turned once. This wasn't right.

Before he could inquire as to what might be going on, a thump interrupted the quiet, and from his periphery, Liam saw his older brother, Sean, fall to the floor. Hands suddenly grabbed Liam from behind, and he was lifted off the ground, carried by someone he couldn't see. Liam struggled to free himself, tried to call for Sean or his mother, but the grip was tight enough that he could hardly breathe, let alone cry out for help.

The bear-claw tub was old and rusted. Liam caught a glimpse of the calm water that had been filled to the rim before he was thrust to the hard tiled floor. His hands were pulled behind his back and tied together so tight he lost feeling in his fingers.

"We're going to visit your father," the voice said behind him. It was his mother's voice, so suddenly full of life and determination. She was strong and vibrant, the adrenaline coursing through her. This new energy scared him the most. "We're all going to be one happy family again. All of us together. Like it should be."

She picked him up and threw him into the tub. Liam thrashed about, kicking and jerking upward, trying to get enough leverage to sit above the waterline, but with his hands tied behind him and the slippery porcelain, he couldn't do much more than keep his face above the surface. He couldn't hear anything under the cold water other than his breathing, which echoed in his ears.

His mother appeared over him. She'd cut large swaths of her hair off so close to the scalp he could see bloody patches of skin. Clumps of hair fell from the collar of her dirty nightgown and onto the water's surface when she moved. Her skin was pale, her eyes sunken and hollow. "I love you, Liam," she said. Her chapped lips cracked as she spoke. "You and your brother. We're going to be with your father now. I'll see you there."

She placed her hand over his face and pushed him all the way under. He held his breath as best he could, but panic set in as he lay on the bottom of the tub, submerged, trapped. He tried to move, turn, kneel up, anything, but his hands were fists stuck under the weight of his body. His mother kept pressing down, her fingers digging into his eye sockets and cheeks, making it impossible for him to move. His lungs burned as he tried to hold on. He squeezed his eyes shut and could see bursts of color exploding in the darkness.

Seconds seemed like hours, and it wasn't long before his tiny body gave in and he involuntarily opened his mouth to take a breath. The water tore down his throat. He tried to cough, but still the water came, rushing into his lungs, choking him. His body regurgitated what he inhaled, but the water had nowhere to go. It kept coming. He was drowning. He was going to die. His mother's maddening promise repeated in his mind.

We're all going to be one happy family again. All of us together. Like it should be.

Liam opened his eyes as he took a breath and began to choke. He jumped up from his sleep, gagging and slapping at the standing water in the tub. He crawled over the side and flopped naked onto the bathroom floor, panting and coughing.

"Jesus!" he screamed between another coughing fit and the wheezing of a damp breath he fought to keep steady.

Footsteps from the hall. His wife, Vanessa, ran to the doorway, where she stopped, frozen by the scene unfolding before her. "Liam! What's wrong?"

The room was blurry for a moment as shapes and colors blended into one floating and twisting image. He sat up and pushed himself against the wall by the toilet, his chest rising and falling as he took deep breaths. "I . . . I . . . how did I get in the tub?"

Vanessa hurried into the bathroom, her blonde hair pulled back in a ponytail, her hazel eyes filled with fear. "What happened?" she asked as she knelt beside him, helping him sit up straighter against the edge of the slippery porcelain. "Why are you screaming? What are you doing in the tub?"

He calmed himself, stared at his wife, then the tub, then back at his wife again. His body began to shake as he was suddenly aware of how cold he was. "Why am I . . . how did I . . . why was I in the tub?"

"That's what I just asked you."

"I woke up, and I was in here. How did I get here?"

"I have no idea." Vanessa stood back up, grabbed a towel from the rack, and tossed it to her husband. "I was sleeping. You scared me screaming like that. I thought something was really wrong. I don't know how you got in there. Last I saw, you were crashed out on the couch."

Liam draped the towel over himself and tried to stop shaking. He stood carefully and shuffled over to the toilet to sit. Ever since the day his mother had tried to drown him, he'd been petrified of water. He never would've voluntarily taken a bath. He hadn't had a bath in twenty-seven years.

Vanessa folded her arms across her chest. "What's going on?" she asked.

"I have no idea."

"You really can't remember how you got in there?"

"I'm serious. I can't remember anything."

"Must've been a rough night last night."

Liam began to examine himself. He was wet and still shivering. A large scratch ran down from his shoulder to his chest. It looked raw. "Wait. You said I slept on the couch?"

"All night, apparently. I woke up around four and realized you weren't in bed. When I went down to look for you, you were on the couch, snoring like a drunken fool. I could smell the liquor on you. Would've been nice if you called to tell me you were staying out that late. You know how I get nervous."

"Sorry. I was planning to call. I guess the night just got away from me." Liam began to towel off. He could sense that familiar tone in Vanessa's voice. She was upset, and he didn't want to fight again.

"What time did you get in?"

And then he stopped what he was doing. Stopped dead in his tracks as his eyes glassed over for a moment. "To be honest, I have no idea," he whispered more to himself than to his wife. "I can't remember that either."

"Oh, that's comforting. Missing the old college days, are we?" Vanessa took a second towel from the rack and started cleaning the standing water on the floor. "You're a grown man, Liam. You're getting too old for blackouts." She looked up at him and pointed. "What happened to your chest?"

Liam didn't say anything.

"Yeah, I know. You don't remember."

She finished drying the floor, then bent over the side of the tub and took the stopper out. He watched as she picked up his boxers from next to the sink, balled them up, and stuffed them in the pocket of her robe. She always cleaned when she was angry. Whether it was a small argument that made her start dusting or a blowout that required a closet reorganization, the cleaning and the anger worked hand in hand. It had been like that since they first met.

"Where are your clothes?" Vanessa asked.

The whistling of the water rushing down the drain made Liam's lungs contract as if he were drowning all over again. He felt as if he might be sick. "The living room?"

"No, they're not."

He surveyed the bathroom, but there were no clothes anywhere.

"Never mind. I don't want to know." Vanessa tossed the wet towel in the hamper and adjusted the tie that had slipped open on her robe. "So who went? No doubt your brother was there."

"Yeah, Sean was there," Liam lied. He couldn't remember anything about the night before. What had happened? How had he ended up in that tub?

"Who else?"

"A few guys from the station. You don't know them."

Vanessa walked to the doorway. "You're a forensic scientist for the Philadelphia Police Department. Don't you think you should be acting more responsibly?"

"It was one night."

"You blacked out, Liam. That's what high school kids do when they steal liquor from their parents' cabinet and can't control themselves."

"I'm sorry."

Vanessa's face tightened just slightly. She paused for a moment and then spun away from him. "Get dressed, and I'll put the coffee on. You're going to be late."

Liam watched her leave. His breathing was starting to steady, and in the solace of the bathroom, he tried to think back and replay his night out. He couldn't recall anything. Not one detail of one moment. How long had it been since he'd gotten that drunk? The tub groaned and wheezed as the water continued draining.

"And clean up your boots," Vanessa called from the hall. "You left them at the bottom of the stairs. Almost killed me when I came down this morning."

"Okay."

Liam got up from the toilet and made his way to the bedroom. His cell phone was sitting on his nightstand, and he grabbed it, touching his thumb to the reader as the phone came to life. Perhaps he could retrace his steps through calls or texts.

"Coffee's on!"

"I'll be down in a minute!"

There were no new texts past four o'clock the day before, the last one being from his brother asking if he wanted in on hockey tickets. Now that he read the text, he could recall being asked about the tickets, but everything since that point was fuzzy. He flipped to his phone records and saw a voice mail that had come in at eight o'clock. It was grayed out, meaning he'd already listened to it, but he couldn't remember the call or the message. He played it again.

"Hey, it's me. I got your text, but I don't see you. Where are you? Call me."

Liam recognized the voice immediately. It was Kerri. She'd called about a text he'd sent her. Again he checked his sent texts and couldn't find anything. He also looked in his trash folder, but there was nothing there either. He walked back through the bedroom, peeked out into the hall, then shut the door. When he was alone, he dialed her number and waited.

"Hey, you've reached me, and if you know who 'me' is, leave a message, and I'll—"

He hung up and tossed the phone back on the nightstand. In the serenity of the bedroom, Liam could hear the birds singing outside the window. A sign of a new day. A fresh start. That was what kept him and

Vanessa going. One day, then another, and still another after that. Their marriage was a work in progress.

Liam had been six years old when his mother tried to kill him. It had happened eleven months after he and Sean had lost their father to a set of bad brakes and a fatal car wreck. Their mother hadn't been able to handle the loss and had spent the majority of that time after her husband's death on a self-destructive spiral that was one of the scariest things Liam had ever seen in his young life. The woman he'd grown to depend on had become dark and intense in her depression, shutting both of her sons out of her life and communicating through a series of muted grunts and head tilts instead of forming actual words. He and Sean had spent most of their time trying to understand what these movements and sounds meant and how they should go about responding to them. Sometimes they guessed right. Often they were wrong. During those eleven months, their mother had stopped eating and cooking and, on that last day, couldn't even rise from her bed in the morning to see them off to school. Their father had been her everything, and he was gone. Over the course of that first year, she'd left with him. There was no way he and Sean could've expected what had been waiting for them that afternoon. That memory, those events, had burned into his psyche like a hot brand.

The birds continued their morning song as Liam got dressed. His head ached, and he fought to recall anything from the night before, but there was nothing. He wondered if his memory would ever return. It had to, right? Probably by the time he got in to work. There was no sense freaking out about it. Besides, Sean would be there. He'd ask his brother for the details and hope he hadn't done anything stupid. If that didn't work, he'd keep trying Kerri. Someone had to know something. Waking up in the tub had scared him. How had he ended up in there? How out of it had he really been?

2

A white sheet covered the body of Alexander Scully. It was the best the responding officers could do until the initial investigation was complete and the EMTs could put him in a body bag for transport to the coroner's office. Sean Dwyer stood over the victim, staring as if the sheet weren't there, as if the corpse would suddenly sit up and tell him who had done it. But there was no need for such a confession, supernatural or otherwise. He knew who was responsible.

The Philadelphia Police Department handled about sixteen thousand violent crimes a year. Of that total number, approximately three hundred were homicides. As a homicide detective, Sean found most of the cases were common enough and forgettable: gang violence, domestic violence turned manslaughter, hit-and-runs. You worked the case when you were up, then moved on in the rotation when you were through. With only twenty-one districts for 350 murders, you didn't have time to be Perry Mason on every assignment. Usually, the person who appeared to be the guilty party was in fact guilty, and the case was solved without much fanfare. Those homicides had no Hollywood flare. They were the real thing, and as with anything authentic, there was a certain percentage of the job that was mundane. This was not one of those times.

Sean rubbed the stubble on his square chin and absently pulled at the shield that hung around his neck. He was twelve years in. Seven with Homicide. He'd thought he'd seen it all by now, but this particular crime scene had stopped him in his tracks. The brutality with which death could be administered was an amazing thing.

The EMTs waited outside in their truck. It was still early, but the morning rush was about to begin. The few pedestrians who bothered to try to sneak a peek were quickly chased away by a police unit parked in front of the shop, but they had been few and far between. For the most part, the city was still rising. They'd have time before the crime scene would be fully exposed.

Don Carpenter, Sean's partner, came in through the front door. He was tall, African American, about fifteen years older than Sean, and good-looking. When he walked, he seemed to float. There were no hard movements about him. The ladies loved him, but he was a faithful husband, which made him all the more alluring. He was the only partner Sean had ever known and had been his mentor since Sean's rookie year. Over time they had formed a bond that grew far beyond the department.

"Sorry I'm late," Don said.

Sean dismissed the comment with a wave of his hand. "How's your mom?"

"She fell asleep last night watching TV. When she woke up, she didn't know where she was. Started panicking. Wouldn't listen to the nurses, so they called me."

"This is happening more and more."

"I know. I might need to move her closer to me if this keeps up. I can't run to Doylestown every time she gets confused. It's getting to be too much." Don pointed to the sheet covering Mr. Scully. "Find anything?"

"Not really. Victim was seventy-two. Owned the store pretty much all his life. We sent a unit to pick up his wife and bring her to the coroner's office for an ID."

Don bent down and pulled the sheet back to take a look. "Jesus," he muttered. "Might as well go straight for the dental records. He doesn't have much of a face left."

"Doesn't seem to be forced entry. UPS guy came to deliver a package this morning and called it in. We're guessing the owner knew his assailant. The store closes at eight, and we're figuring time of death to be around midnight."

"Forensics get any prints?"

"More than they can handle. Between the front door, the glass counter, the shelves, and the back door, they'll have their work cut out for them. This is a stationery store two weeks before Easter. The guy was busy."

Don pointed to a closed-circuit camera mounted in the corner of the ceiling behind the counter. "Any video?"

Sean shook his head. "Camera feeds to a computer in the back. The CPU tower is gone. We also checked and found the registers had no cash. Same with the safe. But we got credit card receipts and checks."

"CPU tower? Who uses a CPU tower anymore?"

"Like I said, he was seventy-two."

Sean walked through the store while Don poked around behind the counter. Other than the murder itself, nothing had really been disturbed. The greeting cards were still in all of their slots next to the glass statues and music boxes, which remained behind their cases. Easter egg cutouts hung from the ceiling and gently swayed in a breeze he couldn't feel. There was simply no sign of a struggle. "They didn't take the checks and credit card receipts because they're traceable. Cutter's too smart for that."

"You think it was Cutter?" Don asked. He was flipping through an invoice schedule that had been next to the register.

"You don't?"

"Could be anyone."

One of the forensic techs walked by, carrying a duffel bag of equipment. Sean peeked into the bag as he passed. There were spray bottles with liquid inside, plastic cases with tape over the tops, and a box of latex gloves. Forensics. That part of the investigation was always so foreign to him. His brother, Liam, worked Forensics. He was the smart one in the family.

"It's Cutter," Sean said when the tech was gone. "He's been terrorizing these shop owners for years, and now he's killing old men two blocks from city hall. He's getting bold, and when he gets bold, he gets dangerous. It was him."

"You're probably right," Don replied. "It fits his MO, but let's keep digging to be sure. You've been up this guy's ass for two years now, and you haven't been able to make anything stick. We get a witness, and suddenly the witness disappears. We get someone to agree to testify, and then at the last second, they change their mind. If this was him, we need to find something that he can't squirm out of."

Sean waited for Don as he retreated from behind the back counter. They walked toward the front of the store. Greeting cards full of well-wishes and celebration surrounded them. Stuffed animals, ceramic dolls, happiness. Happiness among tragedy. Sean's mind clouded with images of what might've taken place between Cutter and Alexander Scully. "He beat the guy's face right off of him."

"That's what it looks like."

"Came in to collect his street tax. That would explain the unforced entry. Maybe the old man was short. Maybe this wasn't the first time. I mean, how much money can a stationery store make these days? I know it's Easter, but he can't be pulling in that much cash. Cutter doesn't care about excuses. He beat the old man until he was unrecognizable. Made him an example to the other stores in the city. It was him. Had to be. There's no doubt in my mind."

"Then we'll get him," Don said. "But it's gotta be by the book. We can't let him walk on a technicality."

"We won't."

The two EMTs came into the store, one of them carrying the folded body bag under his arm. They waved to Sean and Don, who waved back and watched them as they stopped in front of the victim and spread the bag out next to the white sheet. The haunting image of Alexander Scully's brutalized face burned into Sean's memory. No way was this a mundane homicide. This one would leave scars.

3

Raul Montenez hurried into the lobby of the Tiger Hotel, balancing a cup of coffee in one hand and a bag of doughnuts in the other. He glanced through the scratched and dirty bulletproof glass of the cashier's booth and saw his boss, Mr. Guzio, dozing in his chair. The small, overweight man looked as if he'd been sleeping for days. His shirt was soiled and untucked from his pants, the top three buttons unfastened, revealing tufts of black chest hair. He was bald but for sideburns that had grown out. His fingers were ten sausages. A grumble of a snore could be heard through the microphone that had been left on. Even when he slept, his hatred was palpable.

The foyer—most of the day's work for Raul—was littered with empty beer bottles, assorted papers, plastic cups, and a variety of discarded condom wrappers. Cigarette butts were strewn across the black linoleum floor. The already-stained carpet held new spots of mystery. It was going to be another long shift.

"You're late," Guzio snapped. His eyes remained shut, his arms crossed and resting on his oversized gut.

"Good morning, Mr. Guzio. I'm sorry. The bus was running behind. Can you buzz me in, please?"

Guzio opened his eyes and lifted his head, acknowledging the skinny immigrant. "The bus is late a lot," he snarled.

"Yes. It is late a lot."

"I can find others more willing to get here on time if you don't think this job is worth it."

"It was not my fault, sir. The bus was late. When the bus is late, I'm late."

"What bus do you take?"

"The thirty-two."

Guzio struggled to get up from his chair. "I think I'm going to call over to SEPTA and confirm if bus thirty-two was running behind this morning. And if it was, I'm going to give them some crap for sending my help in past due every day."

"That's fine. You can call. If you can get them to fix the problem, I'd appreciate it."

"But if they tell me it was running on time, well then, you and me are gonna have a word about that." The greasy man reached under the counter and pressed the release button on the locked door. "Get to work."

"Gracias."

Raul slipped through the door and put down his coffee and donuts, rushing to begin his day.

"We still haven't heard from B11," Guzio called over his shoulder. "If he ain't down here by the time you finish the first floor, go up and tell him to hit the road. He's already pushing close to checkout time, and this ain't no Marriott. I gotta get these rooms clean before four o'clock. I got a business to run."

Raul pulled a mop and bucket from the broom closet and stood them against the wall with the rest of the things he'd need for the day. "Yes. No problem. If he's not down when I finish this floor, I'll tell him to get out."

———

Two hours of sweeping, dusting, polishing, and mopping had elapsed, and the first floor was finally presentable enough for the upcoming night's customers. The truth of the matter was these patrons wouldn't care if the hotel was clean or if there were piles of cow manure filling the place. The folks who came in were there for one thing and one thing only. Keeping a presentable lobby meant very little. But Raul was told to clean it all up, so he did. Every day.

He took the last trash bag out the disengaged emergency exit to throw in the dumpster. When he came back in, Guzio was standing in the doorway to his booth.

"Our guy in B11 ain't out yet," he said. "Go get him."

"Yes, sir."

"The book says his name's Johnny Cash. Real funny. Says there're two occupants. I want 'em both out."

Fictitious names were common in the hotel sex business, but this one escaped Raul. "I'll tell Mr. Cash to get out now."

"You do that. And hurry. In case you haven't noticed, I'm not a patient man."

Raul made his way up the stairs toward B11. The entire floor was eerily quiet. The sun was shining through a lone window at the end of the hall, and he could see tiny dust particles floating in the air. His steps were muted by the carpet beneath him, and he was suddenly reminded of just how isolated he really was.

When Raul got to the door, he waited, staring at the numbers that were once carefully nailed into place and now hung crooked, reading like the beginning of a website address instead of a room marker: **B//**. The old steel door was peeling flakes of beige paint. Its gold knob was scratched from years of drunken customers blindly stabbing at the keyhole.

He raised his hand to knock, then paused. It dawned on him that he had no idea who was sleeping—or waiting—inside the room. This was not the type of hotel that had **Do Not Disturb** signs to post. One never knew what was going on beyond the many closed doors, and given the clientele the Tiger attracted, chances were good he'd be disturbing something. The idea that the guest had stayed the entire night was in itself strange. The hotel was a by-the-hour establishment, and most guests paid accordingly. Anyone staying the night paid triple and usually had something to hide. Raul's uneasiness grew.

"Mr. Cash, you have to leave now," he called, pounding on the door three times. Paint flakes fell to the carpet. He could feel his breath grow shallow. "Checkout time has passed. You have to leave."

There was no answer. He cupped his ear to the door and listened for movement inside, but couldn't hear anything.

"B11, you check out now. It's morning. You have to go."

Still no movement, no sound.

With his eyes on the door and apprehension about him, Raul slowly pulled a large chrome ring from the waist of his jeans and began flipping through the many keys fastened around it. His hands shook as he passed the numbers, one after the other, until he came upon the master key. "This is your last chance, Mr. Cash. I'm coming in now. You have to leave."

Raul put the key in the lock and turned. "I'm coming," he called, his voice betraying him by cracking. He could feel his face grow hotter as he pushed his way inside.

The same sunlight that was streaming through the hallway window filled the window inside B11. Part of the interstate was framed in the glass, showing cars speeding by on the curved road, then disappearing around the bend toward the city. In the foreground, Raul discovered what was waiting for him.

The woman's body was limp, hung from an extension cord that had been pulled through exposed piping in the ceiling and tied off at the bed. She did not rock or sway but was completely still. There was blood. So much blood. On her legs and feet and down to the floor below. She was naked, her hair shaved with little precision. Her head was tilted to the side, eyes, red and swollen, staring out into nothing. The tip of her tongue escaped through the side of her mouth. She was looking his way, but above and past him. She had been beautiful once. Now there was only the butchery.

"No!" Raul screamed as he fell back out of the room and onto the filthy carpet in the hallway. More flakes of peeling paint fell on top of him as his foot hit the steel door. He blessed himself over and over as tears welled in his eyes and fear overtook him. The devil had come to the Tiger Hotel and left a most gruesome death in his wake. He would never forget this scene, despite the alcohol and the drugs and the sleepless night that would lie ahead. He would remember every detail, every sound, and every scent.

4

Sean sat in the back of an unmarked police van with the rest of the raid team and stared out the small square window, surveying his surroundings while going over the plan in his head one final time. They were parked in an alleyway across the street from a two-story row home. From what he could see, the area was quiet. The houses on the block, like many on the north side, were dilapidated and falling apart. Roofs were caving in. Foundations were crumbling. Windows were covered with sheets or trash bags instead of curtains, their glass panes little pocks of taped-up cardboard. This wasn't supposed to be the type of neighborhood where a wealthy street king would take up residence, but what better place for such a man to keep hidden? Cutter Washington was smart and adept at hiding in plain sight. He knew all the rules and over time had learned police procedures and response times. He was a pro, and he knew every nook and cranny in the city. It was time to take him down.

It didn't happen often, but sometimes luck took a second to smile on the Homicide Division of the Philadelphia Police Department. A couple of college kids from Penn had come to Center City earlier that night and closed a bar on Market Street. When they got outside, they had started walking around the city, randomly snapping pictures on their phones to try to take in the sights and make general asses of themselves to post to social media. One such photograph—of a young man hanging upside down off the street sign marking the way to Independence Hall—had inadvertently caught Cutter in the background, leaving out the back of the stationery store at the same time Alexander Scully was murdered. The kids didn't think anything of it until they saw the story on the morning news and immediately called 911. Their picture, and Cutter's partial print at the scene, was the evidence they needed to get a warrant.

Don closed the case file and tossed it to the side. "Okay, let's go through this one last time."

The sergeant sitting across from Sean nodded. "Right."

"We get to the porch, knock once, then bust in. Be aware that this is the suspect's girlfriend's house and she has two young kids."

"Got it," the sergeant replied.

"Are you set with the uniformed unit out back?"

"Yeah, we're set. He's in position now. Anyone comes out the back door and he's got 'em."

"Good."

Sean pulled himself away from the window. "This guy's no amateur," he said. "This isn't the first time he's been involved with a murder, and it isn't the first time the police have come calling, so be careful. We might bust down that door, and he gives up without a fight, or he might try to run. Or he might try and kill us. Be open for any possibility."

Everyone agreed.

Sean looked out onto the neighborhood one final time. He hated raids. Too many opportunities for things to go wrong. "Okay, radio the unit around back that we're moving out. Let's do this."

The team opened the rear doors, hopped from the van, and scurried across the street with weapons drawn. There were six of them all together with one officer at the back of the house. A lone dog barked somewhere in the distance.

With hand signals and silent confirmations, they spread out on either side of the walkway and ran up the steps leading to the entrance. The men pressed themselves against the house, flanking the entrance, their blue Philadelphia Police Department jackets hiding bulletproof vests. Sean motioned one final time to the others, then pounded on the front door. "Police! Open up!"

He counted to three, then turned and kicked at the door, sending it flying back on its hinges as the team stormed in.

"Police!"

"Police!"

"Come out where we can see you! Come out with your hands raised in the air! We are armed! Cutter Washington, come out now!"

The men broke off in their sweep pattern. The sergeant and three of his officers shuffled through each room on the first floor while Sean and Don took the stairs, Sean first and his partner covering him in the rear.

The house was unnervingly quiet. No one stirred. No children shouted for their mother, nor were there questions as to who might be trespassing. There was no movement of any kind except for the team slipping through each room one floor below.

As Sean and Don crested the top of the stairs, they heard the sudden movement of feet thumping and scurrying about. Sean gripped his Beretta and rushed down the narrow corridor toward the closed door at the end of the hall. "Police! Come out slowly with your hands up!"

The bedroom door flew open, and a woman burst through, running full speed toward the detectives, her hands flailing about, screaming. She was large, dressed in sweatpants and a T-shirt, and came at them quickly, the multicolored curlers in her hair bouncing with each step she took. The detectives couldn't tell what she was saying, but as she continued forward, Sean could see movement from inside the bedroom behind her. He raised his weapon. "Lady, get down!"

The woman ignored him and continued charging. As she got closer, they could hear what she was saying. She was screaming profanities and threats, one after the other. Don pushed Sean to the side and unholstered his Taser. When she got close enough, he shot her in the chest. In one prolonged movement, the woman stopped, grabbed at the wires that were protruding from her skin, then fell to the floor, flopping on the ground as she gasped for breath and rolled into a fetal position. Don disengaged the wires from the Taser and kept moving. "Come on," he said. "In the bedroom."

"Cutter, get those hands up!" Sean screamed.

As Sean made it to the end of the hall, he kicked at the bedroom door to keep it open. Drapes swayed in a breeze brought in by the only window in the room. Their suspect was gone.

"He's heading out back! He went out the window! Get to the back!" Sean grabbed for his radio to alert the officer at the rear of the house, but before he could lift it from his belt, the crackle of gunfire popped in the alley behind him, and he froze in place.

Don ran to the window. He grabbed his radio. "Officer down! We have an officer down at three-fifty-two North Broad Street. Suspect is fleeing on foot. Black male, six foot two, white tank top and jeans. Running east toward North Twelfth Street." He turned to Sean. "Let's go!"

As his partner ran past him and retreated back down the stairs, Sean threw himself out the open window onto a small overhanging roof. He scurried to the edge and used a gutter pipe to shimmy to the ground. When he landed, he could see the sergeant already outside, tending to the officer who'd been shot somewhere near his head and neck. The blood looked unnaturally bright in the early-morning sunlight.

"You stick with him," Sean said to the sergeant as he ran by. He read the name tag on the young officer's uniform. Samson. "Backup and an ambulance are on the way."

The sergeant ignored him, instead cradling his officer in his arms and applying pressure to the wound as his other men finished sweeping the house. He kept whispering in the young man's ear. "Hang in there. Hang in there. Hang in there."

Sean could hear Don behind him but stayed focused on the suspect running up ahead. Cutter was still a good distance away. "Stop! Police!"

As Cutter ran, he turned back and fired twice. Sean covered up when he saw the flashes from the muzzle but never broke stride. He watched as

Cutter hopped a small fence and slipped to the ground when he landed. He was almost out of the alley. If he got onto a busy street, they could lose him among the population and other side streets and cut throughs.

Sean stopped and raised his Beretta, carefully aiming at his fleeing target. A steady finger pulled the trigger, and in an instant, he saw Cutter fall to the ground. "Stay down," he commanded.

Cutter was thrashing about, crying aloud, clutching the back of his leg. Sean approached with caution, his weapon aimed. He climbed the fence and landed on the other side. Cutter's muscles bulged and tensed through his tank top as he rolled around. The oversized watch on his left wrist had cracked when he'd fallen. The diamond-encrusted jewelry around his neck jingled with every motion.

"Where's your gun?" Sean asked.

"Up your ass!" Cutter screamed. His eyes found the detective's for a moment, and then he turned away.

"Give me your weapon, or I end you right here."

Cutter grunted as he pushed his Glock from underneath his chest and slid it across the alley. "Call an ambulance, man. I'm hit!"

Don caught up, climbed the fence, and landed next to his partner. "Nice shot," he said.

"Thanks. Had to get him before he made it to the street. I didn't want to lose him."

"I didn't do nuthin'," Cutter spat. "Get me a doctor, man. I need a doctor. I'm shot. You shot me!"

"Yeah, looks like I caught you in the knee," Sean replied. "That's gotta hurt."

"Screw you, man!"

Sean kept his gun aimed on his suspect and motioned toward his partner. "Cuff him, and I'll search him," he said. "We'll ride with him to the hospital, and I'll sit outside his room until he's ready for transport to Booking. I'm not letting this son of a bitch out of my sight."

Don nodded. "Ten-four."

5

Yellow crime scene tape stretched around the perimeter of the Tiger Hotel, trapping the two patrol cars that had responded to the scene inside the parking lot while keeping all unauthorized personnel at bay. An ambulance and a Forensics van were parked diagonally across from the hotel's entrance. Two officers stationed by sawhorses closed the street in both directions.

There was a particular smell to the Tiger. Liam paused to identify it, but the best he could come up with was an overabundance of Lysol and the stench of wet dog. He held his hand over his mouth and walked to the foot of the stairs with the rest of his team. Sergeant McMullen, the officer in charge, was waiting.

"Ah, Forensics," McMullen said. "We were wondering when you guys were going to show."

"What's up?"

"We got a girl up in B11, hanged with an extension cord, then split open at the gut. Gory, but nothing I haven't seen before. Some of the other guys are having a rough time with it. We're interviewing the owner, trying to get a list of guests or workers who might've seen something. We took a few pictures and cordoned off the area. Other than that, we've pretty much been waiting for you guys to do your thing."

"Okay, we're on it."

McMullen shook his head and looked down at the floor. "Whoever did this isn't playing with a full deck," he said. "Sick bastard left paper flowers at her feet."

Liam stopped. "Paper flowers?"

"Yeah, you know, those flowers made out of tissue paper or construction paper or whatever? Friggin' guy makes like a bouquet of them and leaves them under the body. Weird."

"Who's here from Homicide?"

"Heckle and Keenan. Keenan's upstairs. Heckle's interviewing the owner in the office over there."

"Thanks, we got it from here."

"All yours."

As Liam and his team made their way to the second floor, they pulled on their latex gloves and prepared to investigate.

Detective Keenan met them at the top landing and escorted them to the room. Keenan was a large man, tall and thick. His blond hair was a mop on his head, his face showing old acne scars from his youth. He'd played football all his life and still ran back punts for the department in the fall league. He towered over everyone who walked by. "In there," he said.

The team made its way into B11. Liam stopped to survey the scene. The death had been violent. The smell of Lysol and wet dog was now replaced with the stench of murder that could not, in any way, be mistaken for anything else. Perspiration, bodily fluids, waste, blood—it welcomed him with the repulsion his job had forced him to develop a tolerance for. The bouquet of multicolored paper flowers was under the victim, stained with her blood. For the second time that day, Liam thought about his mother.

"All right," Liam said aloud. "Let's get everything we can. Jane, I want pictures and prints. Rob, get me blood samples. Teddy, you deal with sample fibers from everything in this room. Mattress, sheets, comforter, carpet . . . everything. When we're done, we'll cut her down and bag her. I want an autopsy and tissue analysis once we're in the examination room. Go."

The team broke off and began unloading equipment. Liam had been a forensic detective for the Philadelphia Police Department for the last six years. He was the leader of his team and one of the most dedicated and decorated in his division. With the skill of a scientist and the mind of a detective, he was able to uncover clues to countless homicides throughout the city's jurisdiction by using methods still considered state-of-the-art in the twenty-first century. He was a member of the mayor's Terrorism Task Force and a part-time instructor at the police academy. He'd seen crime scenes as bad as this one and written papers on most of them. Murder intrigued him.

As he watched the others get to work, he pulled a camera from his bag and began snapping pictures. The victim was naked, her body a dark shade of blue. Her head was shaved in random places and hung limp to one side. Drying blood ran from a wound across her stomach and down her legs to the floor. This was violence in the worst way. He stepped closer and aimed his camera, and that's when he saw it. The light that was coming from the hallway hit her in just the right way, and Liam recognized her immediately. He stopped breathing and almost jumped backward, catching himself at the last minute. "Uh, what's her name?" he asked as calmly and as slowly as he could.

Keenan opened his notepad. "Miller. Kerri Miller."

The name shot through him like a bolt of lightning. His knees grew weak to the point he thought he might fall over.

"We took her ID from her purse," the detective continued. "Got ID, cash, credit cards. No cell phone, though."

Liam backed away. Despite all the times he'd run his fingers over her smooth skin, all the times he'd kissed those lips, felt her touch, her embrace, he hadn't recognized her. He looked around the room. There didn't seem to be any sign of a struggle. The telephone, digital clock, and lamp remained in place on the nightstand. The bed was still made and free of any wrinkles. The shades were open. Only two chairs were out from under the table, one on the opposite side of the room in the corner, the other turned over against the bed.

"Where's the victim's hair?" he asked.

Keenan shrugged. "No sign of it. We're guessing the killer took it."

Kerri Miller.

Liam stepped around the body and walked into the hallway. "I gotta make a call. Be right back."

"Everything okay?"

"Yeah. I'll just be a sec."

The hotel was empty but for a few scattered police officers roaming the lobby. Liam staggered down the stairs to the first floor and jogged out the front entrance, almost stumbling his way into the parking lot as his world tilted and sagged. He climbed into the Forensics van and could feel his heart thumping in his chest. His breath caught in his throat, and he let out a noise that didn't sound human. Tears welled in his eyes as he pulled out his phone and dialed his brother's number. Across the street, a small crowd of onlookers and several television vans were waiting to hear something that might tell them what was taking place inside the Tiger Hotel. Adrenaline coursed through him as a shaking hand held the phone up against his ear.

Kerri was dead. Kerri Miller.

His lover.

6

It looked as though the entire Philadelphia Police Department had overtaken the second floor trauma unit of Temple University Hospital. On one side, officers, sergeants, two lieutenants, and a handful of detectives loitered around the main desk, waiting for word on young Officer Samson, who had been shot by Cutter Washington during his attempted escape. The mood was sullen. Voices had fallen to whispers out of respect. Each of the men who waited for an update knew, without a doubt, that it could have been him lying in that operating room. It was a risk they took every day.

On the other side of the floor, there were only Sean, Don, and the two uniforms who had been assigned to guard Cutter when he came out of surgery. None of them spoke. Instead, they looked toward the opposite end of the corridor and hoped for the best as their eyes wandered from cop to cop, the scenes from that morning playing endlessly in their minds.

Lieutenant Phillips walked off the elevator and made his way toward his two detectives. He was thin, and the overcoat he wore swallowed his frame. Long fingers reached into his pocket and came away with a pencil that he twirled in his hand. He always fiddled with something when he was stressed. A ball, a rubber band, a letter opener. This time it was a pencil. The look on his face was steel determination. Like the others, he was angry that a cop had gotten shot, and he wanted answers.

"What do we got?" Phillips growled.

Sean stood from his seat. "Samson's in surgery. It's touch and go. Won't know much for another few hours. Family's been notified. The wife is in a separate waiting room with his lieutenant. Other family's on the way."

"And Cutter?"

"Should be out of surgery soon. Minor. Had to go in and get the bullet out."

"Should've put it between his eyes."

"If I get another chance, I might do just that."

Don joined his partner. "We did it by the book. It's better this way. No mess and no fuss. He ran, shot the kid, and we got him."

"You get a clean look at what happened?" Phillips asked. "Eyewitness account?"

Sean shook his head. "No, we were in the bedroom when we heard the shot. By the time I looked out, the kid was down, and Cutter was running from the scene. We got his weapon, so we'll get a ballistics match from Forensics."

"Anything else I should know?"

"Nothing that I can think of. It was pretty cut-and-dry."

Phillips flopped down in one of the plastic seats and tossed the pencil onto his lap. "Helluva thing," he mumbled. "That kid better make it."

Sean's phone began to vibrate. He pulled it from his pocket and looked at the caller ID. It was Liam. He ignored it.

"We got him," Don said. "If the kid pulls through, we have a victim's account, and like Sean said, we'll have a ballistics match in twenty-four hours. Cutter's going down. And this time we don't have to worry about witnesses disappearing. We got everything we need."

"I hope you're right," Phillips replied. "This son of a bitch has slipped through our fingers too many times before. Even with cases that were as airtight as this is."

Sean's phone vibrated again. Another call from Liam. Again, he ignored it. "I agree with Don. We got him."

"What about the girlfriend?" Phillips asked.

"She's in holding at the station," Don said. "Attempted assault on an officer and accessory attempted murder."

"And the kids?"

"The sweep team found them in their room under their beds. Brother and a sister. The girlfriend's mother took them."

Sean's phone vibrated for a third time. He looked down. Liam. Something was up.

"You gonna get that?" Phillips asked. "That's three times in a row."

"It's just my brother. It can wait."

The phone stopped for a moment, then immediately began vibrating again.

Phillips sighed. "Apparently it can't."

"Sorry." Sean turned away from the others and walked farther down the hall toward the stairwell. When he was far enough out of earshot, he answered. "Liam, what's going on? What's with all the calls?"

"I need you down here at the Tiger Hotel. I'm on scene. Homicide."

Sean could hear the tremor in his brother's voice. "What's wrong?"

"You need to get down here."

"I can't. Me and Don have our own case we're investigating. We're at Temple Hospital."

"But I need you."

It sounded like Liam had been crying. "Why?" Sean asked. "What's going on? Talk to me."

"It's Kerri," Liam replied as his voice shook even more. "She's the victim. Kerri's dead, Sean."

Sean stopped and pressed the phone tighter to his ear. "Kerri? Are you sure?"

"Yeah, I'm sure."

He pushed through the steel door out into the stairwell where he could be alone. "You're positive it's her?"

"Yes, dammit! We have her ID. I saw her. It's her. Kerri's dead."

Sean leaned against the wall and ran a hand through his hair. "Do you know what happened? Can you tell from the scene?"

"She's strung up like some animal. Hanged and cut open."

"Do you have any idea who she was with last night?"

"No. We haven't talked in, like, three months. She broke it off and begged me to fix things with Vanessa. I haven't talked to her since."

"Not a word?"

"Maybe a couple of times on the phone, but I haven't laid eyes on her since we broke up. I have no clue who she was seeing or what she was doing last night."

"Jesus Christ."

Liam sniffled on the other end and took another deep breath. "There was a bouquet of paper flowers at her feet. Just like the ones Mom used to make. And her hair was all chopped up. Like Mom did to herself that day. It's freaking me out. Just get down here."

"Who's there from Homicide?"

"Heckle and Keenan."

"Okay. I'll be there as soon as I can. I'm on my way."

Sean disconnected and let his head fall against the wall leading down to the first floor below.

"You okay?"

Sean looked up. "What?"

Don walked through the steel door into the stairwell. "Everything okay?"

"Actually, no, not really. Liam just got called to a homicide at the Tiger. It's Kerri. She's dead."

"Oh my God."

"I gotta get down there. Can you cover for me for a few hours? I won't be long. I'll meet you back at the station."

"Yeah, sure, I'll cover. Go."

Sean hurried down the stairs and ran out of the hospital toward his car. The air outside had turned warm and heavy. The sun that had been so radiant that morning was now hidden behind dark clouds that had slowly moved in like giant glaciers in the sky. A storm was imminent.

7

The Tiger Hotel was full of police activity. Sean hurried through the lobby, searching for his younger brother. The crime scene looked no different from any other he'd ever been a part of in the past. Why would it? Crime scenes were about procedure. There were things you did during the initial stages of a homicide investigation to preserve evidence and keep the integrity of the circumstance intact. The fact that he knew the victim meant nothing to the others around him.

An officer was leaning against the wall, fiddling with his phone.

"Have you seen the Forensics team?" Sean asked.

The officer scanned the lobby and pointed. "Yeah, some of them are over there by the exit."

"Thanks."

He approached Liam, who was writing something in his pad, and without speaking took him by the arm and guided him away from the others toward the opposite end of the lobby near the back door. Liam kept his head down as they walked. Sean could sense his relief now that he was there.

"Tell me what happened."

"I got called in for a homicide, I get here, and it's Kerri. I couldn't believe it. Then I saw the paper flowers and her hair all chopped up like Mom's. What is that?"

"I don't know. Gotta be something, but I don't know what."

"She's bad, Sean. I hardly recognized her. I wasn't sure what to do, so I called you."

"As usual."

Liam chuckled, defeated. "Yeah."

Sean looked at his little brother. Liam's gaze was distant, the shock of what was happening beginning to take control. "You need to act like this is just another crime scene. No emotions. Keep it together."

"I'm trying."

"Try harder." He looked around and watched the activity around them for a few moments, then turned back to Liam. "Did you ever tell Kerri about what Mom did to us?"

"We talked about it once."

"You think it could be a suicide? Maybe she reenacted a scene from your childhood to get back at you for reconciling with Vanessa?"

Liam shook his head. "This was no suicide. A person can't do that to themselves. Not what's up there. Besides, she broke it off with me. That wouldn't make sense."

Sean leaned in close to whisper. "Does anyone here know about your relationship with her?"

"No."

"Do they know you knew her, even casually?"

"No one knows anything. Jesus, Sean, I thought you'd be a little more shocked or freaked out instead of moving right into covering our asses. I played it as straight as I could. It took me by surprise, you know? Seeing her like that."

"I know. And I am shocked. I just need to know where we stand with things so I can keep everything consistent."

"You think we should tell someone I knew her?"

"Yes, but not yet. These things can get hairy fast. No one else needs to be in the loop for now. Just continue with the investigation, and keep your head up."

"Last night was her birthday."

"Damn."

"Who could've done this?"

"I don't know. We'll figure that out later, and we'll start with the people who knew about you and Kerri and what happened with Mom. Those flowers and her hair are too unusual to be a coincidence. Keep your cool, and we'll be fine."

"Yeah, all right."

"Okay. Let's go take a look."

The two brothers broke from the corner and began to make their way to the stairs. From the bottom landing, they could hear activity and shouts of instruction from B11. The Forensics team had returned to the room.

Teddy and Rob were gently guiding Kerri's body to the floor as Jane released the extension cord from the bed. Keenan remained just inside the doorway, watching. Sean and Liam entered the room.

"Hey, Sean," Keenan said when he saw the detective. "What're you doing here?"

"Liam thought I might know the victim."

"Is that right?"

"Yeah."

Keenan looked at Liam and held out his hands in surrender. "Something you could've mentioned. Pretty important, don't you think?"

Liam feigned a smile and shrugged. "I wasn't sure, so I didn't want to cause a big scene. I just wanted him to take a look."

"Still, you could've said something."

"Sorry."

The two techs slipped the victim into a black body bag that was spread out on the stained carpet as Jane gathered the slack from the cord she'd been holding and stuffed it in the bag with the victim. The makeshift noose remained tied around the girl's neck. No one was to remove it until the transporting team was in the autopsy room with the medical examiner in case there was additional evidence to be found.

Sean walked toward the body bag and bent down.

Liam was right. She was barely recognizable. Her hair had been cut short and then shaved sloppily, clumps in some sections, shaved down to the scalp in others. It was just like his mother had done to herself that day. His stomach seized, and he could feel his face growing hot. He reached out to pull the edge of the bag farther from her face but noticed his hand trembling, so he stopped and put it in his pocket.

"What was the name again?"

"Kerri Miller."

"No. Don't know her." Sean stood back up and cleared his throat. He turned toward Keenan, his head swimming in the vision of the girl in the body bag. "Have you found anything yet?"

"You trying to come in on my case?"

"Relax, I'm just asking."

Keenan glanced at his notebook. "Owner's name is Francis Guzio. He was running the window last night. Says he always runs the window and remembers the woman coming in slumped over a male. The male paid cash for the night, and that's pretty much it. He didn't notice anyone leave, and one of his maintenance guys discovered the girl's body this morning. A Raul Montenez. We took a statement and let him go. Jane lifted a few prints and took some pictures. Teddy took some hair samples off the carpet and some fiber samples for testing. We found half a boot print in the blood. Between all that and the autopsy, we should come up with something."

"You get anything on the camera over the front door?"

"Owner said it hasn't worked for years."

"How about a name on the registry?"

"He signed in as Johnny Cash, so, no, we don't have a name. The owner says he didn't think there was much screaming or carrying on during the murder because he had the other two rooms on either side booked all night, and no one complained or mentioned anything."

"They were probably too busy to notice."

"Yeah, probably."

Sean walked to the bed and picked up the evidence bag that held the paper flowers. He worked to steady his hands as he turned the bag over a few times. "You get anywhere with these flowers?"

"Nope. Seems like normal tissue paper to me. We'll send it out and see if we come up with anything. I'll do some digging on the significance. Could be nothing. Could be something. Who knows?"

"Where's she going?"

"Saint Martin's for the autopsy," Jane replied. "Liam, will you be there?"

Liam shook his head. "No. I'm going to take the prints back to the lab and start the reports. You guys go on to Saint Martin's, and we'll compare notes when you get back."

Teddy and Rob each took an end of the body bag and lifted it off the floor. The others in the room stepped aside as the men shuffled out into the hall. When the body was removed, Keenan grabbed the evidence bag from Sean. "I gotta go process this. We'll catch up later. I heard you had a nice get-together with Cutter Washington this morning."

Sean nodded. "Yeah, we got him."

"The kid gonna be okay?"

"Touch and go right now."

Keenan made his way out into the hall. When he was at the top of the stairs, he stopped and turned back. "Yo, Sean."

"What?"

"For what it's worth, I'm glad you didn't know her."

"Thanks."

The two brothers watched as Keenan followed the procession to the first floor. When they were alone in the silence of the empty hotel room, Sean started looking around, kneeling to search under the bed, crawling around the bloodstains that soaked the dirty carpet. He stood up and snapped his gloves off. "What do you want me to do here?" he asked. "The case has already been assigned. I can't get involved."

"I know."

"I can't step on toes, Liam. Even with something like this. You saw Keenan get pissy just from me showing up. If I start interfering, he's going to go crazy. I'd feel the same way if the situation was reversed."

"I said, I know. I'm not trying to jam you up. I just needed you here."

Sean sighed, looking up at the pipe in the ceiling Kerri had been hanged from. "I'll stop by Kerri's apartment and make sure anything relating to you is gone. That's the best I can do for now."

"You sure I shouldn't just come clean about me and Kerri? If we don't say anything and they find out, it could look suspicious."

Sean shook his head. "Did you see her? This isn't a drive-by or a home invasion gone bad. She was strung up, hanged, and cut. Someone needs to pay for this. Heckle and Keenan will need to clear this case. The lieutenant won't let this one go away quietly. Whether you tell them about your affair with Kerri now or they find out later, you're going to be a suspect. Hell, I could be too. The paper flowers and the head shaving tie us even closer to it. Better to just lay low and see where this thing goes. If they nail a suspect in the next few days, no one has to know anything about your affair. If we have to come clean, we will. Just not yet."

"I figured honesty would work best here."

"Did you kill her?"

"Of course not."

Sean stepped closer to his brother. "What happened to you last night? You were going to the boat to grab the sweatshirt you left on board the other day, and then you were supposed to meet me for drinks. You never showed. Where were you?"

"I . . . can't remember."

"What do you mean?"

"I mean I can't remember. I woke up this morning in my tub, of all places, and I have no recollection of anything from last night."

"How is that possible?"

"I don't know."

"Were you with Vanessa?"

"She said I came home late, drunk, and passed out on the couch. But I don't remember going to any bar or drinking." He paused for a moment. "You think I could've been drugged?"

"Maybe, but who would do that?"

"Same person who did this?"

"Maybe."

"There's something else," Liam said.

"What?"

"Kerri left a message on my phone last night. Around eight. She mentioned that she got my text, but I didn't text her."

"But her number came in on your phone the same night she was killed?"

"Yeah. I called her back this morning. It went right to voice mail. I also tried her when I got to the station. Voice mail again."

"And now your number's on her phone. Twice."

"If you think I had anything to do with this, you're crazy."

"But you can't remember where you were last night."

"I didn't kill her, Sean. How could you even think that?"

Sean grabbed Liam by the shoulder and walked him out of the hotel room. "I don't think you killed her, but you just proved my point. You see how this can look if we tell them up front about your affair? The less they know about you and Kerri, the better it'll be at this point. It'll give us time to figure out what happened. If you come clean now, you'll be their primary suspect, and they'll build a case against you while whoever really did this is running around free. You get it?"

"I guess."

"You need to get those phone records and erase your number before Heckle and Keenan get their hands on them."

"And how does that not make me look even *more* guilty?"

"You won't look guilty if they find the guy who did this. Our priority has to be to keep this between us for now. Otherwise, you become the primary suspect, and the real killer goes free. If they're wasting their time investigating you, then no one is carrying out a proper investigation. You need to stay quiet for now. Can you do that?"

"Yeah."

Sean looked on as the team began to exit the hotel. "Meet me at the dock tonight at seven. We need to think this through, and you need to try and remember where you were last night. Those flowers scare me. Somebody knows something."

8

Sean leaned against the sink and looked at himself in the mirror. His eyes were red and slightly swollen from crying. He splashed water on his face and dried himself with a paper towel. The men's room was deserted. No one was there to see him like this, and he intended to keep it that way.

Kerri was dead. The scene at the hotel was almost too much to bear. Seeing her like that—her body mutilated, her hair chopped off, the blood—was overwhelming, despite how many crime scenes he'd worked in the past. He knew this girl. She had been sweet, kind, and innocent. She had only wanted the best out of life, and now that life had been cut short. She was gone, and although death was an inevitability for everyone, the reality of her death—of her murder—really shook him. Seeing her in that body bag brought it all home again.

Sean crumpled the paper towel and tossed it in the wastebasket. He took one last breath, pulled the door open, and walked back out into the station. It was time to get to work.

———

The sky had finally opened up. The rain was coming down in sheets, hissing like a snake as it slapped the pavement. Cars passed slowly to avoid the water that was rushing along the gutters, minirapids carrying the debris of strewn litter toward the grates that were already beginning to overflow at the end of the blocks. The day was drawing to a close, and with the rain, the sidewalks would be empty soon. Across the street, under the dome of city hall, people rushed to catch the subway.

Don sat alone at his desk, filling out paperwork from the takedown earlier that morning. He liked the quiet. It helped him think with more clarity. He'd often go to the library across town when he had to work through a difficult case. The serenity of the reading room gave his mind freedom to wonder without the constant interruptions he got at the station house. The shouting, the ringing phones, the general noise of movement. The library had none of that. But this was the rare, thin line of time between shifts, when the division was quiet and he could actually get some work done. It was, undoubtedly, his favorite time of day.

Footsteps shuffled up the stairs and into the empty Homicide Division. It was Sean, soaked from the storm. "Where is everyone?" he asked.

"Changeover."

Sean peeked into Phillips's office. It was empty. He came back and sat at his desk across from his partner. "Lieutenant still at the hospital?"

"Yeah. The kid's out of surgery. Gonna be a touchy forty-eight hours, but the doctors are optimistic. They think he's gonna make it."

"That's great news."

"Cutter came out of surgery about a half hour after you left. He was transported to a secured wing where four uniforms are standing with him. He should be able to be transferred to lockup in a few days."

Sean nodded and looked around the empty floor.

"You okay?" Don asked.

"Yeah."

"Shook up about Kerri?"

"Yeah." Sean leaned in toward his partner. "Look, I gotta ask you a favor, but I know you won't like it because it goes against procedure, and to be honest, it could end your career if anyone ever found out."

Don perked up. "This I gotta hear," he said. "Go ahead."

"I need you to go to her apartment tonight, before Heckle and Keenan have a chance to get in there. Remove anything that has Liam attached to it. Notes, pictures . . . anything. I gotta get my firearm discharge report in, or I'd go myself. There's just not enough time. Heckle and Keenan will finish up with their prelim memo tonight, and then it's off to the victim's apartment, so we have to move ASAP. We gotta keep Liam's involvement with Kerri quiet until we find out what happened."

"You're keeping his affair with her quiet?"

"For now."

"You think that's a smart idea?"

"I just need a few days to figure this out. If Liam confesses to his affair, they'll look to build a case against him. Once that happens, it's over. I need to give Heckle and Keenan time to investigate."

"You and I knew her too," Don replied. "Does that put us in the same pickle?"

"It could."

"You don't think Liam had anything to do with it, do you?"

"No way. Not a chance."

"Right, so why not come clean now so it doesn't come back to bite him—or us—if they find out later? I've known that boy almost all of his adult life. Practically raised him alongside you. Inside and outside of this department. I can't see him being involved. Makes no sense not to let Heckle and Keenan know up front."

"I will. But for now we need to keep it quiet. I'd rather face the consequences of not telling them up front instead of telling them everything and have Liam become their prime suspect. I just need to understand what went on before I can decide the next steps. Can you do that? Keep it quiet for a few days?"

"You know I can. I got you. Career ender or not."

"And Kerri's apartment?"

"I'll go tonight."

"No traces of anything involving my brother."

"I understand. I'll take care of it."

The shift change was over. The room began to fill, and the background noise of a busy homicide division was born once again.

9

It was Sean who had saved him. When they had first entered the house, their mother had hit Sean over the head with the Louisville Slugger their father had bought him after he made his first Little League All Stars Team. That single blow had knocked him unconscious. Her plan was to drown Liam first and then his older brother; then she would place each of her children on one of the mattresses, wrap their tiny fingers around the stems of the paper flowers, take an entire bottle of sleeping pills, and lie on the third. One happy family going home to see their father.

But the blow with the bat hadn't been severe enough. Sean had come to and snuck into the bathroom. He had hit his mother across the back of her skull with that same Slugger, using what he called his perfected Mike Schmidt swing. As she lay motionless and bleeding on the bathroom floor, Sean had jumped into the tub, pulled Liam out, and dragged him through the house and onto the front porch, screaming for help the entire time. Neighbors had poured from their homes. Jacob Stevens, a high school kid from across the street who spent his summers as a lifeguard in Wildwood, had given Liam CPR and brought him back before the ambulance arrived. Jacob had got him breathing again, but Sean had saved his life.

———

The dock was just north of Penn's Landing, almost under the Ben Franklin Bridge. Between the rain and the darkness, Liam couldn't see much more than the wooden pier ahead, illuminated only by streetlamps above. The stores that lined one side of the small marina had disappeared with the night. Sean's thirty-foot Bayliner rocked gently in slip 28, its interior lights glowing through the windows. Its captain was already aboard.

His mother had survived. She had been arrested and taken to a mental institution, where she ended up killing herself on the second anniversary of their father's death by drinking rat poison a hired exterminator had accidentally left behind in her bathroom a few days earlier. All she had wanted was to be with the man she loved so dearly. She finally got her wish with a most painful and agonizing death.

The small waves slapping the pier sounded like cannons exploding as Liam inched his way closer to the boat. He walked carefully, always staying in the center of the platform, feeling it sway even though he knew that was impossible. His breath grew short and quick as it always did. His hands began to sweat, even in the rain.

He'd never been out on the boat but often found enough courage to climb aboard and have a few beers with his brother at the slip. The usual joke would entail Sean lowering the motor into the water and starting it, threatening to take it out onto the Delaware River to help Liam overcome his debilitating fear their mother had forever instilled in him. The idling motor would send Liam into a panic that was all too real. Sean seemed to enjoy watching him squirm as he revved the throttle and made as if he were about to untie the moorings. But Liam knew his brother would never really take off in the boat. When all was said and done, he and Sean shared a bond that was stronger than anything he'd ever known. Sean was there to look out for him and protect him. No way that boat would ever leave the slip. He knew that, yet logic would never overtake the panic.

Liam placed a careful foot on the edge of the dock and then stepped onto the back of the Bayliner. He clung to the boat's railing so tightly he could feel it in his shoulders. The black water nipped at the heels of his shoes, trying to grab him from the swimming platform and pull him under. He threw one leg over the side, then slid his body over the railing and brought the other leg around. The rain pelted his face as he balanced himself.

"Sean!"

The door to the interior cabin opened, and Sean appeared, carrying a life jacket. He tossed it to his brother. "Hey. I didn't hear you come on board."

Liam shuffled toward the doorway and fell into it, grabbing the life jacket and throwing it over his neck. "Can't we ever just meet at a bar? Why do you put me through this?"

"Getting on the boat is one step toward your recovery."

"I'm never going to recover."

"Not with that attitude you won't."

The interior cabin was simple. A couch that converted to a bed, a small table that could fold away, a stand-up shower, and the smallest galley kitchen on earth. Sean used it mostly for blue fishing and some-times slept on board when he took it down toward Virginia or up to Cape Cod. Liam made his way into the cabin and took off his raincoat. He put his arms through the life jacket and fastened the clips. The rain pounded the roof, drowning out the radio, which was broadcasting classic rock.

"Seeing Kerri like that today," Sean said. "It scared me. Someone knows something. They know we knew Kerri. And they know about Mom."

Liam walked farther into the cabin. "The only people who knew about all that is me, you, Kerri, and Don. Unless you told someone else."

"I didn't say anything."

"Me either."

"What about Kerri? She could've told her friends."

"Maybe. I never met any of them, so I can't be sure."

Sean sipped his beer.

45

"The paper flowers Mom made for us that day wasn't public domain," Liam said as he sat down on the couch. "It was kept out of the news at the time. How would someone know about that?"

"They wouldn't. But whoever killed Kerri knows it all. You, me, the flowers, the affair."

A heavy silence hung in the cabin.

"Any memories come back from last night?" Sean asked.

"Nothing. I'm going to have my blood run for a tox screen. See if I was drugged somehow."

"You think that's a good idea? I mean, aren't people going to want to know why you're testing your blood?"

"I'll run it through Gerri Cain's office at Jefferson. My team won't know."

Sean put his beer down. "I don't see that sweatshirt you came here to get last night. I assume you picked it up. Did you see it at home this morning?"

"I didn't even remember I was coming here to get a sweatshirt until you told me. Hell, I don't even know which sweatshirt I was talking about."

"What's going on here, Liam?"

Liam shrugged. "I have no idea."

10

With the storm now receding into a light drizzle, Liam sat in his car, staring up at his house as thoughts and emotions compounded, one upon the next. There were several lights on in the windows, but everything else was dark.

It was a simple house in the South Jersey suburbs—a quaint white colonial with black shutters that sat on a quarter-acre lot—and from his vantage point in the driveway, he could see part of the stone wishing well he'd put in last summer. Plants hung in baskets on the front porch, the breeze rocking them ever so gently. Inside the silence of his car, he looked upon all of this as if he were staring at a picture. It felt distant, not part of this reality. Not after what he'd seen today.

He and Vanessa had been happy once and were in the midst of trying to find that happiness again. But so much had happened in between. They'd met in college through a mutual friend. She was in nursing school, and he was studying forensic science. The attraction had been there from the start, but their true bond came from their mutual loss of their fathers when they were young. Vanessa had lost her father to a fatal heart attack when she was ten, and she'd been the first person Liam had known, other than Sean, who'd had any idea what it was like to lose a parent when you were still a kid. Vanessa could relate to the struggles Liam had had growing up without parents in the traditional sense of the term. She still had her mother, but that sense of having lost her dad was always there. Soon, understanding and empathy had grown into love, and he knew he'd found the woman he wanted to spend the rest of his life with. He'd found his soul mate.

They'd married shortly after graduating college. She'd gotten a job at an area hospital, and he'd been accepted into the academy. Their friends saw them as the ultimate couple, but like anything observed superficially from the outside, there were hidden cracks beneath the surface of their blissful existence, and these cracks became deeper and wider as the years went by. Their first test came when Vanessa discovered she was unable to have children. They had talked about adoption, but neither of them really set out to make that happen. The loss that was always there became deeper and more personal as they came to realize they would never have the family both of them had envisioned. The final test had come when Vanessa's mother was diagnosed with terminal brain cancer.

Vanessa's emotional downturn had come quickly and without warning. Liam had seen shades of what he'd been through with his own mother, and it frightened him. He began to turn away as she locked him out of a suffering she wanted all to herself. When her mother finally passed, Vanessa filled her suddenly empty hours with an abundance of overtime shifts at the hospital and an unwillingness to get back to the life she'd known beforehand. Liam tried to reconnect with her, but she shut him out. It wasn't long before the marriage had disintegrated to the point where they'd only see one another while passing in the hallway as one returned from a shift to watch the other leave. Their conversations became mumbled greetings.

When Vanessa had eventually turned to alcohol to help make it through her days, Liam had seen the finality of it all and had contemplated divorce. His decision to stay with her had been based on the reality that despite their problems, he knew leaving would ultimately destroy her, and he couldn't be responsible for that. He'd seen what abandonment had done to his own mother. He couldn't do that to Vanessa. Instead, he had pursued an extramarital relationship with

Kerri. It had lasted for a few years until one night, out of the blue, Vanessa had broken down and asked him to love her again. They'd sought help from a counselor and found ways to rebuild what they had once had. She'd quit drinking, and together they'd begun a new life and found the hint of a passion that had been dormant. She wanted to take care of him, and he would let her. He'd try to make it work. He owed her that much.

His relationship with Kerri had lasted for almost two years. Sean had introduced them, and much like when Liam had first laid eyes on Vanessa, there was an instant attraction, despite Kerri being a little younger than he was. They'd had fun together, laughed, and made love as if they were *in* love. Then one day she'd ended it, imploring him to make things right with Vanessa. She wanted him to go back to his wife to try to make things work again. She didn't want to be the reason Liam's marriage couldn't last. She said he needed a clean slate, and he had reluctantly agreed. But he missed her. He missed everything about her. And now she was truly gone. Dead. It was almost too much to bear.

Sean knocked on the window and snapped him back to reality. Liam grabbed his briefcase and stepped out of his car onto the driveway.

"You okay?" Sean asked.

"Yeah. Daydreaming. Let's go."

The two of them walked along the stone path toward the front of the house. Liam opened the door and was met by a symphony playing on the stereo. The soothing music tried to caress him, to lull him into its arms and protect him from the harsh realities of the outside world, but it fell flat against a headache that was coming on with ferocity. He placed his briefcase down next to a small bench by the stairs and sat to take off his wet shoes.

"That you?" Vanessa called from the living room.

"Yeah. Sean too."

"Dinner's in the fridge."

"I already ate."

Vanessa walked into the foyer. She was dressed in a pair of sweats and a T-shirt. She smiled as she walked over, kissed Sean on the cheek, and gave him a tight hug. "I wish you hadn't eaten. There's enough for all of us."

"Long day today," Sean replied. "Had to grab something while we could."

"Liam bring you by as a peace offering?"

"No. We were in the area going over a new case, and I just wanted to pop in and say hello. See how you're doing."

"That's nice of you. I'm doing fine. Can I get you anything?"

"No, I'm good."

"You boys figure out what happened last night? Did you fill in all the blanks?"

"Just too many drinks," Liam said.

Sean nodded. "Yeah. We started with shots, moved to beer, then ended with shots. I drove him home."

"And your clothes?"

"I left them in Sean's car. Apparently I started stripping on the way home."

"Actually," Sean interjected, "he puked a little, and it stunk, so we threw them in the trunk. I'll bring them by after I wash them. They're at the house now."

Vanessa moved in closer toward her husband. "Are you all right?" she asked. She touched his forehead with the back of her hand the way a mother would do to a child. "You don't look good."

"I'm fine. Caught this new case today, and it has me wiped."

"You wanna talk about it?"

"Not really."

"Tell me about it. It'll feel good getting it off your chest."

Liam looked at his wife, but all he saw was Kerri. For a brief moment, he resented her for being alive, then brushed that thought away as he climbed off the bench and walked toward the stairs. "I don't think so. I feel like crap. I'm just going to head up, take a shower, and go to bed."

"Yeah, I gotta get going too," Sean said. "I'll see you tomorrow."

"Okay."

Sean pecked Vanessa on the cheek. "Good to see you, as always. And go easy on my brother. He can't handle his liquor."

Vanessa chuckled. "So you *were* brought here as a peace offering."

"Maybe."

Vanessa walked Sean to the door and watched him scurry back down the stone path and into his pickup. When he was gone, she turned back to her husband. "Look," she said. There was a hint of desperation in her voice. "I'm sorry I was a bitch this morning. I don't know why I freaked about you going out last night. It's really no big deal. I don't wanna fight. Deal?"

"Deal. I don't want to fight either."

"Good. How about some tea?"

"No. I really just want that shower and to go to bed."

"You want a beer instead? I was hoping we could spend some time together. Talk and hang out. We could watch one of our shows."

"Not tonight."

Vanessa nodded, her lips tightening a bit. "Okay. If that's what you want."

"That is definitely what I want."

"It's just that the counselor said we should spend as much time together as possible when we're both home."

"I'll do a movie or one of our shows some other night. I need to lie down right now. Seriously. I'm beat."

"What about tomorrow? Joyce and I are having lunch in Center City at Talula's. Will you meet me there and have something to eat with us?"

"I promise I'll try."

"I'd like that." Vanessa came forward one last time. She brushed the hair out of his eyes and ran her soft hand down his cheek to his neck and shoulder. "You know, I could come lie with you. I might be able to fix that headache."

Liam didn't answer. He turned away and climbed the stairs to his bedroom, unbuttoning his shirt as he went. All he could see was Kerri's face, blue and swollen. His heart ached more now that he was alone.

Where were you last night? Why can't you remember?

Downstairs, Vanessa called to him one final time. "I love you!"

Again, he didn't answer. Instead, he wiped away tears that began streaming down his cheeks as he made his way into the bathroom, started the shower, and used the noise of the water running to mask the uncontrollable sobs that had finally bubbled to the surface. Kerri was dead. His heart was broken.

11

"Boys? Boys, come take a look at this! Come into the kitchen!"

Sean waited a few beats as he heard the front door close and his mother's footsteps cross the living room into the kitchen. He dropped the bright-yellow Tonka truck he was playing with and ran down the stairs as fast as he could. The sound of Liam's tiny footsteps came up behind him, but they were slower and more deliberate as his little brother climbed down to the main floor, too slow to keep up with Sean.

His mother was standing at the far end of the table they ate at every night. She was wearing a long peach dress with a white blouse. Her dark hair was back in a ponytail, and the sun streaming in behind her from the window above the sink gave her an aura that made her look almost magical. She smiled when he ran into the kitchen, then dug into a large brown paper bag that was sitting in front of her, pulling out several items from inside it and placing them side by side on the green plastic tablecloth.

Liam came in and stopped next to his older brother, panting as if he'd just sprinted in an Olympic race. He instinctively grabbed on to the end of Sean's sweater and pulled himself closer.

"What's all that?" Liam asked.

"This," his mother began as she took the last item from the bag, "is our new project. I'm going to show you how to make my paper flowers, and together we're going to make them and sell them around the neighborhood. People will buy them, and that'll give us a little spare change until the union calls and puts your father on a new job."

Sean walked to the table and could feel Liam tagging along next to him. "We're going to make paper flowers?"

His mother held up a small stack of multicolored paper. "Yup. All kinds. Roses, tulips, daisies. All different colors too. Watch."

The boys climbed up in their chairs and looked on as their mother took a pair of scissors and cut several teardrop shapes out of the colored paper. She then took the shapes and folded them into triangles, attaching the triangles around a long wire.

"Doesn't look like a flower to me," Liam said.

"Be patient," his mother replied.

Sean poked his brother in the head. "Shut up and watch."

His mother secured the paper to the wire with tape and continued to add more paper petals to the bud, taping at the base each time. She kept going—cutting teardrop shapes of paper, folding, taping—until she had a decent bloom of what would become a paper rose. Finally, she twisted fake wire leaves onto the original long wire to create a stem and trimmed the end with their father's wire cutters. She placed the rose on the table and looked up at her boys.

"That's a flower!" Liam exclaimed.

"It's pretty, Mom," Sean said. "I like it."

His mother smiled and grabbed more paper to start again. "We can sell them at church and at bingo and maybe even the flea market. It'll be fun."

"It'll be embarrassing," Sean replied. "All my friends go to those places. They'll rank me out for selling flowers."

"It's for the family," his mother said. "We all chip in around here when it comes to family. Don't you ever forget that. Blood comes first. And I can guarantee if your friends were in the same situation, their parents would have them chipping in too. No matter what. Got it?"

"Yeah, I got it."

"Good. Now come in closer, boys, and grab some of your own paper. We'll make one together. I'll show you."

The boys slid their chairs closer, and each grabbed a wire and paper. "Okay, first you take the wire . . ."

———

The lights of the Ben Franklin Bridge acted like stars in a dark sky that was otherwise absent of them. Sean sat on the back of his boat, listening to the traffic overhead, letting the current of the river rock him. After Liam's house, he had driven back to the marina to sit and think. He didn't want to go home just yet. The rain had stopped, and the air was now cool.

They'd made a bunch of paper flowers that day, and the days and months after. Their father was a union carpenter, and it wasn't unusual to have a job or two and then nothing for a few months. That was the cycle. So they made their flowers and sold them around town. His friends did tease him, but the people in South Philly always stuck together, so their neighbors bought the flowers without question and helped as much as they could. Family looked out for one another. He'd learned that lesson early, and it had stayed with him throughout his life. Being there for Liam was all he'd ever known.

Sean's teenage years had been spent looking after his little brother and trying to be a good student and model grandson for his grandparents, who had taken them in. By the time his friends were sneaking out and going to parties, dating girls, and snorting lines in club bathrooms, Sean was taking care of his ailing grandfather and preoccupying his grandmother with games of rummy and dominos. He stood by and watched his high school days slip away while everyone else had their fun. Liam was lucky enough to have enjoyed the very dances and dates Sean had missed out on growing up. Sacrifice. His life had always been about sacrifice.

But he had been proud when Liam was accepted to Penn State. He'd clapped at graduation and hugged his brother when he landed the forensics position with the department. Sean had attended college at Temple and worked on campus to pay for it. After graduation, he landed a job as a beat cop to help pay for his grandfather's medical bills and what he could of Liam's education. It was a good job that had grown into a nice career. He was the family's foundation, upon which everything else was built. This thing with Kerri would now put him to the test.

Sean stood and made his way to the wheelhouse. He turned the key and lowered the engine into the water. When it was properly submerged, he walked to each dock cleat and untied his boat from the slip. He started the engine and eased out of the marina until he was on the dark open water.

There was nothing out here except the sound of the wind rushing by and the coldness on his face and hands. The boat bobbed up and down in a wake he couldn't see as he made his way upriver toward Rancocas Creek and the Quaker City Yacht Club. At that point he'd decide whether to turn around or keep driving. His mind raced with everything that had happened that day.

He pushed down on the throttle and felt the boat pick up speed. Being out on the water gave him freedom from the city that could sometimes feel claustrophobic. Kerri was dead. His mind filled with the images he had seen at the hotel that afternoon. She was gone. Slaughtered. Somewhere from the depths of a place he thought could no longer exist, he felt another wave of emotion come upon him as he pushed the throttle and felt the boat float on the water.

12

It was late. Almost two in the morning. Don hurried out of his car and crossed a street with no traffic. The moon was hidden behind clouds, making it darker than it otherwise would have been, but the rain had stopped, and the sidewalks glistened. He hopped the steps of the three-story apartment house and went through the unlocked front door.

"Police business" was a term Don often used when his wife, Joyce, wanted to know why he was doing something out of the ordinary and he couldn't give a reasonable explanation or was prohibited to do so because of an ongoing investigation. So when she had caught him rising from bed in the middle of the night to get dressed and slip down to the kitchen, she had asked what he was doing, and he had simply replied, "Police business." After ten years of marriage and a family full of cops, Joyce knew any follow-up questions would be a waste of time, so she had relented with a sigh, fallen back on her pillow, and warned him to be careful. He'd blown her a kiss and left.

Don's relationship with his wife was a bit more complicated than most. His lieutenant was also his brother-in-law. He'd met Joyce, Phillips's sister, at a department charity event, and after a brief court-ship, they'd married with everyone's blessing. Sean had been the best man. Most of the time having the lieutenant as a brother-in-law bought some leeway during investigations, but other times it was a hassle. Phillips was very conscious of not letting it appear favoritism was taking place within his department. Nepotism was bad enough. Every once in a while, he took it a little too far. There was no way he'd approve of what Don was about to do. But Sean and Liam were also family, and the boys needed him. He couldn't say no.

The stairs squeaked as he crept up toward Kerri Miller's apartment. This wasn't really police business. He wasn't sure what it was, but he knew it wasn't proper procedure. If he was being honest with himself, he'd admit this was breaking and entering.

The building was clean but old. At the top of the second landing, he walked the length of a narrow hallway. The overhead lighting was dim, making it hard to see what was ahead. A smell of heating oil emanating from the vents was all around him. He took a small sheet of paper from his pocket and double-checked the apartment number Sean had written under the address. This was it. He looked around once and then pulled a thin metal bar from his jacket to work the deadbolt. The lock sprang, and he slipped inside.

The apartment was small. From what he could tell, everything seemed pretty basic. The bedroom and bathroom were off to his left, down a slender corridor. The kitchen, dining area, and living room were no more than a single space, sectioned off by new pink wall-to-wall carpeting and white linoleum tiles. There was a couch, a tiny entertainment center with a television and stacks of books, and a coffee table with a laptop on it. That was all.

Don slipped off his shoes to make sure he left no wet footprints on the floor and put on gloves he had in his pocket. He turned on his flashlight and walked farther inside. Dirty dishes sat in the sink. Countertops were filled with snack foods and cereal. It was nothing out of the ordinary. He turned on the laptop that was sitting on the coffee table and waited for it to boot up. Framed paintings hung on yellow walls. Silver radiators kept the place warm. Plants hung in front of the windows that flanked the entertainment center. The place looked peaceful.

After a few minutes, the computer was on and waiting. Don sat down and took a flash drive from his pocket. In the silence of the apartment, he could hear the machine's fan spinning. It sounded so much louder than it normally should. He plugged the drive into the USB port and began copying all the files. When he was done, he wiped the files from the laptop's hard drive, leaving the basic functionality systems and her social media accounts. He shut the computer down, knowing that when Heckle and Keenan turned the laptop in for analysis, it would perform like a regular computer but would be absent of whatever these files might contain. He was banking on Forensics concentrating on her social media feeds to try to see who she'd been in contact with versus doing a full top-to-bottom scan. It was a risk, but taking the entire computer would put up more red flags than leaving it as it was. No computer on the premises would look too suspicious. A computer with light use could just be a user's preference.

"Okay," he whispered to himself. "What's next?"

Don snuck his way from the living room area toward the bedroom. He shined his light as he went. Photographs of Kerri with friends and family, housed in a variety of frames, were all around him. He looked at them as he passed and could see the bright-eyed young woman so full of life smiling back at him. She was dead now, and he wondered if any of the people in the pictures were aware of what had happened yet.

There was a bed, a dresser, and a full-length mirror in the bedroom. Not much else. He went to the dresser and began pulling at clothes, moving items to study its contents. He really had no idea what he was looking for and searched quickly, going on to the next drawer and so on until the entire dresser had been turned over with nothing found. He went to the closet. It was small. Clothes hung with no space separating them, pushed together in a mass of hangers and material. He aimed his flashlight behind the clothes. Again, nothing. The shelf above held the same result. When he bent to take a look at the cubbyholes, he found only shoes. The closet was a closet.

"What do you have me chasing, Sean?"

He moved to the bed. A tangle of sheets and blankets hung from the mattress. He flipped them back and peered underneath. Groups of boxes filled the dusty floor. Something gold caught his attention, and he pulled it out. The box was square and shallow, the top gold, the bottom black. He stood and opened it.

The photo album within the box was leather bound with the initials *KM* embroidered in the corner and *Memories* in the center. He opened the album and noticed an inscription.

> To Kerri,
> Fill this album with every memory of our lives together. I love you and will always love you. Happy birthday.
>   Liam

Don flipped through the pictures to find the same couple in every shot. Smiling in each other's arms. Smiling on the beach under an umbrella in Atlantic City. Smiling on the couch he'd just passed in the living room. They were on every page. It was Kerri and Liam. It was the victim and Liam Dwyer.

"Got it." He closed the album, took the now-empty gold box, and carefully placed it back under the bed so there would be no dust markings from something he'd taken. Everything would look as it had been before. That was the trick.

Don remained on his hands and knees, checking every box, the flashlight his only source of light. He wouldn't leave for another two hours.

13

Forensics was on the third floor of the Market Street precinct. Liam sat in his office looking at the set of fingerprints he'd lifted from the hotel crime scene, his thoughts a million miles away. The day had just begun, and already he was feeling the effects of not being able to sleep the night before. His heart ached as he read reports and filed notes into the computer. Each image or description from the units on scene stabbed at him, reminding him of the love he felt for Kerri and how alive he'd been whenever he was with her. He still couldn't wrap his head around the fact she was gone.

The team had found a set of prints on the dresser and a partial print on the crystal of Kerri's watch. Curiously, there had been nothing else anywhere in the hotel room. An area with such high traffic was bound to have more than a single set of prints, so they figured the killer must have wiped everything clean and left what the forensics team had found in error.

Liam took the fingerprints and scanned the card through his computer, watching as the images magnified and displayed on the monitor. The set they'd taken from the dresser appeared to be an index finger and pinky, both full and detailed. The partial on the watch was that of a thumb, a bit smudged but distinguishable nonetheless. He put both sets side by side on the screen and could see similar islands, dots, bifurcations, and ridges. There was no way to be certain, but it appeared the prints were from the same person.

There was a knock on the door. Detective Keenan was standing just outside Liam's office, his giant frame taking up most of the doorway. "You got a minute?" Keenan asked.

Liam waved him in. "Yeah. What's up?"

"Just want to bounce a couple of questions off you based on what we have so far for the homicide at the Tiger. Make sure I'm heading in the right direction."

"Sure."

"What do you think the significance of shaving the victim's head was?"

Liam leaned back in his seat. Images of his mother hanging over the tub, trying to drown him when he was a little boy, slipped into his mind's eye. "My guess would be trophies. Something like that. I've read cases where the killer would have wigs made from the victims' hair in order to stay close to their murders. There apparently is such a rush they get when committing these kinds of crime they need to keep something to remember it by, remember the feeling of that rush. It's not uncommon for a murderer to want to keep something from the victim as a souvenir."

"Yeah, that's what I thought too. And the stomach. I'm thinking cutting her was an act of rage. I mean, she was going to die from the hanging. Why cut too?"

"Maybe," Liam replied. "Could also be the opposite. Maybe he cut her deep across the stomach to expedite her death, make it quicker. Some kind of a mercy kill."

"Yeah, maybe. Helluva way to show mercy, though."

"I'm going to call Gerri Cain and get some time with her. See what she thinks. I'll give you the information when I get it."

"Good." Keenan leaned against the door. He tapped his pen against the butt of his gun that was strapped to his hip. "One more thing?"

"Yeah."

"I just gotta say that I didn't like that your brother came to the scene yesterday without you telling us. I didn't want to cause any trouble with the uniforms there, but just so we're clear, that was crap. You do something like that again, and we're going to have a problem."

Liam nodded and said nothing. Keenan waited a moment longer, then turned and left.

When he heard the door to the lab close and the office was quiet again, Liam picked up the phone and noticed his hands were trembling slightly. He scrolled through his contacts list on his computer and dialed.

"Jefferson Hospital, Psychiatric Unit," a pleasant voice announced.

"Dr. Cain, please."

"Whom shall I say is speaking?"

"Liam Dwyer, Philadelphia Police. She'll know who I am."

"One moment, please."

Music played, and as he waited, Liam pulled up the Automated Fingerprint Identification System from the FBI database and uploaded the prints that were still on his computer screen. The AFIS held millions of fingerprints taken and scanned from countless suspects, convicted felons, law enforcement officials, military personnel, and those in the financial industry. He rose from his chair as the computer searched its files for possible matches. The process would take several minutes.

"Liam Dwyer. Long time since I last heard from *you*."

Liam immediately felt at ease when he heard the gentle caress of Gerri Cain's voice. "Hello, Gerri."

"How have you been?"

"I've been good," he lied. "And you?"

"I can't complain. You know, trying to help as many people as I can in as little time as they give me. Same old story."

"I see Mitchell still has high aspirations."

"I couldn't get my husband off the podium if I tried. Next stop is the White House, as far as that man is concerned."

"Well, tell him I said hi."

"Of course."

Liam gripped the phone tighter. "I was hoping you might be able to help me with a case I just inherited."

The doctor's voice rose in anticipation. "Will we be working together again?"

"I need some questions answered, but only if you can spare the time. I don't want to be a burden."

"You're never a burden. I love getting in on this stuff."

"I need about a half hour as soon as you can spare it."

Shuffling of an appointment book. A pause. "How about my office this morning around eleven? If that doesn't work, you'll have to wait until the end of the week."

"Eleven is fine. Thanks for squeezing me in."

"Shall I call in Nancy Drew or the Hardy Boys? I hear they like this sort of thing."

Liam smiled. "I don't think that'll be necessary. The Hardy Boys'll make it too crowded, and Nancy'll want to do it her own way and then write a tell-all afterward. I hear she's a control freak. I'll just take you and that wonderful noggin full of stuff I need to know."

The doctor laughed. "Sounds good. I'll see you later."

"Okay, see you then. Bye."

Liam hung up and logged the appointment in his planner. Gerri had helped him on cases before, drawing up psychological profiles to assist the team in tracking suspects. Perhaps she could help again. At the very least she would be able to provide some good insight into the questions surrounding the case.

The phone rang.

"Forensics. Dwyer."

"Liam, it's Jane. We've got some preliminary information from the autopsy. Just filed it but thought you might like to hear it."

Liam checked the computer. The database was still searching through the fingerprints. "What'd you find?"

"Victim was pregnant. About two months."

The news, laid out so matter-of-factly, stunned him. He sat, the phone to his ear, eyes staring out into nothing, his throat constricting, almost choking him.

"We found traces of blood under her nails and had it analyzed. It appears there are two types from separate sources. The tests we got back confirmed, showing a type O positive, your typical run-of-the-mill, and a rare type AB negative. The victim had the O positive, so if the AB negative is the killer's, which I would say there's a strong chance, then such a rare blood type could really help with a conviction. We also sent DNA from the two blood samples and a tissue sample from the fetus to see if the killer was the father."

"Excellent," Liam replied quietly, his eyes suddenly locked on the computer screen in front of him. "I'll let you know what I find regarding the prints. Haven't run them yet."

"Okay. Teddy and I will be in soon. We're stopping by Homicide first."

"I'll be here. See you later."

Liam hung up and leaned forward. The colors from the screen danced in front of his face, mocking him, laughing at his confusion. The FBI's system had matched three possible suspects, all three having some of the required ten Galton points for a positive identification. The first possible match was a man named George McPherson. He had a history of violence and had been arrested numerous times for various assaults. Liam ruled him out immediately, as he was already behind bars in South Dakota, serving fifteen years for assault with a deadly weapon. The second possible match was not currently in custody, but Eric Landon was living on the other side of the country, in San Diego, and his short history of offenses were more about being a drug addict than a murderer. There was petty theft, harassment, grand larceny, and prostitution, but nothing that would make him out to be more than what he was. The third match was the strangest. This match had all ten Galton points and came through not because of a prior arrest but because he worked in law enforcement. He was living in the area. Just across the Delaware River, in fact. Liam stared at his own image, his name flashing in red font underneath his picture.

LIAM DWYER

He was a match. His fingerprints had been left at the scene, on the dresser and on Kerri's watch. He tried to remember the last time he'd seen her and if he'd touched her wrist or handled her watch in some way. Perhaps his print had never worn off. No, impossible. There was no excuse to account for his prints being on the dresser in the hotel room. He shut down the database link and pulled up the crime scene photos he'd already loaded into the system. He clicked through each one, hoping to catch sight of himself not wearing any gloves, but in each photograph everyone had his or her gloves on, as was proper procedure. Of course he did. He was a professional. They'd done everything by the book. Always had.

Liam picked up his phone and called Sean. It rang twice before going to his voice mail. He hung up and tried again. Again, it rolled to voice mail.

"Dammit."

Liam shut off the computer and pushed himself away from his desk. There had to be an explanation. He had to think. How could his prints have gotten onto the crime scene? And worse, how could such a rare blood type have gotten under Kerri's fingernails?

Where were you last night? Why can't you remember?

Liam pulled his shirt down and traced the scratch from his shoulder to his chest.

AB negative.

Liam Dwyer was AB negative.

14

The steam from the shower lingered in the bathroom, the light mist floating with the current in the air. Sean did his best to wipe the condensation from the mirror above the sink, but the haze kept returning, smudging the details of his half-shaven face until it once again disappeared behind the thin film. He worked fast to finish up before the shaving cream dried and left his skin to burn. The tapping of the razor against the sink was rapid, thoughts of Kerri Miller taking up most of his morning.

His sleep had been shallow, and he was tired. He'd gotten in from the marina at midnight and was up at four. He'd gone for a run through the neighborhood to try to keep his head clear. When everything was still dark and empty, Sean felt most at peace. He basked in the quiet, the streetlights the only thing watching him as he jogged through the roads and cul-de-sacs. When his legs could no longer carry him, he'd stopped at a roadside breakfast cart and bought himself a bacon-egg-and-cheese and an orange juice, then returned home before the early onset of rush hour began.

Despite how much he would try to keep things hidden, he knew his friendship with Kerri and the relationship between Kerri and Liam wouldn't stay a secret for long. With both Forensics and Homicide working the investigation, someone would eventually discover something, and once they found out about Liam and Kerri being lovers, the news would be passed on quickly. He knew how these things worked. First, it would hit internally and travel through the department. Internal Affairs would get involved, and the brass would try to keep a lid on things, but such news would be too hot to keep under wraps for any extended period of time. It would undoubtedly leak beyond the walls of the station house and out into the streets. The media would have it and then pass it on to the public. At that moment, his brother would become the primary suspect of their murder investigation, and Sean would be chastised for keeping his brother's affair a secret. But for now, no one knew anything. He'd work hard to keep it that way as long as he could.

Sean tapped the remaining hairs from his razor, splashed cold water on his face, and toweled off. From the bedroom, he could hear his coffee percolating. He put on his pants and fumbled with the buttons of his shirt as he walked into the kitchen.

The knock on his door was rapid and light. Sean made his way through the living room and opened the door to find his partner standing before him.

"Jesus," Don muttered. "You look like crap."

"Long night. Thinking about Kerri and everything. I can't believe this happened."

"Yeah, I know. It's crazy. I'm sorry for your loss. Sincerely. I didn't know her like you guys did. I'm sorry."

Sean stepped aside and allowed Don to walk in and take off his jacket. "You find anything?" he asked.

"Enough."

"I was hoping Kerri would've gotten rid of whatever she had of her and Liam after they broke up."

"She didn't."

"What'd you find?"

Don followed Sean into the kitchen. "There were piles of letters in shoeboxes and pictures of the two of them in a bunch of photo albums I found under her bed. The letters were just signed 'Liam,' no last name, but he's in all the pictures. From what I read in the notes and cards, there's no way you'd think they were just friends. There were a lot of shots showing them hugging and holding hands and planting cute kisses on each other. Puppy love kind of stuff."

"What about pictures of me? Or you, for that matter? You've been out with all of us more than once."

"No. Just Liam."

"And these were pictures of them together?"

"Yeah."

"Then there was someone else who knew about their relationship. A third person had to be there to take the pictures, right?"

"Maybe," Don replied. "But really, anyone could've taken the pictures. I get asked by tourists all the time to take their picture. A lot of the photos looked like selfies, anyway."

"What else?"

"I also found a toothbrush, a hairbrush, a few shirts, and a pair of pants. I don't know if they were Liam's, but they were men's things, so I took them just to be safe." Don fished the flash drive out of his pocket. "I also downloaded all the files from Kerri's computer and then wiped it clean. I doubt Heckle or Keenan would get the tech unit involved to back trace her hard drive, but if they do, they'll find whatever I deleted. I didn't have the proper equipment to do a total purge." He tossed it to his partner. "There was no time to go through anything in much detail, but I did notice an encrypted file on her hard drive. Not sure how sophisticated the encryption is, but we can have Rocco take a look at it if you want."

"Not necessary."

"You sure?"

Rocco was a local hacker who'd been busted on drug charges several years earlier. In exchange for probation, he'd agreed to help the department with suspects' computers and encrypted files from known gang members. The agreement was kept off the books and confidential. Only the most trusted cops were in the loop.

Sean held the drive between his fingers, studied it for a moment, then tossed it in the garbage disposal. He flipped the switch under the window and listened as the drive was churned into nothingness. "I don't want to see what's on that file," he said. "I'm afraid of what I might find, and we already know too much."

"What if it's proof Liam is innocent?"

"Liam is innocent."

Sean stared into the sink where tiny shards of plastic had been tossed back up from the disposal. "I just can't see my brother doing something like what I saw in that hotel room. I mean, you should've seen her hanging there. It was a mess. I'm talking torture. I don't know how else to describe it. It was . . . evil."

"I can't see it either," Don replied. "Not Liam. But we've been through too many cases like this over the years, and they've all ended the same. The person most likely to commit the crime is usually the one who's guilty. You and I both know that. From what I've seen on this job, I think anyone is capable of anything. You need to look at this like a cop for a second and not as Liam's brother. Ask yourself who this crime points to right now."

"I can't."

"You need to look at this like Heckle and Keenan are going to be looking at this. They're good cops. They're going to find out about Liam's affair with their vic."

Sean turned back around to face Don. "Why are you so eager to pin this on Liam?"

"I'm not. I'm just saying we can't be blind to what's in front of us. If he was trying to rebuild his marriage and Kerri was getting in the way of that, there's motive. You know that."

"Kerri broke up with him."

"What if she changed her mind and was trying to get back together with him? What if she became relentless, and he had to make her go away?"

"This is all speculation," Sean said. "We don't know anything. Kerri could've been dating six other guys. That's why we need to stay quiet and let Heckle and Keenan do their thing. You're right. They are good cops. They'll find something, because I know it wasn't my brother who did this. Liam hadn't seen Kerri in months. Why would he kill her now?"

"Because she was pregnant. Maybe that's why."

"What?"

"Two months pregnant. They found it in the autopsy. I called Jane on my way over to check on the ballistics test from Cutter and innocently inquired about the Tiger Hotel homicide. I got her talking, and she told me about the pregnancy and that they also figure the killer used an extremely sharp instrument to cut her stomach. The medical examiner thought it might have been something like a scalpel. Vanessa keeps medical instruments like that in her workbag, right? Something Liam would have easy access to?"

Sean covered his face with his hands.

"And Liam saw Kerri two weeks ago. It hasn't been months." Don reached into his coat pocket and came away with his notepad. He flipped through several pages and pushed it across the table. "After I left Kerri's apartment, I got home and spent some time taking down all the dates on the letters and photos I found and put them in chronological order. Their last picture together was two weeks ago. Heckle and Keenan are going to get her phone records today or tomorrow. Could've been even sooner than two weeks ago. I'm just going by the photos. Your brother lied to you. Why would he do that?"

Sean crossed the room and took the notepad from his partner. He read through the list. There had been three dates after the time Liam had told him he'd last seen Kerri. "She called him the night she was killed," he said. "Left him a voice mail."

"That's going to be on the phone records, Sean."

"Why was she calling him?"

"I don't know."

The rotating fan hanging from the kitchen ceiling spun lazily above the men. Sean watched it turn in circles. "Maybe buying time was the wrong idea," he said. "We might have to make this go away."

"You sure about that?"

"He's my brother. He's family. The only family I have."

"And you're okay turning your back on murder?"

"I'm not turning my back on murder. I'm protecting Liam. It's what I've always done." He looked at his partner. "You with me?"

Don nodded. "Always. You know that."

Sean walked out of the kitchen and into the living room. "Where are the items you took from Kerri's place?"

"In my trunk."

"Let's check them out."

The two men walked to the front door, and Sean stopped, his hand on the knob. He didn't turn around. "We're going to let Heckle and Keenan investigate. Hopefully they'll find who really did this. It wasn't Liam. Couldn't be. But at the same time, we'll look into things on our end quietly. That work for you?"

"Yup."

"You sure? I don't know where this is gonna lead, and I can't have you second-guessing what we're doing here if things go sideways."

"Not gonna happen."

"I'm sorry I got you involved."

"Don't be. It's cool."

Sean opened the door and walked out into the morning air. There was nothing left to say.

15

"It's Jane again. I got some additional results back from the lab."

Liam felt his stomach turn as he bounced down the steps from the station house. His mind was racing. What had she found? He swallowed the lump in his throat. "Yeah, I'm here. Go ahead."

"DNA came back way quicker than I thought it would. It's a match between the fetus and the traces of AB negative we found under the victim's nails. Looks like the father was the killer. We figured that."

"Okay."

"They also found ketamine hydrochloride in her system. It's a heavy sedative sometimes used on horses. Normally it wouldn't be traceable, as the body absorbs it quickly and flushes it through the liver, but when she died, her body stopped functioning, so they found it. The ketamine hydrochloride would explain how whoever did this was able to get her out of the club and into the hotel without her kicking and screaming. She'd be doped up, but nothing too out of the ordinary for a place like the Tiger. A second dose inside the hotel room, however, would have knocked her out and allowed the killer to string her up without much of a fight. It's hard to tell just how much she had in her system prior to death."

"Interesting." He didn't know what else to say.

"We also found microscopic grains of something under her nails when we scraped the blood. Same stuff was on her skin. Sent it out to be analyzed and turns out it's padding from a seat cushion. We checked the hotel, and no seats were torn. The mattress was okay too. Rob's going to go back to the club and see about ripped seats there. Not sure if this could lead us anywhere. The FBI lab is running further tests to see if they can narrow the materials that made up the cushion to help us pinpoint what we're looking for."

Liam got into his car and started the engine. "Good finds. I'm heading over to Jefferson Hospital to talk to Gerri. Get her perspective on this. I'll see you when I get back. We'll talk more then."

"Okay."

He hung up and closed his eyes. The DNA from the blood matched the fetus, which meant if that was, in fact, his blood they found under Kerri's nails, then the baby was his. She'd never said anything to him about being pregnant. He wondered if she'd known and had been protecting him.

A phone rang.

The ringing was muffled, but it was there. Liam looked at his own phone for a moment, then turned and looked in the back seat. Nothing. The ringing stopped, then after a few seconds, started again. The trunk.

Liam threw open his door and ran around to the back of the car. He pressed the button on his keychain, and the trunk's lid disengaged. He lifted it and looked inside. Kerri's white phone sat atop a pile of bloody clothes. His clothes.

"Where are your clothes?"

"The living room?"

"No, they're not."

He felt faint, swaying from side to side as his world went out of focus for a moment. He looked at the caller ID: Tina.

Kerri's phone stopped. Before it could ring again, he grabbed it, shut it off, and stuffed it in his pocket.

The wind was picking up.

Liam fell against his car and dialed his brother. For a third time that day, it rolled to voice mail. He didn't leave a message.

16

The Psychiatric Unit of Jefferson Hospital was quiet and out of the way from the general traffic. The loudspeaker overhead played soothing tunes, the volume turned low. A nurse sat behind a desk answering calls that were routed in succession, one after the other. Liam stepped off the elevator at the fourth floor and followed the yellow dots to the main desk.

"Yes?" the nurse asked.

"Liam Dwyer to see Dr. Cain."

"Have a seat. I'll let her know you're here."

He walked to the waiting area and grabbed a magazine. His mind was still racing after finding Kerri's phone in his car. And his bloody clothes. He still couldn't remember anything about what had happened that night and refused to consider what the voices within were screaming at him, what logic was dictating. He loved Kerri. He'd never do anything to hurt her. Why couldn't he remember? What had happened that night?

A woman was sitting across the way, tearing tiny strips of paper as she rocked in her seat, exhaling heavily. The paper fell gently to her feet, covering her slippers. She was mumbling something, but it was too quiet for Liam to hear. A male nurse came from beyond one of the three closed doors of the waiting area and approached her. "Greta," he said.

The woman looked up at the nurse. "That's me. I'm Greta. Greta Feely."

"I know. Dr. Mecca is ready for you." The nurse guided the woman to a standing position. "Can you come with me?"

"I want to see Dr. Mecca."

"Okay. Come along with me, and we'll see him."

Greta Feely dropped what remained of the paper and allowed the nurse to take her away. Liam could hear her asking questions as they walked through the door, her voice eventually trailing off. He turned his attention back to his magazine and flipped through the pages without reading any of it.

"Liam!"

Liam looked up to see Gerri Cain walking toward him. He smiled and stood. "Hey, Doc. How are you?"

They hugged.

"Come inside. I'll get you a cup of coffee."

"Lead the way."

Gerri Cain was an attractive woman, forties, well-built, in shape. Her dark hair held natural curls that hung above her shoulders and bounced when she walked, but it was her confidence that magnified her attractiveness. Liam had always thought she was beautiful, and his respect for her made her all the more alluring. Her husband was a lucky man, indeed. From time to time she worked for the department doing evaluations of recruits and first-year rookies, but most of her practice was private.

Gerri walked into the office and went for her coffee maker, grabbing two mugs from a shelf near a mini refrigerator. "It's been a little while," she said.

Liam found a seat on one of the leather couches and allowed his body to relax a bit. "Yes, it has."

"How're things going with you and Vanessa?"

"Good, actually. I think we're really doing good. That counselor you recommended is fantastic."

"That's great to hear." She handed one of the mugs over. "Like I said, it takes a while, but if both of you are committed to making it work, it will. Two partners who are in it together make all the difference."

"I think you're right. I can sense the change for the better. We're not totally there yet but so much better than we were."

Gerri smiled as the conversation died. "So what brings you to see me today?" she asked. "Sounded kind of urgent when we spoke."

Liam placed the coffee down on a table in front of him. He grabbed his briefcase, opened it, and pulled out a folder. "We came across this victim at the Tiger Hotel in Center City last Sunday. She checked in with a man that Saturday night and was discovered by the owner the next day. The killer paid cash and left a phony name, so we don't have much to go on. I need to know what the significance of some of this mutilation could represent." He extracted the crime scene photographs from the folder, placing them side by side on the table. He desperately wanted to tell her more. He wanted to tell her about the affair with Kerri, waking up in the tub on Sunday morning, unable to remember anything about the night before. He wanted to tell her about the phone and his clothes in the trunk, the scratch on his chest. And he wanted her to reassure him that he had nothing to do with Kerri's death. But he knew he couldn't. He didn't know her well enough to trust her with such information.

Gerri picked up each photograph, studied it, and placed it back with the rest. "What exactly were the mutilations?" she asked. "All I see here is a big mess."

"The victim was two months pregnant. According to the autopsy, she was hanged, her head was shaved, and her stomach was slit with her placental sack being pierced, not necessarily in that order."

"Were there signs of healed wounds or bruises that were fading?"

"I'd have to check with the medical examiner. Why do you ask?"

"At first blush, I'd say the fact that she was pregnant and the nature of the injuries all point to spousal abuse. The extreme measures that were carried out at the hotel paint a picture of ongoing abuse reaching its final breaking point. I'd look into a boyfriend or spouse."

"She wasn't married."

"How about a boyfriend?"

Liam's face reddened. "None that we know about, but we're still looking into it."

Gerri picked up another picture. "The way I see it, this woman had a significant other who was a control freak. Power over women can be very enticing, very addictive to someone like this. I hesitate calling him a sociopath because this could be anything from a psychotic break to a serial killer and everything in between. We just don't know yet.

"I'd envision him beating her or ruling over her, always the one needing to be in control, always secretly scared to death that he may lose that control. The hanging could be simply the suspect's need to scare the victim, to hold her in suspense until he kills her. Again, this all stems from the killer having the power and controlling what takes place next.

"Perhaps the pregnancy was unplanned, unexpected. She told the man about the baby, and that represented his loss of control. He killed her by hanging her and then slit her stomach in both an attempt to scar her as well as to make sure the baby was dead. *He* was going to be the one who controlled life and death. Him killing her made the unplanned loss of control go away. Him killing her made everything all right again."

Liam looked at the pictures on the table. He'd never tried to control anything about Kerri. In fact, it was her loose spirit that had made her so attractive. They'd had a few superficial arguments, but he'd never touched her. The person Gerri was describing was not a person Liam could ever be. "What about the hair?" he asked. "What does that tell you?"

Gerri took a picture that showed a close-up of Kerri's shaved head. She studied it for a few minutes. "What's the one thing that makes or breaks a woman in our society?"

"I don't know."

"Beauty. Our makeup, our bodies, our nails, our eyebrows, our figures, and our *hair*. Hair is probably *the* greatest self-defining, first-impression characteristic both women and men have, but for women its significance is much greater. Our hair defines us, like it or not. I hate the fact that society makes us obsess about our hair and all these other things, but we do, all of us.

"Shaving the head is this guy's way of making the victim ugly in his mind. He's using his power to take away her beauty. That's what he's trying to do here. It's all about the power. The killer and his power." She handed the pictures back. "What was the victim's name?"

"Kerri Miller."

Gerri took a pen from her breast pocket and jotted the name on a notepad. "If you get me her social security number, I'll do a search to see if she was ever admitted to an ER for something that would indicate abuse."

"That would be great."

"You should also do an off-line search through NCIC to see if there have been any other murders with these trademarks. The slashing of the stomach. The hair. The hanging. A combination of the three. As I said, I don't know what we're dealing with here. Wouldn't hurt to tap NCIC."

"Will do." Liam took the photographs and opened the folder. As he began to drop them into the file, he stopped. "Let me ask you something. Is it possible for someone to commit a crime like this and not remember it? I mean, not have the faintest idea they were ever near a hotel, let alone do all this. Is it possible to forget everything?"

"Absolutely. If this guy had a psychotic break, his mind could shut down, and at that point he becomes a machine, his body just going through the motions with his subconscious leading the way. He then would repress the memory, and he could wake up the next day and not remember anything. Not even the tiniest little detail. He could forget it all. Repression is a defense mechanism. Women who've been raped have been known to repress so deeply that they'll pass a lie detector test. They have no recollection of the rape ever taking place."

"Really?"

"In a psychotic break, the memories are usually triggered as time goes on. Could take days or years, but the memories surface after a while. Why do you ask?"

"I was reading a case study the other day. Guy committed murder and had no memory of it. I thought it was strange."

"It's more common than you think."

Liam slid the folder into his briefcase and climbed off the couch. "Thanks, Doc. This helps a lot."

"And we didn't need Nancy Drew after all."

"I told you."

Gerri walked Liam to the door. "Don't be a stranger," she said. "Call me, and we'll do lunch. And keep going strong with Vanessa. I know you'll be fine."

"I will. And I'll have Jane send you Kerri's social security number so you can check with the hospitals."

They said their goodbyes, and Liam made his way out of the office. He walked down the hall slowly, thoughts cascading one after the other. Technically speaking, it was possible he could have killed Kerri and not remembered it, but there was no way he ever laid a finger on her in the past. He wasn't a control freak. There were suddenly more questions than answers.

"Hey, Liam," Gerri called as he was about to turn the corner for the elevators. Her voice was darker now, serious. "Find this guy. He's dangerous, and if he did all that to this woman, he can do it to another. Find him."

"We're trying," Liam said as the burden of his secrets consumed him. "We're doing our best."

Gerri disappeared back into her office, and Liam made his way toward the elevators. He had one more stop to make before leaving the hospital.

17

The nurse was quiet as she wrapped the rubber tourniquet around Liam's bicep and tapped the inner part of his arm to get a good vein. The lab was only one floor down from Gerri's office and around the corner from Radiology. His team had used it many times before in various investigations where speed was a priority, so he was familiar with the personnel manning the floor, and they were familiar with him. But this particular nurse was new. He'd never seen her before.

"And what are we sending this out for?" the nurse asked as she slid the needle into his arm and began attaching the vials that would hold his sample. She was short and middle-aged and worked quickly. There was no doubt she had years of experience behind her. He'd hardly felt the needle break the skin.

"General tox screen. Anything that might come up."

"Am I sending the results to the department?"

"You can send it directly to my attention. Dr. Fleece has my contact information. I'm using my blood as a baseline test in a comparison we're working on back at the office."

"Couldn't get this done there? Seems like a hassle to come all the way over for a baseline draw."

"I needed it high priority, and I figured if we take a sample somewhere other than the precinct, no one can challenge its validity. Neutral playing field. Plus you guys can deliver faster than we can."

The nurse was only half listening. No doubt she had other patients waiting. She leaned down to switch out one vial that was full with another empty one. "You can relax your grip," she said. "And they'll always challenge the validity of the test. If it's between a conviction and a challenge, it won't matter where you got this baseline drawn from. And, for the record, I don't want to be called to no witness stand."

"I'll do my best to keep you out of it."

"Please do."

Liam let his fist go and looked up at the nurse. She concentrated on her task and said nothing more. There was a desire to try to explain further, but anything else that came to mind seemed like overkill. Instead, he sat in silence as the seconds ticked away in a prolonged awkwardness.

When everything was complete, the nurse capped the last vial, pulled the needle from his arm, and attached a piece of cotton with a Band-Aid. "All set."

"Thanks."

"We'll send this out in a few. Should have something for you by tomorrow. Next day at the latest."

Liam rolled his shirt sleeve down and buttoned the cuff as he walked out of the lab and back into the hall. When he got to the elevators, he grabbed his phone from his pocket and dialed his office.

"Forensics. Jane Campelli."

"Jane, it's Liam. I'm at Jefferson. Just finished up with Gerri, and she suggested we call in an off-line search through NCIC."

"Okay."

He stepped onto the elevator with two other people. "We need to search for homicides involving any combination of hanging, lacerations to the stomach, and head shaving."

"Isn't that something Heckle and Keenan would handle?"

"I just spoke to them before I called you," he lied. "They were busy following up on interviews from the club, so I told them we'd do it."

The other two elevator occupants took a step back when he began explaining the search criteria.

"Start with Philadelphia and build out from there. Gerri seems to think there might be a chance our perp has done this before. Maybe not to the extent we saw at the Tiger, but perhaps a variation of it. It's worth looking into."

"Okay," Jane replied. "I'm on it. You heading back here?"

"Yeah, later. I need to check in on a few things across town first. Call me if you need anything."

The elevator doors opened as Liam was hanging up his phone. The other two occupants rushed past him and scurried across the lobby out onto the street. He had missed the connection between his graphic description of the search criteria and their hurried escape. His mind was too preoccupied with other things.

The NCIC was the National Crime Information Center. It was a nationwide computerized information database that included millions of records, ranging from petty theft to murder. Through the NCIC, local, state, and federal law enforcement had instant access to all available records and could cross-reference past offenses, outstanding warrants, and crime trends. Most police departments had the NCIC system in their patrol cars to aid officers during traffic stops and other calls to determine if the suspect had warrants or past offenses. What he needed was an off-line search, which was a very specific cross-referencing of key terms that the regular database wouldn't have built into the system police departments used. Jane would have to reach out to their local FBI office to conduct the kind of search he was asking for. Results would most likely be back in a few days.

Liam walked out of the hospital toward his car, which was parked in a lot adjacent to the main entrance. He thought about his fingerprints at the scene, the scratch down his chest, his rare blood type found under Kerri's nails, and her phone being in his trunk on top of the clothes he'd been wearing the day she was killed. He thought about the animal Gerri had described in her office while profiling the type of person who could commit such a crime. A man who was capable of doing such savage things was foreign to him. There was no way he'd be capable of the kind of violence he'd seen at the hotel. So then why was there suddenly so much evidence to the contrary? Why was everything pointing to him and no one else? He tried desperately to think about events from the night she was killed. Still, there was only blackness. Why couldn't he remember?

18

"Hey, sorry I'm late."

Liam walked through the maze of tables as he approached Vanessa and Joyce. Joyce was Don's age, tall and thin, and had mesmerizing eyes that seemed almost iridescent. She was a kind woman and had become as much a part of their lives as Don had. She always dressed nicely and today had on an aqua-colored dress and radiant red heels. Vanessa was in her scrubs, as she'd be heading straight to work from lunch. The two of them were sitting at the small table for three and couldn't have looked more opposite, yet their friendship was a strong bond.

Joyce rose from her seat and kissed Liam. "If you're working the same hours as my husband, it's no wonder you're late. What they got you involved with that takes up all your time?"

"Everything," Liam replied. "And all at once."

"Up and gone Saturday night. Up and out last night. Always running around, that man."

Vanessa kissed Liam. "I had no idea what you were in the mood for, so I told the waiter you'd decide when you got here. We started without you. I gotta get back for my shift."

Liam looked at the half-eaten salads and sandwiches spread out on the table. Nothing looked appetizing. His stomach had been in knots all morning.

"Take a load off," Joyce said. "Tell us about this mega case you and Don are working on."

Liam poured himself a glass of water but remained standing. "I am on a new homicide, but not with Don and Sean. They're working something else. And I'm sorry, but I can't stay. I just stopped by because I knew you'd be waiting. If I wasn't already in the area, I would've called and canceled, but I figured I'd see you for a quick hello."

Vanessa stared at him for a long time, then turned away and began playing with the napkin on her lap. "You can't stay? You said you'd join us for lunch."

"I'm sorry. And for the record, I said maybe."

"Can you at least have a sandwich or something? You have to eat."

"I can't. The day is already getting away from me."

"But you shouldn't work on an empty stomach. That's all I'm saying."

"Vanessa, I can't."

Vanessa looked back up at him with a combination of sadness and anger in her eyes. "You promised."

"I didn't promise. I said I'd try, and I did try. Things are too crazy today."

There was an awkward silence that fell between them until Joyce spoke up. "It's okay," she said. "Go do what you have to do. We understand. I'm going to finish eating with my favorite girl here, and we're going to take a walk around Independence Plaza to chat. Just us ladies."

Liam placed his water back on the table. "Okay."

Joyce pointed at him. "But let the record stand that you owe her. If you promised lunch and there's no lunch, then it goes on the ledger as an IOU. You got that?"

"Yes, ma'am."

"Good, then go. We got some gossipin' to do. Can't talk behind your back when you're standing right there in front of us."

Liam looked down at Vanessa. "I really am sorry. If there was a way I could make more time, I would. It's just one of those days."

Vanessa nodded. "You can make it up to me later."

"I will."

"I love you, you know. You realize that, don't you?"

"Of course. I love you too."

"You sure?"

"Positive."

As Liam walked back through the maze of tables, he could hear Joyce start talking about one of the women they were friends with from a cooking class they used to take together. Something about her oldest son going to rehab after an overdose. Their voices faded with distance, yet in his mind's eye, he could still see the look of disappointment on Vanessa's face when he had told them he couldn't stay. He hated that this case was taking him away from a marriage that needed to be cared for and cultivated. But there was a truth out there that he had to find before others within the department discovered their own version of it. His freedom depended on it.

19

The outside of the art museum was packed with people. Tourists sprinted up the famous steps and leapt in victory as Rocky Balboa had done so many years before. Although Rocky's statue was gone, the treads of his sneakers were cemented into the concrete, and those same tourists took their time snapping pictures and posting videos because, as everyone knew, if you couldn't post it, it didn't really happen. Others walked past the fountains and beneath the oversized stone columns to get into the museum itself, more interested in the works of art inside than what pop culture offered outside. It was the perfect place to meet, surrounded by so many strangers.

Liam stood at the midway point of the stairs and looked out at the city's skyline toward Eakins Oval. The very tops of the tallest buildings were hidden in a fog that had rolled in after the temperature dropped. The stone and marble around him still glistened with moisture from last night's rain. It was beautiful. He dug into his pocket and came away with a gold pendant, holding it up, twirling it in his fingers, looking at it from different angles, front to back, side to side, all the while thinking of her. Kerri had given him the mini–magnifying glass as a gift when things were still fresh in their relationship. After he'd returned home the night before, he'd uncovered the lost memory and was struck to find the thoughts and emotions the pendant had attached to it were still as fresh as the day she'd given it to him. She used to call him the Great Inspector and would tease him in what she called her Sherlock Holmes accent.

"Hey, little brother."

Liam quickly palmed the pendant and looked up. "You're late."

Sean was one step below him. "Had to finish my reports on Cutter Washington. They put me on mandatory leave for a weapon's discharge, but more importantly, it looks like we finally got him."

"How long you out for?"

"A few days."

"Any word on the kid who got shot?"

"He made it through the night okay, so that's a good sign. Docs think he'll make a full recovery. Has a tough road ahead of him, though."

Liam put the pendant in his pocket. "Come on—let's walk."

The two brothers made their way down the rest of the steps and followed the sidewalk that would bring them around the back of the museum and into Fairmount Park. The trees in the park were budding, small white flowers popping from the tips of the branches, all lined in a row.

Liam watched two kids running around a tree, chasing each other while their mother looked on. The sound of drilling and hammering filled the air, and he looked up to find a maze of scaffolding fanned out across the back of the museum. He couldn't tell what the men were working on, but it appeared to be a sizeable project.

"I think I'm being framed, Sean. It's the only explanation."

Sean nodded. "How do you figure?"

Liam took out his phone, pulled up several pictures of the crime scene, and handed it to his brother. Tiny circles were drawn around several objects in the hotel room. "We got some preliminary results back from the crime scene. The prints we lifted are mine. Two from the dresser there, and one on her watch. The blood we extracted from her fingernails matches my blood type. My rare blood type."

"Are you serious?"

"I talked to Gerri Cain this morning, and she said it's possible for someone to have a psychotic break and not remember long stretches of time, but if I really did do it, even in a state where my subconscious had taken over, wouldn't I know how to clean up a crime scene and not leave any traces of anything that would point to me? Everything had been wiped down but the dresser and her watch. Those were the only things that point to no one *but* me. It doesn't make sense. I felt no ill will toward Kerri. We ended the affair mutually. Why would I do something like what you saw at the Tiger? And the paper flowers."

Sean looked at the pictures on Liam's phone, then handed it back to his brother. "So who's doing this, then?"

"I don't know."

"And why?"

"Don't know that either. Whoever it is, they know a hell of a lot more than most people do. They know about Kerri, and they know about Mom. The paper flowers she left for us weren't in the news back then. Neither was the way she cut up her hair."

"So who else knew about you and Kerri? We need to start there."

"Just me, you, Don, and Kerri." Liam stopped walking. "I just saw Vanessa and Joyce. They were having lunch. Joyce mentioned Don was out Saturday night on a case. Last night too. Where was he?"

"He was with me at the stationery store. The Cutter case."

"No, that was the morning. Joyce said he was out all night."

Sean laughed. "I think we can erase Don from our list of suspects. He's the most honest guy I know. He wouldn't take a pencil home from the department if it wasn't authorized. No way he could do what we saw at the Tiger."

"But where was he Saturday night?"

"His mom's. She had an episode, and he had to go see her."

"Any way we can confirm that?"

"He has no motive, Liam. Why would Don kill Kerri and frame us? There's no reason."

"Can we confirm it or not?"

"Yeah, I think so."

"Then do it."

The boys playing around the tree ran over to their mother, laughing. A street performer began playing a guitar and singing.

Sean took a breath. "I heard about the autopsy results."

Liam didn't respond.

"She was pregnant."

"I know."

"Is it yours?"

"The DNA from the fetus matches the DNA from the blood found under Kerri's nails, so . . ." Liam couldn't look at his brother. He stared at the crowd walking up the path toward the museum. "I found Kerri's phone in the trunk of my car this morning. My clothes that were missing too. There was blood all over my clothes."

"What?"

"Someone was calling her, and the damn thing started ringing in my car. How did it get there?"

Sean looked out beyond the park as cars rushed by beyond the iron railings. "I think you might be right. I think someone might be trying to frame you. I'm not sure why, but we have to find out who's doing this. Things are starting to spin out of control. All we need is for this guy to start contacting the department or a newspaper, and then we're all suspects."

"You think they're going to try and blackmail me?"

Sean chuckled. "If that's the case, they picked the wrong family." He looked at his brother. "We need to be honest with each other. About everything. Starting now."

"I am being honest."

"Last night, Don went to Kerri's apartment to try and get anything related to your affair out of there so we could buy some time to figure out what was going on. He got some pictures of you two, and they were time-stamped. You told me it had been three months since you last saw her, but the pictures say it's been two weeks. Why would you lie about that? To me? I'm trying to help you."

Liam could feel his face flush. He shook his head and started walking again. "I was freaked when I saw her at the scene. Truth is I didn't want to tell you we were still seeing each other because I know how much you helped me patch things up with Vanessa. It wasn't romantic. Not really. We were friends. I needed her company, I guess. I didn't want you to be disappointed with me. I had no idea all this other stuff would come up."

"I need the truth from now on," Sean said. "All of it. No matter what you think my reaction might be. You have to let me know what's going on. This affects me too. We're in this together."

"Okay." Liam walked behind a row of bushes, hiding himself from the other people walking through Fairmount Park. "One more thing." He unbuttoned his shirt to reveal the scratch that ran down his chest. "If that really is my blood under Kerri's nails, I'm assuming this was how it got there."

Sean studied the scratch, carefully reaching out to trace it with his finger. "Jesus Christ, Liam. What is happening?"

"I don't know."

"Think for a second. How could Kerri scratch you and you have no memory of it?"

"The same way I woke up in the tub and have no memory of how I got there. The whole night's just gone."

"But if someone's framing you, they would've needed to come in direct contact with you to make that scratch. With what? Kerri's dead hand? That means you could've been at the Tiger that night. Or the club."

"I know."

Sean reached into his coat pocket and rummaged around for something. He came away with a pair of sunglasses and pushed them into Liam's hand. "Hold these." He searched through his pocket again and finally pulled out his phone. He looked at the screen, read something, then put it back away and grabbed the glasses. "Don downloaded a bunch of files from Kerri's computer onto a flash drive and then wiped it clean so no one would find anything connected to you."

"What was on the flash drive?"

"No idea. I destroyed it."

"Why would you do something like that? There could've been something on there that could've cleared me."

"Or there could've been stuff on there that sealed your fate. I made a gut call and did what I thought was right. We don't need any more evidence that points to you." A crowd of tourists walked past them, fingers pointing in all directions. When they passed, Sean spoke again. "What else did you find from the investigation so far?"

"The shoe print on the rug came back. Nothing out of the ordinary. It's a Timberland boot. I forget the model number off the top of my head, but it was common enough to know it'd be a long shot. It's one of their bestselling boots."

"You have a pair of Timberlands," Sean replied, again watching the traffic round Kelly Drive. "This just keeps getting better."

"What should we do?"

"Don said Heckle and Keenan already ordered her phone records from the apartment and her cell. Your number's going to be on them. She called you the night she was killed, and you called her back the next day."

"Yeah."

"They're going to trace your number back to you, and when they do, the dominos start to fall. I'm telling you, you'll be charged with murder, and they'll stop looking for who really did this. No one's going to believe you're being framed when you have a goddamn scratch down your chest and your blood in Kerri's nails. You need to find a way to intercept those records, delete your number, and get them back to Heckle and Keenan. If you can bury that side, we can make this go away. Shred the fingerprint report and tell them it came up empty. If we let this go long enough without anything concrete, they'll file the case away unsolved."

"I don't want to make it go away. I want to find out who's trying to frame me. I want to find out who knows about me and Kerri and arrest them."

"We will," Sean replied. "But we have to do it on our own time. We don't need an open investigation that points to you and only you. As soon as someone catches wind about your affair, it's over. If there's this much evidence against you, they'll get a conviction. We need to make this go away, and then we can investigate on our own. Get the phone records."

20

The ride from the city to his home across the Delaware River normally took about thirty minutes, but tonight Liam sat in bumper-to-bumper gridlock as traffic crawled methodically across the Walt Whitman Bridge. Three lanes had been merged into one because of an accident involving multiple cars.

He dialed the technology division of the police department. Up ahead, he could see the flashing lights of emergency vehicles as the scene unfolded before him.

"Tech. Nelson here."

"Yeah, Nelson, this is Detective Heckle," Liam said. His voice shook as he spoke. "I'm lead on the Kerri Miller homicide. You guys were supposed to have some phone records for me. You get anything from the carriers yet?"

Tapping of computer keys.

"Nothing yet," Nelson replied. "Should have them before the night's out, but they're not in at this point. I'll email them to you when I get them."

"I need them as soon as possible. If I come in early tomorrow, you think they'll be there?"

"Yeah, should be. I'll get in touch with the phone company and light a fire."

"I'm counting on you, Nelson. My boss is up my ass about this report I need to complete."

"I'll get 'em to you by morning. I'm on it."

"Thanks."

"No sweat."

He hung up and flipped on the radio to listen to chatter while his mind wandered. It had been a few hours since he'd left Sean at the museum. There hadn't been much more conversation after they'd walked through the park and ended up back at the steps. What more could have been said? They needed to find out who was doing this before Heckle and Keenan found out about his affair.

He gripped the steering wheel, inching closer toward the flashing lights on the side of the bridge. His blood had ended up under her fingernails. He rubbed the scratch on his chest as a small whimper of doubt questioned how it had really gotten there. This was a game. A sick game. It had to be. But still, he couldn't remember anything from that night.

When he'd gotten back to his office after the museum, he'd erased the computer history of his identification match in the database and shredded the computer printout as Sean had instructed. Jane had called several times, but he had never answered. Tomorrow. He would handle it all tomorrow.

Horns sounded behind him as other drivers grew impatient now that the finish line was in sight. He was in the single lane, inching closer. He crawled past the flashing lights of the accident and stepped on the accelerator, merging with the rush of traffic, heading into the night, toward home, where Vanessa waited. He pulled the gold pendant from his pocket and let it sway back and forth between his fingers as he drove. The mini–magnifying glass represented another life, another time. He opened his window and threw it out onto the road. There was already far too much connecting him to Kerri. He needed to walk a fine line from now on.

After the traffic had spread out, the commute home was mundane. The sports chatter on the radio helped distract him for a few more minutes, and it wasn't long before he was pulling into his driveway as the sun was setting and turning the sky a brilliant combination of blue and pink.

Liam entered the house and was immediately surrounded by hundreds of votive candles dancing in the darkness. His senses were engulfed by lavender while R & B played from the stereo in the living room. He dropped his briefcase and stood dumbfounded in the foyer, staring at the tiny flickering flames strewn across the floor, balanced on tables, and lining the hallway. The rest of the house was dark. He followed the candles down the hall into the living room, where the fireplace crackled with romance. Vanessa was lying on the couch dressed in only a silk robe, the robe open and falling off her thin and toned body.

"Hey, stranger," she whispered seductively. "I thought you weren't gonna make it."

Liam feigned a smile, trying his hardest to get into the moment but knowing full well he wanted to be anywhere but there. "I hit some traffic. Accident on the bridge."

"Well, I'm glad you're home. Come over here, and let me show you how much I missed you today."

There was a time, years ago, when Liam wouldn't have been able to contain himself, but as he looked on, disinterested and distracted, he felt nothing. He wasn't turned on or shocked or appalled or disgruntled. He wasn't happy or sad or confused or ungrateful. He wasn't anything. Standing in front of his beautiful wife lying naked on the couch, waiting for him to take her, Liam wanted nothing more than to turn around, climb the stairs to his bedroom, and go to sleep. All he could see was Kerri's mangled body hanging from the pipes in that hotel room, and he fought off the tears that wanted to come. He heard the instructions from their marriage counselor echoing in his mind.

Be spontaneous.

Learn to love one another again.

Find each other.

Remember why you decided to spend your lives together, and let that fuel your newfound romance.

He walked toward Vanessa and knelt beside her. "I'm glad you're feeling better."

Vanessa smiled. "Like I said yesterday, I'm sorry for being a bitch. I wanted to make it up to you, and I figured since you owed me for lunch, this'll make us even."

"You didn't have to do all this. The candles and the music."

"I want to. I love you, Liam. No matter what we've gone through, I love you. You're the man I want to be with for the rest of my life. You and me. Forever."

She leaned in and kissed him slowly. He felt her lips touch his, but there was nothing he could do to take his mind off of Kerri. A part of him wished it was Kerri who was on that couch instead of his wife, and it pained him to admit that to himself. There was no love Liam could offer Vanessa that would be genuine. He backed away and stood. "I can't," he muttered. "Not tonight."

Vanessa looked stunned. "Wait, what? Why? What's wrong?"

"I just can't do this right now. I'm sorry. I love you, but I want to just go upstairs and go to bed."

In one swift motion, Vanessa sat up on the coach and pulled her robe closed. "You want to go to sleep?"

"I know it sounds crazy."

"Yes, it does."

"I'm sorry. It's not you. There's just too much going on at work, and I'm exhausted."

"Work? Is that what this is about? What's wrong with you? I set all this up, and you're not into it? You're tired? Last night you come home and didn't want to be bothered. The counselor said—"

"I know what the counselor said."

"If we're going to rebuild our marriage, I need you here with me. I love you. Don't you understand that?"

Vanessa tried to take his hand, but he pulled away. "I can't. I'm going to bed."

"You promised me. You promised you'd make it up to me for missing lunch."

"I know. And I will. Just not tonight."

He walked out of the living room and past the candles that had showed him the way. He could feel her staring at him, but he didn't care. All he could think about was Kerri and the fact that he was being framed for her murder.

21

His mother opened the front door, and already the house felt different. There was a silence he hadn't experienced before, a void of some kind. His father was dead—he knew that. But this was a different kind of emptiness. It was as if the spirit of the house—the good times and laughs and love and playfulness—had been snuffed out like the last embers of a fire that had burned for too long. There was a nothingness now, a desolation he couldn't comprehend at his age. But he knew it was there. He could sense it, smell it. And that scared him most of all.

She walked inside without saying anything, her black heels clicking on the hardwood floors. She took off her black coat and laid it across one of the wingback chairs in the living room and then dropped her black purse on the same chair. Sean came in behind her with Liam clutching his hand so tight it made his fingers white. Both boys stopped in the foyer. Sean watched his mother as she took off the small black hat and veil that had been bobby pinned to her head and tossed it on the coffee table, where piles of bills had been strewn about. As she staggered farther inside, she stripped herself of the remaining black clothes she'd been wearing until only her satin slip and stockings covered her. He didn't move until she disappeared into the kitchen.

Sean turned and closed the front door. The streetlights that lined the block were just beginning to come on. Dusk was upon them. The day was coming to a close. He pulled his brother upstairs and into his room to get him changed.

Liam had been quiet for most of the day. Neither of them had been allowed to attend their father's wake, so the funeral was the first time they'd had the opportunity to experience what had been, up to that point, only words and tears from others. They hadn't seen their father since he left that morning a few days ago to go to work. The casket at the funeral was closed. They hadn't had a chance to properly say goodbye.

During the funeral, Sean began to cry when the woman in the balcony of the church started singing her sad songs, but Liam was quiet. Even when friends and relatives tried to console Sean, Liam was off to the side, distant, detached. Perhaps he was too young to fully understand what was happening. He knew their father was dead, but how much could a five-year-old really comprehend death? Liam hadn't known him like Sean had, so the pain and the sadness would be limited. His little brother had been lucky in that regard.

Sean helped take off Liam's jacket and pants and unbuttoned his tiny white dress shirt. He fished his Rugrats pajamas from one of his dresser drawers and walked over to the bed where his little brother was sitting.

"Here," he said. "Put these on."

"I want Mom to help me," Liam replied quietly.

"She can't right now. We gotta do it."

"Why?"

"Because."

"Because she's sad?"

"Yeah."

"That Dad left her?"

"Yeah."

"I'm sad too."

Sean shook his head. "What do you know about being sad? You hardly knew him."

"I knew Dad! I loved him."

"Not like me and Mom. You're too young."

"I still miss him."

"I know."

Liam hopped off his bed and shuffled over to Sean in only his underwear. He hugged him and squeezed until Sean had to pull him away.

"Don't ever leave me," Liam whispered as he finally began to cry. "Don't die, Sean. I don't want you to die."

Sean knelt down so they were face-to-face. He used his thumb to wipe away Liam's tears. "I'm not going anywhere. And I'm not going to die. I won't leave you."

"Ever?"

"Ever. I'm your brother. You're stuck with me."

Liam tried to smile. "You're stuck with me too, then. Forever."

Sean rumpled Liam's hair. "Forever sounds good to me. It's a deal."

———

Sean pulled his red pickup truck into the driveway of his home in Blackwood, New Jersey, and shut off the engine. The house was an old craftsman, a little beat up from years of minimal upkeep. The grass was slightly overgrown with spring dandelions beginning to dot the landscape. He hopped out of the car and walked to the front, never noticing the imperfections his neighbors couldn't help but see. The house had been given to him after his grandparents died, a reward for helping raise Liam. It never felt like his, though. It was just a place he grew up in and now occupied mortgage-free. Just another hand-me-down. The busted front window and rusted doorframe remained.

The front door shut with a thud as he stepped into the empty house. He walked into the kitchen and turned on the light. Everything was so quiet. He'd been the one to meet Kerri first. He'd seen her leaning against the wall outside the women's room of a club, waiting for a friend, and had made his move. The conversation was quick but friendly. He'd offered his usual line about being a cop, and she'd bitten with the intrigue he was accustomed to. They talked and drank until the bar closed and the hours turned over the day. Numbers were exchanged, and an on-again, off-again relationship was formed. No sparks, just a little chemistry. A little fun.

Liam had met Kerri about two months after his brother, and unlike Sean's experience, the expressiveness of sexual attraction between the two of them was both unmistakable and immediate. Liam, deep within the trenches of a failing marriage and looking for a light at the end of his tunnel, had fallen head over heels for his brother's girlfriend, and Kerri had responded accordingly. Neither of them could help what they felt for one another, and both knew they were hurting Sean, but love conquered all, and they were no exception. Their relationship began the moment their eyes met.

Sean never had trouble dating women, but lasting and concrete relationships were few and far between. He did his best, but the inevitability of a breakup always seemed to preoccupy him until he used it as a crutch to let the relationship crumble.

Although he thought he could've loved Kerri, Sean convinced himself their relationship would've fizzled within a few months as all the others had; so giving her to Liam was fine. He was used to sacrificing for Liam. Kerri was no different a sacrifice from anything else he'd had to give up. It was all part of being a good brother and the leader of their little family.

Sean pulled his phone from his pocket and scrolled through his contacts list. When he found what he was looking for, he dialed.

"Tender Cares," a voice said on the other line. "How may I help you?"

Sean cleared his throat. "Yes, hi. I need to make an appointment to see Marisol Carpenter and her primary caretaker at the facility. I'd like to come tomorrow if I can."

"Are you family or friend?"

"Family," Sean replied. "We're family."

22

Back in 2008, during the peak of the financial crisis, Liam's team had been brought in on a homicide involving a young financial advisor who had been skimming his clients' accounts for almost a decade, while at the same time creating quite a lifestyle for himself. As the market declined, his clients had begun to withdraw their money from funds that were losing millions by the day, and it was then his scheme was discovered. It wasn't long before the man was found shot three times in the foyer of his home.

Partnering with Homicide and Forensics was the tech team from the police department. They had used a hacking device called rainbow tables to bypass the victim's password and gain access to his computer, thus providing client lists, emails, ledgers that tracked the amounts of stolen money throughout the years, and whatever else they needed. In the end, it had been an older woman, six years into retirement, who'd killed the financial advisor with her husband's illegal handgun. The tech team had uncovered several email exchanges between the woman and the advisor that had ended with threats, which ultimately steered the homicide detectives toward the woman, who eventually confessed. The investigation had lasted about three weeks, and Liam had ended up keeping a copy of the hacking software on a CD-ROM one of the team members had given him. He'd never imagined a scenario where he'd have to use it, but then again, he'd never imagined a scenario in which he'd be a murder suspect.

Operating systems didn't store a user's passwords in plain text. It would be too vulnerable to attack. Instead, they executed calculations through an algorithm called a hash and put the passwords through a one-way hash function for storage. Even if someone were to obtain these hashes, they would be rather useless as they'd be no more than symbols that meant nothing. The password would still need to be entered, after which the hash would need to be calculated and compared to the stored password hash. A rainbow table circumvented this requirement in a matter of seconds by matching against an enormous list of passwords with the respective hashes included. This allowed a hacker to get into a person's computer without having to delete or change a password. The victim would never know his or her system had been compromised, which was the beauty of the rainbow table. It was the skeleton key to a person's protected data, and it was exactly what Liam needed to pull off his latest move.

As dawn broke on a new day, the Homicide Division was relatively empty. There were a few detectives at their desks, but for the most part, the floor was dark and quiet with changeover from the midnight to day shift still about an hour away. Liam quietly slipped through the double doors and hid behind a row of filing cabinets. He made his way to the opposite end of the room and sidled up to the last row of desks in the far corner. Keenan's desk was one in from where he stood. He looked from behind the cabinets and saw two detectives, three rows away, hardly moving, their heads buried in their computer screens. The entire floor was deadly quiet. There was no way he could come out from where he was without being seen. One wrong step on the ancient hardwood floors and all heads would turn. It was too dangerous.

Plan B.

Liam retraced his steps, walked back out into the hallway, and made his way down to the first-floor back entrance, where he was alone. He leaned against the wall and ran through his contingency plan once more in his head.

There wouldn't be much time once things began. He'd have to act quickly and with purpose. The next few minutes could dictate the rest of his life.

The fire alarm was just outside the stairwell that led up to the second and third floors of the department. The nearest fire department was five blocks away, which meant arrival time would be about ten minutes. He'd have ten minutes to get this done. Anything more, and he'd be caught. And if he were caught, things would be revealed, which would mean the end of him trying to find the truth. Trembling fingers wrapped around the alarm's tiny glass handle. One more breath, then he pulled it.

Somewhere in the back of his mind, Liam knew the siren ripping through the station house was deafening, but his focus was solely on the metal stairs he climbed two at a time. When he got to the second floor, he was met by about a dozen officers and detectives making their way out of the green steel fire door and onto the stairs that would bring them to the lobby and out onto the street, where they would await further instructions. Liam could hear some of the men mumbling profanities under their breath while others wondered if the alarm was a drill or the real thing.

It took some effort to swim against the current of bodies pouring against him, but he stepped to the side and moved ahead as they passed by without so much as a glance. He waited until the last man remaining from the second floor began to make his descent and then ran down the hall into the Homicide Division, which was now void of anyone other than himself.

The clock was ticking. Liam scurried to Keenan's desk at the far end of the room and turned on his computer. In the moments it took the computer to boot up, he finally noticed the volume of the alarm as well as the flashing strobe lights coming from the fire monitors that were mounted on the walls.

The computer was on.

Unlike the simple method of copying files from a computer that Don had done on Kerri's laptop, this process required complete stealth and had to leave files intact. Keenan couldn't know Liam had ever touched his keyboard, let alone been inside his system. Therefore, this was a procedure that needed to be done physically at Keenan's desk. There was no other way around it, and time was of the essence.

Beads of perspiration slipped down his forehead as Liam took the CD from his pocket and placed it in the disc sleeve on the side of the laptop. He pushed the sleeve back in and checked his watch. Eight more minutes. By his estimation, the emergency responders were already suiting up, and an EMT unit was being dispatched from one of the area hospitals. This had to work quickly. Police personnel would stay out of the building until the fire department gave them the all clear, so he didn't need to worry about anyone else sneaking up on him. Still, the clock was ticking.

As soon as the CD loaded, a series of numbers and letters flashed onto the screen too fast for the human eye to keep up with. Alphanumeric combinations came, one after the other, in nanoseconds. After about two minutes, the screen went black, and then Keenan's desktop appeared. Liam slid the mouse over to the email file and clicked on it. The computer opened the file, and Keenan's inbox appeared. He was in.

Just as Nelson had promised, the phone records sat at the top of the list, unread. Liam clicked on the email and forwarded it to himself.

"Floor Captain!" a voice cried over the unrelenting alarm. "Anyone up here?"

Liam's heart skipped a beat as he slid off the chair he was sitting on. He hid the best he could while trying to delete the email from Keenan's inbox as well as delete the email he'd sent himself from the Sent file.

"Hello! Anyone here?"

The department had assigned several officers to be floor captains in the event of a fire drill. Their job was to be the last people out to ensure everyone else was evacuated and accounted for. He'd forgotten about them.

"Hello!"

Both emails were deleted. Fumbling hands moved the mouse over to the deleted files, and with a few key strokes, he purged those as well. Almost done.

The beam of a flashlight bounced off the wall as it approached from down the hall. It was time to go. Liam ejected the CD from the sleeve and shut down the computer. Just as he stood up, the flashlight hit him square in the chest.

"What're you doing here?" the floor captain asked.

The man behind the flashlight was an older sergeant he recognized by face, but he couldn't place the name. Liam made a circular motion with his hand. "All clear," he replied.

"What?"

"I already checked this floor. All clear."

"You're not a floor captain."

"Just trying to help. That alarm came out of nowhere. Wasn't sure if it was a drill or not."

The sergeant dropped his flashlight. "All right, let's get out of here. Follow me. FD's on its way. ETA one minute."

Liam followed the sergeant back down the hall, out the green fire door, and down to the first floor. When they got out into the street, he turned and walked in the opposite direction of where the rest of the precinct's personnel had gathered. He'd done it. The phone records were now in his inbox and deleted from Keenan's. He'd need to edit the records and resend to Keenan before noon. Otherwise, he'd risk Keenan calling down to place a rush himself. Timing was everything. His life depended on it.

23

There were still a few hours before he was due to show up at the station house, and with the extra time, Liam found himself turning off of Broad Street and onto Passyunk Avenue. The brick row homes he passed by brought a sense of joy as well as the familiar weight of dread. He'd spent the beginning of his childhood playing out on these very streets in endless games of stickball and tag and touch football and hockey. But with those memories came the nightmares of his father's death and his mother's attempted murder-suicide. South Philly always had an air of both joy and misfortune. Whenever he traveled through the streets here, he never quite felt at home, but he couldn't deny the comfort that was also there. It was unmistakable.

South Street Mission was nothing more than a redbrick facade, a metal door, and a small sign fastened to the side. There was ten-minute parking out front, so Liam knew there'd be a spot when he pulled up. The mission's tow policy was no joke. Outside, a few kids played hopscotch inside chalk boxes that had been drawn on the sidewalk. The chalk itself had almost been washed away by the recent rain, leaving a ghostly outline instead. Small puddles splashed up as the kids jumped from one end to the other. Liam pulled over, turned off the car, and decided, without really thinking, to go inside.

The aroma from inside the mission was always the same no matter how many times he'd walked through those doors: bleach, finger paint, and paste. It was one of the most distinctive smells in the city, and it hadn't changed for more than two decades. The mission had originally been founded as an after-school program, daycare facility, and meeting room for support groups or hobby clubs or whomever wanted to rent the space. After the tech bubble burst in 2000, and then again after the housing crash in 2008, the mission had converted itself into a homeless shelter and food pantry, eliminating the space for clubs but keeping the after-school program and half of its daycare. It was a place of peace. There was a sense of calm here.

Liam walked down the hallway into the administration office to find Father Brennan sitting alone behind a desk filled with stacks of paperwork—so much so, the desk's wood surface was completely hidden. Father Brennan was short and pudgy. He was pushing seventy. His face looked like pink Play-Doh, with cheeks so round the older women in his congregation couldn't help but squeeze them as they exited his service each week after Sunday mass. A full head of silver hair was still intact. His green eyes shone. The priest was beloved in the neighborhood, a staple at Saint Agnes, and helped run the mission. There wasn't a soul in South Philly who had a bad thing to say about him.

"Liam!" Father Brennan shouted when he saw him standing outside the office. He rose from his chair and scurried around to wrap his boy in a giant hug. "How are you?"

Liam couldn't help but smile as he was engulfed in the old man's embrace. "I'm good, Father. I'm good."

"Come in. Sit! Sit!"

For a brief time after their father died, and on a more regular basis after their mother had been taken away, Liam and Sean had been enrolled in the mission's after-school program. At that time, Father Brennan had still been fairly new to the parish, but his overwhelming sense of joy and ability to see the good in every situation had made him someone the boys had gravitated to and admired. As the years passed, despite living across the river with their grandparents, both brothers had become altar boys at Saint Agnes, and they still kept in touch through letters and an occasional visit. Liam hadn't been back in years. It felt good to be there again.

"So what brings you by?" Father Brennan asked as he sat back behind his desk, sliding one of the paper stacks to the side so he could face his visitor. "It's been so long. You passing through the neighborhood?"

"I guess you can say that, although truth be told, I pass by the neighborhood every day on my way into work. I guess I just decided to pop in this time. Sorry to come unannounced."

"Nonsense! You never have to be sorry about coming here. You're always welcome. How's Sean? And Vanessa? Tell me!"

"Good. Everybody's doing good."

Father Brennan took his glasses from the desk and put them on. He stared at Liam for a moment. "Well, now," he said. "That's a half-truth if I ever heard one. Something's troubling you. I can see it. Just like I was able to see it when you were little. Nothing's changed. Talk to me, boy. What's on your mind? Consciously or not, you wouldn't have stopped by unless you wanted to talk. You might've driven here, but trust me, God steered. Out with it."

Liam's head sank. "You always could see right through me."

"A gift."

"I recently lost someone close to me. A friend. She was killed."

Father Brennan bowed his head for a moment. "I'm sorry to hear that."

"I'm completely torn up. I can't sleep. Can't think straight. When I close my eyes, all I see is her face. I have this void in my soul, this emptiness."

"It sounds like she meant a lot to you."

"She did."

"When did you hear the news?"

"Couple days ago."

The priest shrugged. "Give it time. Don't run from the memories you had with this person, but don't let them cripple you either. You'll mourn her the way you're supposed to, but you can't allow it to take over your life."

Liam closed his eyes and rubbed his forehead. He could feel a headache coming on. "There's so much violence in this world. So much death. The way she was killed got me thinking about my own life. Like, what drives people to commit these acts? This is the kind of stuff I investigate all the time. Homicide shouldn't be something you build a career off of. You ever stop to think about the evil in this world?"

Father Brennan chuckled. "Of course. The evil in this world can seem quite overwhelming sometimes, but we have a choice to give in to it or not. For example, you choose to see evil because you're tasked with bringing murderers to justice. People who watch television see evil because that's what sells, so that's all the media shows them. Me, I choose to see life. I see the joy of a new mother holding her child for the first time. I hear the laughter of newlyweds as they walk down the church aisle together as husband and wife. I see the joy of a family getting together for the holidays. These are the things that give me hope. I've seen the dark side too. More times than I wish to count. But I balance it with the good. I suggest you do the same. Evil is part of this world, as it's part of your job, and it will remain so until the end of days, I'm afraid. You need to counterbalance it with the good. Find the good."

Liam met the priest's eyes. "You ever notice a violent side of me growing up? Like a darker side? A side that might've been affected by how my dad died or what happened with Mom? Anything like that?"

"No. Never. Not once."

"What about Sean?"

"No. Sean can be more serious, but his heart is pure. What I've seen from the both of you are caring, nurturing, mature young men who are still full of love. You're a good person, Liam. Sean too. Always have been."

Liam checked his watch and rose from his chair. "I think that's all I needed to hear, to be honest. I need to get to work."

"You and Vanessa okay?"

Father Brennan didn't know about the issues he and Vanessa had gone through. Liam was determined to keep it that way. "Yeah, we're fine. I think I just needed to hear you say it was okay for me to mourn in my own way. I also needed to hear that I'm a good person. The stuff I see, it can throw you for a loop."

"Don't doubt yourself. You're a fine lad, and you'll find peace in your friend's memory."

"Thanks for always being there for me. For me and Sean."

"I serve the Lord," Father Brennan replied with a beaming smile plastered upon his pink face. "Anything you need for as long as I'm on his planet, I'm here."

"Thank you."

"And don't forget to find the good. That's the key to everything."

Liam's phone rang. He pulled it out of his pocket and stared at the screen. It was Sean.

"I gotta take this," he said.

Father Brennan waved him away. "Go. Do what you need to do. Bring justice to the world."

Liam walked out of the priest's office and answered on the third ring. "Yeah, I'm here."

"Where are you?" Sean asked.

"South Street Mission."

"What the hell are you doing there?"

"To be honest, I'm not sure."

"You get the phone records?"

"Yeah, I got 'em." Liam pushed through the metal door out onto the street. "I'll download them when I get into the office. It's still too early for me to go in. It'll look weird if I show up now."

"Meet me at the Liberty Diner in ten minutes. I got us an appointment to talk to Marisol and her nurse. You wanna know if Don really did go see his mother Saturday night?"

Liam climbed into his car and started the engine. "Yes."

"Good. We're going to go there and ask her. You and me."

Liam put the car in gear and pulled out into traffic. "Liberty Diner, ten minutes. I'm on my way."

24

Tender Cares Adult Living Facility looked like a typical condo complex from the outside, uniform and plain with beige siding on all the structures and black shutters on all the windows. Each door was red, and every front yard had a flagstone walkway that cut through the grass to the sidewalk. The roads were fresh blacktop, and the trees were all still in their infancy. The place had been built only three years prior and hadn't begun to show the wear and tear of seasons gone by. Everything was still so sterile.

Liam pulled around the man-made lake and noticed a cluster of geese floating atop the glassy surface. The scene looked peaceful with the backdrop of budding cherry trees stretching out into a small forest. He made a left onto the first street and stopped in front of 1432, a corner unit that was two stories and adjacent to the community pool area.

Sean got out of the car without saying a word. They hadn't spoken much since Liam picked him up at the diner. The ride to Doylestown had been long and awkward with only superficial questions being bandied about to dot the otherwise endless landscape of quiet.

Marisol Carpenter, Don's mother, was standing at the front door, arms outstretched, waiting to embrace her boys. Her hair was a cluster of white curls, grown down past her ears but not quite touching her shoulders. She was old-age slender, her skin hanging in places it hadn't when she was younger. Her lips were thin, and the way her cheekbones poked out from under her glasses made her face seem longer than it really was. She looked fragile, but at the moment, she seemed very much alive.

"My boys are here!" she cried as she scooped Sean into a mighty hug. "It's so good to see you! Been too long. Too long!"

Sean hugged her back and rubbed her shoulders. "It's good to see you, Marisol. You're right. It's been way too long."

"And my Liam is here. Hello! Come give Mama a hug and a kiss."

Liam did as he was told, and she pulled him close. "How's Vanessa?"

"She's fine."

"I'm so glad to see you."

"Me too, Marisol."

She grabbed Liam by the hand and pulled him inside. Sean followed and shut the door behind them.

The inside of the condo looked as if it was still in the process of being moved into, despite Don having moved his mother from her home in Cherry Hill over a year ago. It had the essentials—seats to sit in, a table to eat on, utensils to cook with, and pots and pans to cook in—but for the most part, the place was bare. Aside from an oversized picture collage of Marisol's family hanging above a gas fireplace, the walls were empty. A love seat, two wingback chairs, and a round coffee table took up the small living room. A kitchen table and an antique secretary's desk she'd taken from her home filled the dining area. Other than that, there was nothing.

"Can I get you boys something to drink? You hungry?"

"We're fine," Liam replied.

He followed Marisol into the living room and thought about bringing her up some things to decorate with next time he visited. A few picture frames. Some art for the walls. Curtains. Something.

A younger woman sitting in one of the wingback chairs stood when they entered. She looked to be in her late thirties and had olive skin, black hair that hung to the midway point of her back, and brown eyes. She was wearing green scrubs with a white lab coat over them.

"This is my nurse," Marisol said, pointing to the young woman. "Adena Khan. She takes very good care of me."

Adena extended her hand, and Liam shook it.

"It's nice to meet you," she said.

Liam smiled. "We appreciate you meeting with us."

He sat down on the love seat, and Sean sat next to him after also shaking the young woman's hand. Marisol plopped into the other wing-back chair, and Adena returned to hers.

"How have you been, Marisol?" Sean asked.

The old woman shrugged. "Good, I guess. I can't complain. I mean I could, but no one would pay me no mind."

"They treating you okay here?"

"It's an assisted living facility. I call them when I need them. They assist. It's fine." She reached over and patted Adena on the knee. "And my nurse has been wonderful. The things she puts up with. An angel!"

Sean leaned forward in his seat, resting his arms on his knees. "Marisol, we need to ask you a few questions about this past Saturday night, and I'm hoping you can remember. Because of the HIPAA laws and patient confidentiality, I couldn't get any information over the phone. We're not family."

"Nonsense," Marisol replied. "You're family as far as I'm concerned."

"Not blood. But that's okay. I just need to ask you these questions, and if you give your permission, I can ask Ms. Khan a few as well."

"You know you can ask me anything you want. Go."

Sean cleared his throat. "I want you to tell me about the episode you had on Saturday night. You woke up confused? Had to call Don?"

Marisol looked away from Sean for a moment. An expression of determination overcame her as if she was willing the memory to come, forcing it back into her mind. She looked back at the brothers. "I think I remember. Yes, I'm pretty sure my Don had come to see me."

"So Don came up?"

"Yes, I think so." She turned to Adena. "Did my son come up Saturday night?"

The nurse opened a file that was sitting on her lap. "It looks like your son checked in on Saturday night at 11:16 and checked out at 1:34."

"So he was here a few hours," Marisol said.

"Yes," Adena replied. "He helped get you back into bed and then stayed to make sure you weren't waking up again."

"I had an episode?"

"You woke up and were confused where you were. You were scared and rang your call button, but you wouldn't let the night nurses help you. You kept asking for Don, so we called him."

Marisol shook her head. "I'm so embarrassed. I make such a fool of myself sometimes. I cause these good people too much trouble."

"Nothing to be embarrassed about," Sean replied.

"I guess one of the perks of Alzheimer's is you can't remember every time you act like an ass."

"I think we're good here," Sean said. "We just needed to double-check where Don was that night."

"Why?" Marisol asked. "He in trouble?"

"No. We got a case that morning and just have to verify his whereabouts. Standard procedure."

"All this way just for a few questions?"

"I'm afraid so."

"Stay for coffee."

"I'm sorry, but we can't. We have to get back to the city. This case can't wait."

The two brothers got up from the love seat and made their way to the door. Marisol followed them out, gave them their hugs and kisses, and walked them all the way to their car. When they were driving back past the pond to leave the complex, Sean spoke.

"So I guess that rules Don out."

Liam shrugged. "Yes and no."

"How do you figure? We just confirmed his whereabouts."

"His visit still is within the general time frame of Kerri's time of death. Plus you said he was late to your crime scene that Sunday morning."

"It's a long drive."

"Maybe."

Sean shook his head. "Look, Don's clean. There's no way he killed Kerri. Why would he? Think about it. He has no motive for any of this."

"Okay, but we don't have many suspects who know what we know about Mom and what she did to us and my affair with Kerri."

"We need to find motive. Who has motive to kill Kerri and do all this?"

Liam turned onto the main road that would lead them back to the turnpike. "So far, the only person I can see who has motive to kill Kerri is me. That's the scary part. She breaks it off. I want her back. She won't take me, so I kill her. Or she tells me she's pregnant, and I kill her to keep it from Vanessa."

Sean leaned his head back on the seat. "You just recited the two oldest motives in the book."

25

Liam dropped Sean back at the Liberty Diner and went to the station house. Don was on the far end of the Homicide Division, next to the wall of file cabinets. Liam made his way through the floor and tapped his friend on his back.

"You got a minute?"

Don turned around and closed the drawer he'd been flipping through. "Yeah, what's up?"

"I wanted you to hear this from me or Sean, and since Sean's on mandatory leave, I'm here."

"Okay. What is it?"

"I know you've been in on this Kerri thing, and I appreciate you helping us out."

"It's fine."

"I'm not sure how much Sean told you about what's happening, but it looks like someone is trying to frame me for her murder. I don't know how, but they have my prints at the scene and my blood type in Kerri's nails. We're trying to find out who could know about our past with my mother and why they're trying to tie Kerri's murder to me. So far, I'm coming up empty."

"So you need my help?"

Liam shook his head. "No. You're one of my suspects."

"What?"

"There aren't many people who know about what happened with my mom and that I was having an affair with Kerri. Whoever killed

Kerri keeps leaving clues that tell us they know everything. You're one of those people."

Don fell against the file cabinet. "Hold on. After all we've been through, you think I could kill someone in cold blood and then try and pin it on you? Why would I do something like that? I hardly knew Kerri."

"I don't know why, but only you, me, Sean, and Kerri knew everything. Kerri's dead, and I'm the one being framed. Sean's working his ass off to get me out of this jam. That leaves you."

"That's the biggest crock of bull I've ever heard."

"Me and Sean went to see your mother this morning. We confirmed you went to see her Saturday night, but the time you were there and left makes you available in Kerri's TOD window."

"You went to see my mother?"

"Yeah."

"Are you even listening to yourself?" Don asked. "I'm the one helping Sean make this all go away. If I killed her and wanted to expose you, I could've done it with all the stuff I took from her apartment. You're not making any sense."

"Why were you late to the Cutter Washington homicide Sunday morning?"

"I got home from my mother's and fell asleep."

Liam said nothing.

Don leaned in and lowered his voice. "Listen, you son of a bitch, I'm helping you and Sean make this go away. For you. Whether you really are being framed or you had some kind of massive break and killed Kerri, I'm helping to make this go away so you don't become a suspect in your girlfriend's murder. Isn't that enough? What more loyalty do I need to prove? And why would I kill her? What do I have to gain from it? You were the one having an affair. You're trying to rebuild your marriage with Vanessa. Kerri tells you she's pregnant. Now she's dead. That's motive, Liam. Textbook."

"I know, I—"

"Get away from me."

Don pushed off the cabinet and walked back to his desk without saying anything further.

Liam watched him go. There was nothing more to say. Everyone he loved was trying to help him, but he wasn't sure whom he could truly trust.

26

The computer screen was the only light on in Liam's office. He'd drawn the shade over his window and turned off the overhead fluorescents. His door was shut. He needed to be alone and give the illusion that the office was empty. The screen showed Kerri's phone records. His cell must've been on there more than twenty times, and her outgoing calls and texts also included his information, with the most recent being the night of her murder. He went through each line, deleting his number and any trace that he knew the victim of his own murder investigation. When he was done, he'd pass the records to Heckle and Keenan and have them investigate whatever else was on there. It would appear as if everything was moving status quo with the case. In a matter of weeks, if not days, they would find nothing and close the case unsolved, putting this all behind them. Sean was right. Better to be done with it and move on quietly so they could investigate on their own and find whoever was doing this.

Liam clicked though the phone records, line by line, deleting evidence as he went. The next number he saw stopped him in his tracks as he sat up and stared at it. He recognized it instantly, his cursor flashing on and off in front of it, waiting for its next command.

Sean's number.

Liam traced the dates. Sean had called Kerri two days before she was murdered. Why? They hadn't talked in a long time. At least, that's what Kerri had told him. He scanned through the earlier portion of the month and saw Sean's number three more times. Kerri's outbound calls had Sean's home number once. They'd been talking throughout the month. Neither of them had ever mentioned anything.

Only you, me, and Don know about everything.

Liam hit the button to activate the printer and then deleted his brother's numbers along with his own. Tampering with evidence was a crime. This was beyond that. This was tampering to clear his name as a primary suspect in a homicide. If anyone found out what he was doing, he'd be sent to jail for a long time. But now there was something new to investigate. He had to find out why Sean had been calling Kerri.

The cell phone rang. Liam fished it from his pocket. "Liam Dwyer."

"It's Jane. Where are you?"

"Uh, almost at the office. Where are you?"

Jane's voice was excited. "I'm at the bureau. You're not going to believe this, but NCIC got a hit already on our off-line search."

"Talk to me."

"Like you said, we started with Philadelphia as a drop point and circled our way out. The system picked up a match in Delaware. Two hours away. Prostitute was found six weeks ago, hanged in a motel in a downtown section of Wilmington."

"Yeah, hanged is common enough. We don't know—"

"No," Jane continued. "Let me finish. She was hanged *and* her hair all cut off."

Liam fell back into his seat. "You're kidding me."

"It's him. It's gotta be. Nothing about a stomach slashing, but this is too much of a coincidence for it not to be our guy. Wilmington Homicide filed it away unsolved. As far as they were probably concerned, it was one less hooker on the street they needed to deal with. It was filed and forgotten."

"Almost an exact match," Liam whispered more to himself than Jane. "So I assume no autopsy was done?"

"No."

"Wondering if she was drugged like our vic."

"You want me to call down there? Have her exhumed and autopsied?"

"Yeah. And tell them we're heading down there ourselves. I think you're right. This could be the same guy. Let me write it up, and then we'll take a ride tomorrow. Gonna start making calls now."

Liam hung up the phone and sent the edited phone records back to Heckle and Keenan through an email. He told them that he'd inadvertently gotten the records instead of them and he was forwarding. They wouldn't ask any follow-up questions. Things like that happened all the time. When he was done, he let the silence of his office envelop him. Another victim. Sean's number in Kerri's phone records. Why? The questions continued to mount.

27

Liam walked along the dock slowly and carefully, searching for something that could help him remember where he was the night Kerri was murdered. After he'd sent the phone records back to Heckle and Keenan, he'd driven to the marina to see if something could help him put the pieces of that night back together. It was raining again, and small whitecaps crested, one after the other, as the wind howled and the river turned rough. The air was cool, and he was shivering, but he continued on, moving methodically, still feeling the wooden platform shifting underneath, still knowing that such movement was impossible.

Sean had mentioned the sweatshirt he had supposedly come back to the boat for the night Kerri was killed. He hadn't seen anything that Sunday night when he was with his brother, but it had been dark then, and he hoped something inside the cabin might point him in the right direction now that there was daylight. He was well aware he was grasping at straws, but he was desperate to gain some piece of his memory back.

Along the dock, on the way out to the boat slips, there was a tackle shop, a small café, and a souvenir shop lined up side by side. In front of the café, under the protection of a somewhat tattered awning, an old Asian man sat on a milk carton with a young Asian boy, his grandson. They were both dressed in bright-yellow parkas, the man snapping pictures with a Polaroid as folks passed by, the young boy calling out to them to purchase the picture his grandfather had just taken. This was Grandpa and Kiki. They were a staple at the dock, and he and Sean had grown to know them over the years as many of the boat owners had.

One picture, one dollar. Everyone got their photo taken. Not everyone bought. Rumor had it that Grandpa had a way of getting free film from a warehouse that housed audio and visual equipment. Liam wasn't sure how Grandpa pulled this off and was certain he didn't want to know. Let the man and the boy make their living. This wasn't what he would consider a crime worth looking into.

Liam passed them without looking up. The rain was stabbing at him now as it blew sideways. He pulled his hood tighter and made his way down the steps to slip 28, where the boat was waiting. Sean had put the cover over the wheelhouse and fishing platform to protect it from the weather. In order to come aboard, Liam would have to unsnap the corner and climb through. His hands were slippery on the rope that acted as a railing.

"What are you doing?" he asked himself aloud.

His feet refused to move any farther. He shook with adrenaline, staring at the boat's hull as it rocked up and down in the heavy surf. One slip and he would fall into the water that knew of his fear and so relentlessly reached out for him time and again. He closed his eyes into slits and stepped onto the rear platform of the boat, balancing himself as he rocked with the waves. His fumbling hands unsnapped the corner of the cover as fast as they could. The whitecaps nipped at the heels of his shoes again as he stood on the swim platform, catching him on the ankle so he could feel the icy temperature of a winter just past. He steadied himself as he slid under the canopy, belly flopping on board. Outside, the rain thumped against the plastic. Inside, his heart thumped much louder.

He used the flashlight on his phone to look around, trying to recall anything, but again nothing came. The boat rocked in the angry current as he continued into the cabin. No memory was triggered that could help him in his quest. He looked at the couch that converted to a bed and thought about his time there with Kerri. They had come to the boat to make love on several occasions. Despite his fear of the water, she'd always made him feel comfortable, safe. He shut his eyes and thought he could still smell her perfume and their sweat floating in the air. Oh, how he missed her. He searched for a single spark that might tell him something, but it was as if he were seeing the boat for the first time. No memories from Saturday night came forth.

As Liam was turning to leave, his flashlight caught a piece of metal shining in the corner of the hull where the tabletop folded down into the floor for the bed. He leaned in and saw something sticking out from between the cushions on the couch. It looked like a small metal chain or perhaps one of Sean's fishing lures. He reached over and untangled it from the fabric, then held it up to the light.

It was Vanessa's charm bracelet.

The chrome from one of the charms was what had caught his eye. He turned it around in his hand and recognized the tiny medical bag that represented her profession, the cross that reminded her of her mother, and the angel that represented her mother watching over her. What had Vanessa been doing on Sean's boat?

Vanessa doesn't know about Kerri.

Motive.

Only you, me, and Don know about everything.

Liam carefully climbed out of the boat and refastened the cover to keep the rain out. He scurried back up the stairs toward land and hurried into the tackle shop. Inside, Bud Statler, the owner, sat behind the counter watching an old tube television that was propped up on a stool. There was no one else in the store.

"Hey, Liam!" Bud called when he walked in. "Where's Sean?"

"Just me today."

"Trying your luck in the rain? I hear they've been biting."

"You know I don't go out on the water."

Bud smiled. "Oh, yeah. Right." He hopped off his seat and leaned over the counter. "What can I get for you then? T-shirt maybe?"

The store was quiet. "Listen," Liam began. "I gotta ask you a strange question, so bear with me."

"Go ahead."

"Was I here the other day? Do you remember seeing me on Saturday?"

Bud shook his head. "No, I don't think you've been in here since last season. I haven't seen you. Why?"

Liam tried on a smile he was sure didn't work. "Had a good time drinking and can't remember a thing. Trying to retrace my steps. Sean thought I might've come to the boat."

"A blackout!" Bud shouted. There was a hint of admiration in his eyes now. Perhaps the land lover wasn't so bad after all. "Oh, man, I've been there before, my friend. Been there too many times." He laughed and smiled. "But no, didn't see you. If you came by the dock, you didn't come in here."

"Okay, thanks."

"If you find out what happened, let me know. We'll trade stories."

Liam waved and walked out as Bud was still laughing. The traffic from the bridge above was a constant droning. He had started back to his car when the Asian man, Grandpa, began calling to him in his native tongue. Liam waved but kept moving. He wasn't in the mood to pay for pictures in the rain.

Kiki ran up to him. "Mr. Liam!" he cried. "Mr. Liam, wait!"

"No pictures today, Kiki. Maybe some other time."

"My grandfather is asking where your lady is?"

"She's not here."

Kiki stepped in front of Liam to stop his progress. "She promised to buy our pictures when you were here on Saturday, but we haven't seen her. Is she still going to buy them?"

"What lady are you talking about?"

"The lady you come here with."

"She was here the other day?"

"Yes."

"When?"

"Saturday. With you."

"Show me the pictures."

Kiki walked Liam over to his grandfather and spoke to the old man in Cantonese. Grandpa picked up a metal box and opened it, rifling through what must have been hundreds of pictures from people who'd refused to pay.

"It's one dollar for one picture," Kiki explained.

"I know how much it is." Liam took out a five and handed it over. "Are you sure it's me you want?"

"Mr. Liam and his girl. No Mr. Sean."

The old man pulled out two pictures. Liam took them and couldn't believe what he was seeing. In one picture it was just him. The other showed Kerri, both taken without them realizing it. Kerri was looking past the camera at the water, and in his, he was almost completely turned away. The sky above each of them in the photo was clear and blue. He'd been with Kerri four days ago. The photographs confirmed it.

He'd been with her the day she was murdered.

"You're sure these were taken four days ago? On Saturday?"

Kiki nodded. "Four days. Grandpa take picture, and your girl says she will buy them next day. Now we don't see her. Cost is two dollars. One picture, one dollar. You have two pictures there. Two dollars."

Liam nodded and turned to walk away.

"Wait! You want change?"

"Keep it."

"Thank you! Come again!"

Kerri was smiling in her picture, just as she'd always been. She was with him the day she was murdered. He was with her. Now she was dead.

What was happening?

28

Don climbed the winding driveway toward the sprawling six-bedroom colonial that sat perched atop a rocky hill. The rain had subsided, and the sky was gray with thick clouds hovering low in the atmosphere. He was angry about Sean and Liam going behind his back to check on his whereabouts with his mother, but he was furious that Liam thought he could have anything to do with Kerri's murder. All the years spent nurturing those boys, and now one of them—if not both of them—thought he could be capable of such a heinous act. If he had to clear his name, so be it. He had nothing to hide. He'd clear up any lingering suspicion they might have. Not a problem.

The file he'd pulled was from Heckle and Keenan's witness list. There was no question he was stepping on toes coming up here without anyone knowing, but it was time to do some digging himself.

He parked at the foot of the pathway that led to the porch and climbed out of the car, taking a final look at the sheet of paper in his hand and matching the number on one of the pillars with the address from the computer printout. Satisfied, he folded the paper back in his pocket and walked along the path toward the front door. He ascended the stairway, then listened as his heels scraped and clicked on the porch's hollow flooring below. He had no idea what to expect or how much information he could uncover after Heckle and Keenan had already been through here. But he had to do something.

He rang the bell and could hear noise inside. A middle-aged man opened the front door and stepped forward. "Detective Carpenter?"

"Yes, sir."

The man shook Don's hand. "Russ Wilcox. Tina's father. Please, come in."

Don followed Russ through the small foyer. "I appreciate you seeing me."

"The other detectives have already been by, and the girls told them everything they knew."

"I understand. I just have some follow-up questions that might help in the investigation. This won't take long."

"Anything we can do. The girls are inside."

"How are they holding up?"

Slumping his shoulders, Russ stopped and turned around. "This was a shocker," he said. "I don't know that they'll ever be completely okay. They were close friends. I don't think it's really hit them yet."

"I see."

"They seem to think it's their fault Kerri's dead. They think if they didn't leave her at the club, she'd still be alive."

"What do you think?"

"I think young people do dumb things, and if that means going off by yourself with someone you don't know or leaving a friend at a club without calling the police, then those are the unfortunate lessons others learn from. Makes me sick to know Kerri had to learn her lesson the way she did." Russ shook off any remaining thoughts. "Look, I didn't get a lawyer. You think I'm going to need one?"

"That won't be necessary. This is just routine."

"They're in the living room."

Tina Wilcox and Megan Curry were sitting together on the sofa when Don and Russ entered. They looked up at him as he sat on the love seat, opposite the girls. The two young women held one another, their shoulders touching, their hands clasped together. They waited as Don read over his notes in silence. Megan held a picture of Kerri in her free hand, absently rubbing it with her thumb. It was clear they were both devastated. Crumpled and discarded tissues, black with mascara and moist with tears, created a small pile next to the girls on one of the end tables.

"My name is Detective Carpenter," Don began.

"I'm Tina, and this is Megan," the first young woman said, grabbing another tissue from the half-empty box.

Don pointed to Tina. "You were the one who left the messages on Kerri's voice mail? The investigating officers pulled it from her home phone."

"Yes. I called once at the club and once when we got home. We also left a bunch of messages on her cell. I even called her the other day, after they told us what happened. I know it's stupid, but I needed to hear her voice again, so I called her cell and waited for it to go to her voice mail."

"You stated you guys got into the club around nine o'clock?"

"Yes, around nine. We got something to eat in Center City at, like, six and had to wait on the line for about twenty minutes, so I think nine o'clock would be a pretty good guess."

Don finished writing and turned his attention to the other girl. "Megan, tell me what happened when you entered the club. I know you already went through this with the other detectives, but think for a moment. Did you see anyone you knew? Did you go for a drink? Tell me what happened while you were all together."

Megan rubbed Kerri's picture as she rested her head on Tina's shoulder. "We got in and went to the bar. We each had a drink and hung out for a few songs. We danced together, got another drink, and then these two guys came up to me and Tina and asked us if we wanted to dance. We said yes and went. That's the last time we saw Kerri. When we got back to the bar, she was gone. We figured she was dancing. We spent the rest of the night dancing too, figuring we'd run into her eventually. The place is pretty big. It's not unusual to get separated during the night. I guess we started to wonder where she was by midnight."

"When did you start to look for her?"

"We hung out at the bar for, like, four songs and looked around the place from where we were. We didn't see her. Then we went into the lounge and onto the dance floor to find her. We checked the bathrooms and even got a guy to check the men's room. She wasn't anywhere. That's when I called the first time."

"You didn't call anyone else?"

"No."

"What then?"

"Me and Megan spent the rest of the night looking for her. We checked the parking lot and in the backs of cars. We couldn't find her anywhere. When the place closed, we got a bouncer to help us look, but he didn't seem to care. He told us she probably hooked up and to go home and call her in the morning. I called when I got home that night. I didn't want to wait until morning."

"Did it ever occur to either of you to call the police?" Don asked.

Both nodded. "That's what I said on one of the last messages," Tina replied. "We wanted to call the police but decided against it. I mean, what if she did go home with someone? How embarrassing would it be to be having sex and the cops come knocking on your door because your friends got worried? I told her to call us. Next thing I know, the police came here to tell me what happened. I called Megan, and the police were there too."

Tina began to cry again, and Megan held her. Don sat back and waited to ask his next question. This would indeed be a life lesson neither would ever forget. "Girls, do you remember seeing anyone there who looked familiar? Someone who might've had an interest in Kerri?"

Megan shook her head. "No."

Tina did the same. "No."

"Do you know if she had a boyfriend?"

"She was seeing some guy, but we never met him. Never even saw him before. We used to tease her that he never really existed."

"So you have no idea what he looks like?"

"No."

"Not even a name?"

"Sorry, no."

Kerri had kept her affair with Liam quiet. To not even know his name was unusual. "Did she see this mystery boyfriend a lot?"

Tina blew her nose and shrugged. "Enough, I guess. Not every day, all day, but a few times a week. She said they broke up, but they still hung out sometimes."

"Did you ever find it funny she wouldn't tell you his name or introduce you to him?"

"The guy was having an affair with Kerri. He was married. That's all she'd tell us and asked us not to pry. We let her keep her secrets."

"Interesting," Don replied.

"Do you think the boyfriend did it?" Megan asked.

"I don't know."

"The other detectives think it might've been the boyfriend. They said that was where they were starting their investigation. I wish we could tell you more about him."

It was clear the girls couldn't shed any new light. Don rose from his seat and gathered his papers. He handed them each a business card. "If you think of anything else, I want you to call me."

Tina rose. Megan remained seated. "Thanks," Tina said. "Please find the person who did this. I know Kerri won't rest until they're caught, and we won't either."

"We're trying."

Megan sighed and tried to steady herself. "Have you talked to Kerri's parents yet?" she asked.

"No. I think the other officers are handling that."

"If you do talk to them, tell them we're praying for them."

"I will."

29

Liam took a step back when he saw his brother's face. Sean was standing on the threshold, leaning against the door he'd just opened, his eyes dreary and red. The porch light reflecting off the shadows of the dark afternoon made his skin look pale.

"What happened?" Liam asked. "You okay?"

"Yeah, I'm fine. Come in."

The house was neat but dusty. Sean kept very few items above and beyond the necessities. When their grandparents had passed, he'd called the local library and had them send a truck over so he could donate all of their grandmother's books. Then he'd called for a dumpster and trashed anything he wouldn't need. There was a coldness to the house amid all the emptiness. Liam had never quite gotten used to that.

"I called you a few times," Liam said. "Where'd you go after I dropped you off at the diner?"

"Came back here. I was in the yard most of the day. Didn't have my phone with me. Was doing a lot of thinking."

"About what?"

"What do you think? I can't believe all this is happening with Kerri. And you. It got to me."

They made their way into the living room, where Sean sat on the couch and grabbed for the bottle of Jack Daniel's on the coffee table.

"We got a hit on NCIC. Found a victim in Delaware. Homicide was from six weeks ago. Prostitute. Same MO that was in Kerri's homicide except no stomach laceration."

Sean stared at him for a moment, then slowly took another sip from the bottle. "And?"

"And what?"

"Were you in Delaware at the time of the homicide?"

"Of course not. I haven't been to Delaware in years. Last time we passed through was on our way to the Outer Banks. What was that—six years ago? Seven?"

"That helps with things, I guess. Can you think of anyone who's been to Delaware recently?"

"I've been wracking my brain since I heard the news. Nothing."

"What was the date when the murder down there took place?"

Liam clicked through his phone to see the notes Jane had sent him. "Body was discovered February fifteenth. Homicide took place the night before, February fourteenth. Valentine's Day."

Sean shook his head and took another sip. "Back to square one."

"What do you mean?"

"I hate to break it to you, but Vanessa was in Atlantic City at a medical conference that weekend. I remember because you went on and on about how you guys were going to miss your first reconciled Valentine's Day. You were alone that weekend."

Liam let the facts sink in. "I can't catch a break here. This is unreal."

Sean looked at his brother, who was still standing. "Can I ask you a question? Man to man?"

"Yeah, sure."

"Are you messing with me?"

Liam stared back at Sean. "What do you mean?"

"I mean, are you messing with me? Think about all the evidence we've found that links you to Kerri's murder. Think about how few people know about the details of the paper flowers and all the other stuff. Can you really not remember what happened that night, or are you messing with me?"

Liam reached for the bottle and took it out of Sean's hand. "I can't believe you just asked me that," he whispered. "Drunk or not."

"Well, I did ask you, so answer."

"I am not messing with you." Liam could hear his voice shaking with both adrenaline and fear. "I'm very aware that the evidence points to me, and I'm not lying to you when I say I can't remember what happened that night. All I know is how I felt about her, and I can't reconcile those feelings with what we saw at the Tiger Hotel. I can't make that leap. So it has to be someone else. It has to be."

"Then who?"

"I don't know!"

Sean sat up in his seat. "If there really is someone else out there doing this, and we don't figure out who it is soon, Heckle and Keenan are going to find something. They're going to find something we missed, and when they do, you're screwed. At that point it'll be our word versus a stack of evidence that points only to you."

"It points to you too."

"No," Sean snapped. "I get banged for trying to help my brother find out if someone else killed his girlfriend and not coming clean with my department. Slap on the wrist. Probably suspended, but that's about the extent of it. Maybe Phillips sends me to another precinct. You get banged for murder, Liam. Life sentence. Big difference."

Liam put the bottle back on the table and sat in a recliner across from his brother. "I got Kerri's phone records like you told me. Cell and home."

"Good. Did you erase your entries?"

"Yeah. I erased yours too."

The two brothers stared at one another for a long while, neither saying anything. The house was still, the quiet overwhelming.

Liam took a breath. "Why was your number on her records, Sean?"

"You sure you want to know?"

"Positive."

Sean grabbed for the bottle and took another sip. "The baby was yours. No more secrets, right? That's what we agreed to? Kerri was scared and had no one else to turn to, so she called me and asked for help. I had to play dumb when they caught it in the autopsy. Had to pretend I was hearing it for the first time, but there's no sense in pretending anymore. We're way too far down the rabbit hole. The baby was yours."

Although he'd already figured as much, the confirmation of this news shook Liam. He put his head in his hands, contemplating what he'd just been told. "Why didn't you tell me she was pregnant with my baby?"

"She asked me not to. She knew you were fixing things with Vanessa and thought if she told you, it would screw everything up. She had your best interests in mind. We talked a few times about what she was going to do, and then the next thing I know, you call me and tell me she's dead."

"What was she going to do?"

Sean stood up. "She was going to keep it. She was going to have your baby. But you'd never know. Not as long as you were still with Vanessa. She wouldn't have allowed it." He wiped the top of the bottle with his shirt and held it out. "You want some? Makes the news go down better."

Liam reached over and took a sip. The alcohol stung his throat. He coughed, handing it back. "I can't believe you didn't tell me."

"I'm good at keeping secrets. As you can plainly see."

"But that was my child."

"So you wouldn't have killed her if you knew she was pregnant?"

Liam jumped off the chair and grabbed his brother by the collar of his shirt. "I didn't kill her!"

Sean pushed Liam away. "Yeah, you keep saying that. But we're running out of suspects."

"What about you?" Liam cried. "You knew everything I knew about Mom and Kerri. You could've done this."

"Yeah. I'm risking my career going behind Heckle and Keenan and trying to kill this investigation while protecting the primary suspect, but I'm actually guilty. That makes sense. Come on, Liam. You need to figure out what really happened that night. I'll help you, and I swear, I'll bury this if it was you, but you need to come to terms with what might have happened before anyone else gets hurt. I can get you help if you need it."

"I don't need help because I didn't do anything."

"Then find out who did!"

Liam was angry and scared. Sean was making sense, and that frightened him the most. He had come to tell his brother about Kiki and the pictures, but decided not to. Not like this when his only ally was accusing him of murder. Instead, he turned to leave. "I loved her more than you know," he said over his shoulder. "There's no way I could've killed her."

"I don't think you killed her," Sean replied. "But you gotta come to terms with this in case you did. If it was you, we can get you some help, but I can't be there every time. Not when it comes to things like this."

Liam threw the front door open and left the house, climbing down the stairs and running toward his car, which was parked in front. When he got in, he began to scream, his vocal cords tearing against his throat, a mixture of pain and fear and anger combined in the inhuman sound that filled the small space. He knew now that there was no one he could ever turn to with this. No one would be willing to help him find the truth. Too much evidence was stacked against him. It was clear now.

He truly was alone.

30

Sean waited until his brother drove away and then walked into the kitchen. He rifled through his cabinets, pulling out a glass and carrying both it and the bottle of Jack back into the living room. He placed them on the coffee table, then made his way into the foyer and stood at the bottom of the stairs.

"You can come out now," he said. "He's gone."

"You sure?"

"I'm sure. He's gone."

31

It was early evening when Liam returned home. He made his way up to the front door as Vanessa was pulling into the driveway. Headlights illuminated the house, and he turned, surprised to see her.

"Hey," he called as she climbed out of the car. "I hope I didn't wake you this morning. I had to get in the lab a little earlier than usual."

"I heard you, but I had an early shift anyway." Vanessa shut the car door. "Thought you might've called at some point."

"I wanted to, but I wasn't sure if we were on speaking terms. I know I screwed up last night. I'm sorry."

Vanessa walked up the path toward him. "You think one day we could clean out the garage so we can actually park our cars in there?"

Liam smiled. "I'll call in the dumpster tomorrow." She'd ignored his apology, which meant the argument was most likely over. That was how it usually went.

"They asked me to work a double again," Vanessa said as she pushed past her husband and unlocked the front door. "But I said no. I was hoping we could just stop fighting and curl up in bed and watch some television or something."

"Yeah, that sounds good."

Liam and Vanessa walked inside. The house was quiet. They kicked off their shoes and placed them in the corner, next to the closet. Vanessa dropped her pocketbook on the small bench under the staircase, unzipped it, and pulled a stack of envelopes from inside.

"I got the mail," she said. "Do we really owe this many people money?"

"I'm sure we do."

She handed her husband the bills and made her way into the kitchen, where she opened the refrigerator and grabbed a beer. "You want anything?"

"No, I'm good."

"How about Chinese tonight? I don't feel like cooking."

"Okay."

Liam stood in the hallway flipping through the envelopes, reading none of them. He hadn't been expecting Vanessa so early, and now she'd be home the entire night. He glanced at the closet door. He'd have to be careful.

She appeared from inside the kitchen, her hair up in a neat little bun, her scrubs still on, her stethoscope hanging from her neck. "It was funny," she began. "Today I'm at work, and I'm pissed about last night, then all of a sudden I start missing you. Can't really explain it. Just a feeling that came over me. By lunch, I don't care about being mad anymore and start thinking how much I wanted to be with you. I couldn't wait to get home."

"I missed you too. I'm sorry I've been in such a crappy mood. This case at work has my head all screwed up."

"You wanna talk about it?"

"Not really."

"It's okay." Vanessa took a sip of her beer. "I'm sorry too. I haven't been around lately, and then when I am, I expect you to drop everything so we can spend time together. That's not fair. I promise I'm not hiding in my work. Some of these extra shifts are mandatory. The census really picked up over the last week, and we're understaffed as it is."

Liam put the envelopes on the table and walked over to his wife. "It's okay. No more apologies."

Vanessa giggled uneasily. "If the counselor finds out about us working like this again, she's gonna flip."

"This is life. Some days are going to be busier than others. When things get to be too much, we drop what we're doing and come home to each other. Like tonight."

"Yeah, like tonight." Vanessa smiled and kissed her husband. "You think we can save us, right?"

"Absolutely."

"I love you, Liam. I don't want to lose you."

"You won't."

They kissed again, and then Vanessa pulled away. "I need a shower. Order the Chinese, and I'll meet you upstairs. I'm in the mood for a comedy. I have enough drama in my life."

"I have something for you."

"What?"

Liam reached into his pocket and came away with the charm bracelet. He held it up so she could see it clearly.

"My bracelet!" Vanessa cried. "I've been looking all over for it. Where'd you find it?"

"Sean's boat."

It was subtle, but Liam could see his wife's jaw clench for a moment. She looked at him and smiled. "Sean's boat. Of course. I went over there the other night, about a week ago now, I guess. I wanted to talk to him about us. Get some advice. You don't realize this, but sometimes you're so hard to talk to. I needed to get some things off my chest, and Sean offered to be a shoulder to lean on."

"Did it work?"

"I guess. We're about to spend the night together watching movies and eating Chinese, right?"

"Right." He handed her the bracelet. "Go take that shower."

Vanessa nodded and made her way upstairs. Liam followed her to the bottom floor landing.

"Can I ask you something?"

Vanessa stopped on the first step. "Sure."

"Did you work Saturday night?"

"No, I was off."

"So you were home when I was out with Sean and the guys from work?"

"Yup. I watched *Jaws* on the DVR like I do every spring, and then I went to sleep. Woke up in the middle of the night, and you were a crashed-out drunken mess on the couch. Why?"

"Just another opportunity for us to spend time together, and I screwed it up."

Vanessa began walking up the stairs. "You can make it up to me with some sweet-and-sour soup. Go."

"Yes, ma'am."

Liam watched his wife walk up the stairs. For a brief moment, he forgot about Kerri and the case and his fingerprints and only thought about his wife. But when she was gone, his world was his again. He didn't have much time.

The bathroom door closed upstairs. Liam scurried to the front door, eased it open, and ran out to his car, where he reached into the back seat and retrieved a small black bag. He was back inside within seconds.

The shower upstairs was running. Liam placed the bag on the bench under the stairs and unzipped it, quickly pulling out a small spray bottle. He'd have about ten minutes. Not much time.

After leaving Sean's house, doubts had begun to creep into his mind about his innocence and his theory that he was being framed. He still couldn't recall anything about the night Kerri was murdered, and although his heart wouldn't let him believe he could do such a thing, facts were facts. Everything pointed to him.

Liam walked to the closet and pulled his Timberlands out into the hall. He remembered Vanessa yelling about him leaving them out the morning after he woke in the tub. That could only mean he'd been wearing them the night before. Part of him wanted to run from whatever he might discover, but he had to know. There was no other way.

Inside the spray bottle was luminol. He sprayed each boot, covering every inch of surface and sole, a process he'd done countless times at countless crime scenes. Now he was doing it in his own home. He rushed back to the bag and pulled out a black light that he plugged into the wall next to the side table and knelt down. He took a deep breath and then turned on the light.

Luminol was a substance that bonded with the hemoglobin in blood and created a light-producing chemical reaction that made traces of blood glow. Without special chemicals to thoroughly wash it away, blood could remain on things for years. Liam watched helplessly as both boots glowed in the black light, the blood illuminating his guilt. A feeling of helplessness overwhelmed him. How could he be innocent? After everything he'd found, how was it possible at this point?

"What're you doing down there?"

Liam quickly straightened up. "Nothing," he replied. "Cleaning my boots."

Vanessa was at the top of the stairs, watching him. "With what?"

"Leather cleaner." He cleared his throat. "That was a quick shower."

Vanessa came down a few more steps. "I had to get my brush from my pocketbook." She was at the bottom landing now. "What's with the light?"

"Nothing. I wanted to make sure the waterproofing stuff I put on hadn't come off. It's an old trick I learned from work."

"So you need a black light for that?"

"It helps."

"Is all that glowing stuff the waterproofing?"

Liam shut the light. "Yup."

Vanessa stared at him for what seemed like an eternity, then shrugged and pointed. "You missed a few spots."

"I know. That's why I was checking with the light."

She walked over to her pocketbook and retrieved her brush. "What happened to the Chinese?"

"I thought I had a few minutes. I'll order it now."

"Are you okay?"

"Yeah," Liam replied, forcing a grin he knew looked both fake and stupid. "Why?"

"You look like you're about to have a panic attack or something."

"I'm fine. Sometimes the fumes from the cleaner get to me. Hard to breathe."

"You know you can talk to me about anything, right?"

"Of course."

"Whatever might be bothering you. We can talk. That's what we need to do to keep us going. If you need me, I'll be there for you. From now on I'll always be here for you. You're all I have, Liam. You're all that's left in my life. If something's bothering you or you need to talk, please. I'm here."

Liam nodded but said nothing more. Finally Vanessa turned away and started back up the stairs.

"I'll meet you upstairs. With Chinese."

"You got it."

He watched her as she went and then listened for the bathroom door to close again. When it did, he threw his shoes back in the closet, unplugged the black light, and placed the items back in his bag. He ran to the television and turned it on, flipping through the memory on the DVR until he got to Saturday night. Just as Vanessa had said, *Jaws* had been viewed from nine thirty until eleven thirty. He dropped the remote and fell onto the couch. His life was crumbling, and he had no idea how to stop it. His boots had Kerri's blood on them. With everything else, what more proof did he need? How could there be any doubt? His only hope was to find something when he traveled to Delaware tomorrow to look at the other victim. But he was clearly running out of tomorrows.

It looked as though Liam could, in fact, be guilty of murder.

32

The screams sent shivers down his spine, freezing him in place as he sat up in bed. Even with his eyes still half-closed and his mind still somewhat dormant, he knew it was Liam. He was having another nightmare.

Sean pulled the covers away and hopped onto the floor as his brother's cries pierced the otherwise quiet house. He half jogged, half stumbled out of his bedroom and down the narrow hall, pushing himself to keep moving forward when what he really wanted to do was cover his ears, curl up in a ball, and yell at his brother to shut up. But he knew he couldn't do that. His grandmother hadn't been feeling well this past week, and getting woken up like this wouldn't be good for her. It was Sean's job to get in there and stop the screaming. It always was.

Sean threw Liam's bedroom door open and rushed inside, his bare feet slipping on tiny Matchbox cars and hard plastic superhero figures that were scattered across the floor. He fell onto Liam's bed and took his brother by the shoulders, shaking him.

"Liam! Liam, wake up! Wake up. It's just a dream."

Liam continued with a few more screams that then turned into whimpers.

"Wake up, buddy. You're okay."

A ten-year-old Liam finally opened his eyes and focused on his big brother. Perspiration matted his hair to his forehead, his skinny chest rising and falling with deep, ragged breaths.

"Sean?"

"You were having another bad dream."

"Did I wake Grandma and Grandpa?"

"I don't think so."

"And this is real life?"

Sean smiled. "Yeah, this is real life."

Liam propped himself up on his elbows and looked around the room. "Can you turn on the light?"

Sean walked back toward the door and fumbled in the darkness until his fingers found the light switch. He turned it on and could now see the booby traps of toys that he'd tripped over on his way in. The room was a mess. Clothes that should've been in the hamper were thrown over his desk. Liam's extra pillows had ended up against his closet. Picture books lay open on the floor, the pages dog-eared and worn. A small stack of photos was on top of the desk, next to the clothes. Their mother and father.

"I had a dream about Mom," Liam said.

"Yeah, no kidding. You been looking at these pictures before you went to bed."

"I found them in one of my books. I didn't do it on purpose." He fell back against his pillow and stared up at the ceiling as he spoke. "She was like she was . . . that day, you know? All sick and scary. She was chasing me around the living room, and Grandpa was on the couch reading the paper, and you were at the dining room table doing your homework, and Grandma was making spaghetti in the kitchen. None of you would help me. I kept calling out, but it was like you couldn't hear me. Or you were ignoring me. And Mom kept coming. She kept chasing me and wanted to throw me in the tub. You wouldn't help me."

Liam started to cry, and Sean came over to the bed. He pulled his little brother against him so he could hug him.

"I would never do that. I would never ignore you. It was just a dream. I'll always be there for you. Always. Whenever you need me, you call me, and I'll be listening. I'll hear it."

"You promise?"

"Of course I promise. We only have each other, Liam. So because of that, we only have each other to count on. I'll be there for you, and you be there for me. Got it?"

"I guess."

Sean kissed his brother on the head.

Liam looked up at him, his eyes still glassy from crying. "Do you think you can stay here with me until I fall back to sleep? I keep thinking about Mom. I'm scared."

Sean maneuvered himself next to Liam on the small twin bed and kicked his long legs under the blankets until they were covering both boys. He pulled half the pillow over to his side and flopped an arm over his brother's chest.

Without another word, Liam and Sean closed their eyes and fell asleep. The night pressed on, unimpeded.

———

Sean was in the basement sitting at his workbench when his cell phone rang. He pulled it from his pocket, glanced at the number. Vanessa.

"Hello?"

"We need to talk."

"What's wrong?"

Vanessa spoke in a whisper. There was an urgency about her. Her breath came in short bursts. "It's about Liam."

Sean closed the toolbox he had open in front of him and pushed himself off the stool he'd been sitting on. "Where are you?" he asked.

"I'm at home. In the bathroom. Liam's downstairs."

"What's going on?"

Again, there were a few short breaths before she spoke. "His boots."

"What about them?"

"Wait, I think I hear him coming. I have to go. I can't talk now. Meet me tomorrow."

"What's happening?"

"I said I have to go. I'll call you tomorrow. He's coming."

"Tell me!"

The line disconnected, and Sean was again in the silence of his basement. He redialed and waited, but it immediately went to voice mail. He hung up and dialed again. Voice mail.

"Dammit."

He tried one more time. Vanessa didn't answer. He hung up and stared at his phone, waiting to see if she'd call back. After a few minutes, he knew she wasn't calling, so he stuffed it in his pocket and sat back down on the stool in front of the workbench. What had she seen? What was going on?

33

There was a bit of traffic, so the drive from Center City to Wilmington took a little over an hour. During that time, there wasn't much conversation with Jane, who kept busy by studying Kerri's file and comparing it to the victim they were about to see. The victim was known on the streets simply as JB and had been working a certain section of the city for about four years. She'd been arrested several times for loitering and solicitation, but nothing heavy. On the night she was killed, she was working the corner of Hay Road and East 12th Street, just under Interstate 495. She worked that area alone, and no street cameras were operational in that section of the city, so who she went with, and at what time, remained a mystery. She was found the following morning in a motel on Bowers Street, several miles away from where she was picked up. There had been no next of kin, so JB was buried near the railroad tracks in a city cemetery primarily used for inmates with no families, homeless people who couldn't be properly identified, and the occasional Jane and John Doe the department came across.

Liam drove in almost absolute silence. He thought about the mounting evidence that pointed to him, the fact that he still couldn't remember anything from the night Kerri was killed, and the latest discovery that his boots were stained with blood. Even the victim they were driving to see was surrounded in more mystery than he could handle. Sean was right; Vanessa had been at a medical convention for her hospital the weekend of Valentine's Day, and Liam had been alone at the house. Theoretically, a drive to Wilmington and back, even with a brutal murder crammed in between, wouldn't have been that big of a time crunch. He strained to try to recall exactly where he'd been that weekend, as the thought of someone else framing him for Kerri's murder began to fade. All he could remember was watching TV alone at the house. No way that would hold up in court.

Detective Grimley was standing outside the medical examiner's office when Liam and Jane pulled up. He was a portly man, forties, whose thick beard swallowed the rest of his face, leaving only tiny black dots for eyes recessed in the back of his skull. He smelled of cigars and cheap cologne. Strands of thinning brown hair tossed about in the morning breeze. His dress shirt had the remnants of an old stain under the breast pocket. Exploded pen, no doubt. Happened to the best of them.

Introductions were brief but friendly, made in the parking lot before the local detective led the way inside the building. They walked down a narrow corridor made up of sky-blue subway tiles and what had once been a bright-white grout that had stained to a nasty mustard yellow over the years. Fluorescent lights hovered above. The space was completely functional. No room for anything other than the task at hand.

Grimley pushed through a set of double doors and ushered his guests inside. The medical examiner was standing over the exhumed body of JB, who was lying on the stainless steel operating table, a sheet covering her body.

"Here she is," Grimley said. "Just like you asked."

Liam walked toward the girl and could feel his heart beating in his chest. His body was shaking, so he kept moving. He didn't want the others to see.

The medical examiner took out his file and opened it. "I know you guys wanted a tox screen and autopsy," he said. "We didn't do one originally, and she's been embalmed, so we're going to have to take bone samples and go from there. Results will take a bit longer, but that's the only option we have at this point."

"No tox at all when you first found her?" Jane asked. "Not even a general screen?"

"No."

"That's too bad."

"It was coded as a homicide when she came in with clear cause of death being strangulation. She was a prostitute, and we could see how she died. At the time, we didn't think anything more was necessary. Obviously we had no idea this could've been a part of something bigger."

"I get it," Liam replied. "Hooker with no next of kin to care that she's dead. No one to ask any follow-up questions. Get her in the ground and move on. Don't waste the taxpayers' money. We would've done the same thing."

Liam pulled back the sheet that was covering the girl. A small squeak of breath escaped from his pursed lips. It was as if he were staring at Kerri all over again. The haphazard nature of the hair cutting. The neck that was just slightly out of place from the noose. It was all so horrifically familiar.

"According to some old ID we found at an apartment she shared with a handful of other girls, her name was Jamie Buffucco," Grimley said from the edge of the room. "She was found hanging from a ceiling fan in the motel room by the cleaning crew the next morning. Uniforms cut her down, and my partner and I spent about a week following up on leads that went nowhere. No one saw anything. She worked her area alone, got picked up, and was found dead the next day. We went to the address on her ID, but no one there knew who she was, and no one in the area knew her, either."

"And nobody saw anything at the motel?" Jane asked.

Grimley shook his head. "No. Guy who checked in paid cash and left a fake name. Elvis Costello. No one saw the girl."

"Elvis Costello," Jane said. "Sounds like our guy."

Liam couldn't take his eyes off the victim. "She was probably unconscious in the car. This motel the type of place you drive right up to your room? No lobby to walk through?"

"Yup."

"Then no one saw anything."

"We did the best we could with what we had," Grimley said. He closed his file. "The trail went cold at the motel. We filed unsolved soon after."

Jane walked up and stood next to Liam. She pulled pictures of the crime scene at the Tiger Hotel from her file and held them up next to JB's body on the table. They were almost identical. "I think he was practicing," Jane whispered to herself.

Liam turned. "Say again?"

"He was practicing. This girl was a nobody. She was a hooker, a throwaway as far as he was concerned. Kerri wasn't. Kerri had a family, a job, a life. The killer had one chance to get it right with her, and he didn't want to screw it up." She looked at Liam. "So he drove down here, picked an anonymous woman no one would miss, and practiced on her. He did everything to this girl he would eventually do to Kerri to make sure he got it right. This girl was the sketch before he put actual paint to canvas. He cared enough to want to murder her exactly the right way. After all, she was the mother of his child. She was special. He didn't want to screw anything up."

Liam slowly reached down and brushed a few strands of the girl's hair from her brow. He tried desperately to recall her features, to see something that might be familiar, but there was nothing. He was certain he'd never seen this girl in his life.

"You might be right," Liam replied. "He was either practicing, or we have a serial killer no one's picked up on yet. Kerri Miller could've been the prize, or she could've just been another victim like this girl here. Could be a crime of circumstance instead of one where he was working his way up to a victim who counted for something. We just don't know." He walked to Grimley, who was still standing near the examination room doors. "Can you take us to the motel and the area of town where this girl normally worked?"

"Sure. Not certain what you think you're gonna find, though. Must've been a dozen rain- or snowstorms since then to wash away any evidence."

"I'm not looking for evidence. Just want to get a general sense of the town. Put myself in her shoes. See what she saw."

"Okay, let's go."

What Liam wasn't telling any of them was that he needed to see the motel and the area where JB worked to see if there was a memory that would jog loose or if his world would continue to drown in waves of amnesia.

He needed to see if this girl's death could, in any way, point to him.

34

The men sat around a large conference table on the executive floor of the precinct. Sean, Lieutenant Phillips, and Sean's PBA lawyer, Paul Brown, sat on one side. The detectives from Internal Affairs, Farmer and Nix, sat on the other. Paul Brown was an older man, perhaps in his sixties. He had a thick mat of white hair and a matching white mustache that dominated his face. Nix was short, balding, and slightly unkempt. His tie was pulled down a bit, his top button unfastened. Farmer was taller and more physically fit than his partner. His suit fit him well, his tie appropriately up under his collar. Cuff links glistened in the overhead lighting.

Nix folded his hands on the table and cleared his throat. "Detective Dwyer," he began. "As you know, it's standard procedure to interview our officers after a weapons discharge. Detective Farmer and I would like to ask you a few questions about what went on during your arrest of Charles, a.k.a. Cutter, Washington a few days ago."

Sean nodded. "Yes, I'm familiar with the procedure."

"Good. Then let's begin."

Detective Farmer began speaking, but Sean's mind was elsewhere. He hadn't heard from Vanessa since the night before and wasn't sure what she'd been talking about when she called him about Liam and his boots. He'd tried her several times when he woke, while he was getting ready, and on his way into the station. All of his calls had gone to her voice mail.

"Detective Dwyer?"

Sean blinked and shook his head. "I'm sorry."

"Are you with us?"

"Yes."

"I'm glad. Now, as I said, can you please tell us, in your own words, what happened during the apprehension of Mr. Charles Washington?"

Sean looked at his lawyer and was given permission to begin. He sat up in his chair. "Well, we caught a break from a bystander's picture that put Cutter at the scene of the stationery store at the time of the vic's death, so we got a warrant and served it at his girlfriend's house. We had an arrest team enter through the front with one squad sweeping the ground floor and myself and Detective Carpenter taking the second floor. We also had a uniformed officer out back for additional backup.

"We entered with force, identified ourselves repeatedly as Philadelphia PD, and were met on the second floor by the girlfriend, who tried to block our access to her bedroom, where the suspect was trying to escape from a second floor window.

"Detective Carpenter subdued the girlfriend with his Taser, and we proceeded to the bedroom, all the while instructing the suspect to come out with his arms raised and identifying ourselves as police officers."

"What about the children?" Nix asked.

"A brother and sister. My partner and I didn't see them, but they were found by the other team who was sweeping. By the time we got to the bedroom, we heard a gunshot outside in the back. The officer we had stationed there was down, and the suspect was on foot, fleeing the scene. I went out the back window, and Detective Carpenter took the stairs. I pursued down the alley, and the suspect fired two rounds at me while running. I shot him in the leg to stop his progress before he hit the busier streets. I didn't want to lose him." Sean fell back in his seat. "I placed the suspect under arrest. By then, units were rolling for backup, and EMT had been dispatched for the officer who was shot. We called in a second ambulance for the suspect. That's about it."

The room was silent. Farmer and Nix looked at one another, then back toward Sean. "Have you seen the psychologist?" Farmer asked.

"Yes."

Nix flipped through a folder that was sitting in front of him. "Psych eval cleared him. He's good."

Farmer nodded. "I agree. I'm going to classify this as a good shooting. You're clear to resume duty. Do you have any questions?"

"No."

"Does your PBA rep have any questions?"

Paul shook his head. "I'm good."

Nix closed the folder and motioned toward Phillips. "He's all yours."

As the men all stood and shook hands around the table, Sean's focus was back on getting in touch with Vanessa to find out why she'd called him the night before. What did she want? What did she see?

35

Joyce was at work and wouldn't be due home until later that evening. Don took advantage of the empty house and sat on the couch of his living room, placing his computer on the coffee table in front of him and powering it up. He plugged the flash drive he'd made from Kerri's computer into the USB port and waited.

A man's conscience is a funny thing. As much as Don wanted to help, knew he should help, and was willing to help, his conscience had ended up getting the better of him. The Dwyer boys were family. He'd watched them grow up within the department and was there with them celebrating countless holidays and family vacations. He was Sean's mentor and Liam's confidant. He looked at them as if they were related through blood, and they looked at him the same way, but the brutality in which Kerri had been murdered had caused a speck of doubt to creep into Don's mind until that speck grew into a mass of uncertainty and finally a cancer of conscience. Walking through that empty apartment and sensing the finality of that young girl's life gave his heart pause. He was certain Liam wasn't capable of murder, especially the kind of murder he'd seen in the crime scene photos Sean had shared with him, but he had to know for sure, so he'd made an extra copy of Kerri's files when he got back that night. The first copy had been destroyed in Sean's garbage disposal. Don was the only one to know about the second copy. An affair, and a pregnancy on top of that, could cause a person to do things well outside of his or her circle of normalcy. He'd seen it so many times before. Some people would go to extremes to keep a secret hidden forever. He was sure Liam wasn't one of those people, but if those boys could suspect him of such a crime, couldn't he do the same? If he didn't find anything, his conscience could rest, and he would help them root out whoever was framing Liam, but if he did find something . . . well . . .

Don went through Kerri's files, which were listed alphabetically, clicking on each one. Most were work-related memos and saved emails. The memos contained information about upcoming analysis that was needed and dates to save for future staff meetings or client presentations. He moved on to the emails, and it was more of the same, mixed with a handful of personal messages from friends and family. Birthday wishes seemed to dominate her inbox. Everything was as it should have been with nothing pointing to Liam or the circumstances surrounding her death.

After about an hour, it was apparent there wasn't anything in regular files or email that could point him, or anyone else, in the direction toward her killer or a motive. He moved on to the encrypted files.

As the first decade of the twenty-first century had come to an end, a priority within the department had become the emerging use of computers and the technology available to commit cybercrimes. These crimes ranged from online stalking to identity theft to general hacking to financial manipulation, and almost everything in between. Don had been one of three homicide detectives chosen for a pilot program aimed at teaching the good guys some of the tricks the bad guys used in order to infiltrate and trace a criminal in cyberspace. The eight-week class had taught him a few techniques in tracking, tracing, and tagging online. Within those lessons was a brief introduction to encrypted files and the art of decrypting.

Don uploaded the first of Kerri's encrypted files. He knew he wouldn't be able to open it with algorithms or encryption methods. The department hadn't given him that level of training. What he could do was try loading various passwords that might have meant something to Kerri to see if he could hit on the right one and gain access. If that didn't work, he'd have to pay Rocco a visit.

A white box popped up, asking for a password. The cursor blinked on and off, waiting. Don started firing off key words, one after the other. KERRI, MILLER, KM, KERRIM, KMILLER, 3592, 351992, 1992, 92, KERRIMILLER, DWYER, SEAN, LIAM, LDWYER, LIAMDWYER, SDWYER, SEANDWYER, DWYERBROTHERS, DWYERBROS, SECRET . . .

A gentle chime came from the inside of his jacket pocket. He reached in and grabbed his phone. It was Sean. "Hello?"

"Hey, man, we're all set. The report on Cutter is filed, my meeting with IA is over, and I'm cleared."

"That's great," Don replied. He continued typing whatever he could think of into the computer as he spoke. Nothing would take. "So now you can continue investigating me for killing Kerri *and* get paid for it. Nice."

"Liam told you we visited your mom?"

"Yes. And just for the record, that's crap."

"I'm sorry, man. We had to cross you off the list. It wasn't my finest moment, but it was necessary. I was sure someone was setting Liam up, but now I don't know. So much evidence points to him. It's hard to ignore. Why would he do that?"

"I don't think he would."

"Me either. But everything is pointing to him. I'm thinking we let Heckle and Keenan file this away; then we figure things out on our own."

Don said nothing. He kept typing passwords into the computer.

"I really am sorry about going behind your back."

"I got news for you. Liam isn't convinced I'm innocent."

"He's scared—that's all."

"I get it," Don replied. "But if I'm going to help you guys, Liam needs to be able to trust me."

"I'll talk to him."

"And if you go behind my back like that again, we're gonna have a problem."

"Understood."

The first file was a bust. Don moved his mouse over to the second and tried that one, repeating the numbers and words he'd tried with the first file: KERRI, MILLER, KM, KERRIM, KMILLER, 3592, 351992 . . .

"Phillips put you back on the board?"

"Tomorrow. We're back in the rotation come eight a.m."

"Good."

"Come out for a few beers with me later. I owe you a drink. I feel bad for what we did. I'll meet you at the Hard Rock. They'll have the game on, and we'll grab a bite."

1992, 92, KERRIMILLER, DWYER, SEAN . . .

"Yeah, I'll come by. But just a couple of beers. If we're back on the board at eight, I don't want to be hungover and falling asleep at my desk."

"Tell Joyce I'll have you home by ten."

LIAM, LDWYER, LIAMDWYER, SDWYER, SEANDWYER, DWYERBROTHERS, DWYERBROS, SECRET . . .

Access denied.

"I have a few things to wrap up here at home, and then I'll be by. Meet you around seven?"

"Sure, that's great."

The second file failed as well. Don shut down the program and pulled the flash drive from his laptop.

"Look," Don said. "I gotta go, but I'll see you tonight. Meet me at the bar."

"I'll see you there."

Don hung up and fell back against the couch cushions. It was a long shot he'd be able to come across the right file on his own. He'd have to let an expert take a look at it, and that meant he'd have to stop by Rocco's on the way to the Hard Rock and drop off the drive. What Rocco uncovered would determine the next step he'd take.

36

"Yeah man, come in. Make yourself at home. You want a Red Bull or something? I got the Bull, I got a 5-hour Energy, I got beer, but you're probably on duty or something. Oh, I got some Mountain Dew."

"I'm all right, thanks."

"Something to munch on instead? Pretzels? Cheetos?"

"Nothing."

"Cool."

Don walked inside the cramped studio apartment and was instantly consumed by stacks of hard drives that climbed halfway up to the ceiling, countless processors that lined one wall, and wires that snaked the entire length of the floor to the point where he could barely see the carpet underneath. The rest of the space held a bed, a stained black futon that acted as a couch, and a small flat-screen television balanced on a stack of books. In the far corner he could see a refrigerator but no stove. Everything else was covered by some kind of technological hardware.

Rocco turned and walked to a desk that had three laptops on it, each one running some kind of code. He was dressed in an army green robe that looked like rags sewn together and white boxer shorts. He was pale and thin but for a belly that protruded from the robe. His shoulder-length hair looked greasy, as did the goatee that had grown out of control.

"I was in the middle of a killer hack when you called," Rocco said, his voice raspy from the cigarettes he constantly smoked. "A new airline out of Cairo hired my firm to try and infiltrate their booking system."

He pointed to the laptop on the left. "That's what that one's doing. Shouldn't take me too long to get in. Some places in the Middle East have a long way to go when it comes to cybersecurity. They're still using technology from the eighties. Cracks me up." He sat in his seat, took a long drag from his cigarette, and spun around to face his guest. "So what'd you bring me?"

Don handed over the flash drive. "There are two encrypted files on this drive. I need to get in there as part of a murder investigation."

"You get a warrant, or is this gray-area classified stuff?"

"Gray area. Just between you and me. You get something, you call me."

Rocco studied the flash drive. "Part of a murder investigation, huh? Cool. Do you know when the file was created?"

"No. I tried a bunch of random passwords to see if something clicked, but I couldn't get in."

"Was the person who made this a techie?"

"Not sure."

"Okay," Rocco replied. "It really doesn't matter either way." He spun back around, plugged the flash drive into the middle laptop and began to make a copy. "Sometimes, if the user is new to encryption, they just take whatever they can find off the internet, buy it, and encrypt. The newer the encryption service, the less tested it would be, which means people like me haven't found all the vulnerabilities in it yet, which then means it should be relatively easy to manipulate and gain entry."

"How long you think it'll take?"

"Depends on the encryption service that was used. If it's one that's been around awhile, it could take a bit longer. Maybe a week or two. If it's new, shouldn't take more than a few days. I'll hit it with blunt force to find a way in, and if that doesn't work, I'll look for a back door. Either way, I'll get what you need. That's what I do." The laptop made a few noises, and Rocco leaned forward to extract the flash drive. He turned back around in his chair and handed it to Don. "Copy made. You keep the original. Anything else I need to know?"

"Nothing that I can think of." Don took the drive and put it back in his pocket. "Just remember, you get anything, you call me. Don't read through it, don't make any more copies, don't tell your friends what you're doing. Just call me."

Rocco laughed. "Don't read it. Yeah, okay. I'll break into a file that's linked to a murder, but I won't read it. You crack me up, man."

"We don't even know what's in there," Don said. "Could be plans for a new marketing campaign or an upcoming summer vacation. I just need to know for sure."

"No problem. But just so you know, I'm gonna look."

"Call me when you get in."

"Sure thing."

Don checked his watch and made his way toward the door. The afternoon was drawing to a close, and he'd have to run home to get ready to meet Sean at the Hard Rock. "This is between you and me, Rocco. Got it?"

Rocco took a drag of his cigarette and let the smoke seep from his teeth as he put on a broad and obnoxious smile. "Your secret's safe with me, Detective. I ain't saying nothing."

37

As dusk began to take hold, Liam walked through the front door of his home and collapsed onto the bench beside the stairs. He was exhausted, both mentally and physically. The ride back to Philadelphia from Wilmington had taken longer than expected due to an overturned tractor trailer on I-95, and as the minutes had passed in an unrelenting gridlock, the images of Kerri and JB had continued to invade his every thought. Even with the radio on and some mundane conversation Jane was able to offer along the way, he couldn't stop thinking about the two victims and the fact that he could've had something to do with them.

Liam opened the manila file that was on his lap. Glossy crime scene photos from JB's murder stared back up at him as he began flipping through them, one after the other. Jane could be right. The killer might have been practicing on a girl no one would miss before moving on to the primary target. But the way the rope was tied through the bedpost, up into the exposed piping in the ceiling, around the ceiling fan, and back down to the victim told him this could also be the telltale sign of a serial killer. What he'd seen in Delaware was exactly the same as what he'd seen at the Tiger, only there was no fan at Kerri's scene. JB had been placed on a chair just as Kerri had been, and the chair had been taken from under each victim for the actual hanging. The way JB's hair was cut so randomly not only reminded him of how Kerri's hair had been cut but also of how his mother had cut her own hair the day she had tried to kill him and Sean. These were patterns. There was ritual to it, a cadence. The only thing missing in JB's homicide was the stomach slashing and the bouquet of paper flowers. Everything else was pretty much the same.

Liam closed the file and tossed it onto the bench next to him. He stood on weary legs and made his way into the kitchen, crossing to the refrigerator, where he grabbed a beer, twisted the cap off, and took a long sip, almost finishing it in one gulp.

The front door opened, and Liam could hear Vanessa shuffling inside, dropping her bag on the bench, and slipping off her raincoat.

"In the kitchen," he called as he took another sip of his beer, finishing it.

There was no answer.

He walked into the hall and found his wife untying her sneakers. "Hey."

Vanessa didn't look up. "Hey."

"Something wrong?"

"Yes, something is definitely wrong." Vanessa looked at him, and now he could see she'd been crying. Black mascara had run down her cheeks. Her eyes were red and swollen.

"What happened?"

Vanessa kicked off her sneakers and brushed past him, into the kitchen. "I called your office today on my break. I was going to surprise you and stop over for a late lunch. Our census dropped, and they let some of us go early. I thought it'd be a nice opportunity to spend some time together."

"I was in Delaware today. Wilmington. We had a lead we had to follow up with. I just got back."

"Yeah, that's what they told me. They said you went to Wilmington with Jane Somebody."

"Campelli. Jane Campelli. She's on my team." Liam followed his wife. "What's going on?" he asked. "Why are you so upset?"

Vanessa threw open a cabinet next to the stove and took out a wine glass. She walked over to the pantry and retrieved a bottle of merlot.

"If you had to cross the state line on a lead, wouldn't the FBI have to get involved?"

"No. It was just a lead. We were following up on it from our jurisdiction."

"Are you lying to me, Liam? After everything we've been through, I need to know. Are you really trying to make things work? To make us work? Or are you lying about loving me and making our life together work again?"

A mixture of confusion and anger began to boil within Liam. He knew it was the result of this ridiculous accusation but also the fact that she wasn't totally wrong. It was as if she could somehow read his mind and make him see things for what they were, and he wasn't ready for that.

"Where is this coming from?" Liam asked. "What are you even talking about?"

Vanessa poured the wine into her glass and took a sip. She put the glass down and stared at her husband. "I need to know the truth," she said. "Are you having an affair with Jane Campelli?"

Liam couldn't help but laugh. "Are you kidding me? Jesus, this is all I need. You're all worked up because I went to Wilmington with Jane on a lead? And now you think I'm having an affair with her?"

"Answer the question!"

"Of course not! That's the most ridiculous and childish thing I ever heard. I was working today. Doing my job. The only reason why you know where I was is because you called to go to lunch. I have news for you: I travel all around the area during investigations, and this isn't the first time I've crossed a border. Look, I've been patient, and I've been willing to reconstruct this marriage, but if this is how you're going to act every time I'm not where you think I should be, then we have a lot more work ahead of us." He stormed out of the kitchen, grabbed the file from the bench in the hall, and came back. He tossed the file across the marble island and watched as it landed in front of Vanessa, the glossy photos spilling from beneath the cover. "This is what I was doing today. Not an affair. A homicide."

Vanessa looked at some of the pictures and then pushed them away. "Tell me you love me," she said.

"Why are you—"

"Tell me you love me!"

Liam could feel everything crashing down on him. His anger intensified as he tried to reconcile his wife's irrational reaction to the fact that he wasn't at his office when she'd called. The two things didn't mesh. The entire situation was so completely bizarre. "Why didn't you call my cell?" he asked.

"I did."

Liam pulled out his phone and checked the log. Two calls from Vanessa's phone had posted. He hadn't heard either of them.

"Tell me you love me. That's what I want to hear. I need to hear it."

"Why are you acting like this?"

"Tell me you love me and you'd never do anything to hurt me."

"What's wrong with you?"

Vanessa slammed her wine glass down on the counter, and it shattered all over the photos and file. "Tell me!"

"No, I can't." Liam backed out of the kitchen, shaking his head. "Not when you're like this." He turned, walked through the hall, and opened the door.

"Where are you going?"

"Away from you."

"Tell me you—"

He slammed the door and ran out into the cool, silent night. His anger was getting the better of him, and he needed to get away. There was no particular destination in mind. Just away. He had to think.

38

Liam backed out of the driveway and whipped the car around onto the street. He drove for half a block, his anger fueling him to the point where he thought he might burst. His breathing was shallow, so he pulled over to the side of the road, sat back in his seat, and closed his eyes. He concentrated on his breathing. In, out. In, out. After a little while, he steadied himself and felt better. A thought flashed through his mind.

Were you this angry when you killed Kerri?

"No," Liam said aloud as the thought vanished as quickly as it had come. "No."

He took a final breath and sat up, glancing into his rearview mirror in order to pull back out onto the street. He wasn't exactly sure where he was going or where he'd end up, but he knew he had to get out of there. His mind was still spinning from what had just happened with Vanessa. Her emotions frightened him.

And that's when he saw Vanessa's car pulling out of the driveway.

It maneuvered its way out onto the road and drove off in the opposite direction, its red taillights outlining the sedan as it cruised to the intersection, then turned left. Liam immediately whipped his car around and followed. Where was she going now?

He knew as it grew darker outside the night would give him the cover he'd need; however, the sun was still setting, which made him vulnerable to being spotted. He kept a safe distance between his car and Vanessa's. Tailing someone hadn't been part of his training as a forensics tech, so he relied on common sense and the movies he'd watched with his brother where Sean would point out when the Hollywood director had gotten police procedures right and when they were laughably wrong. The safest way to play it would be to stay a few cars behind and track her as best he could from there. If she turned, he'd speed up to find out where she was heading and then fall back again. If she stopped, he'd drive past her or turn onto another street. That was the best plan he could come up with.

He followed her as she turned onto Route 42 North and took position in the left lane about four car lengths back. A truck in front of him helped disguise his position while, at the same time, he was able to keep his eyes on her car. It wasn't until she turned off 42 and onto Interstate 295 North that he had an idea of where she was going.

Sean's house.

Liam thought about the bracelet he'd found on his brother's boat and Vanessa's reaction when he'd told her where he'd gotten it from. Did Sean have more secrets than he was letting on? He tried to recall the other times they'd all been together. So many times. Had either of them acted strange, or were there signs he'd been missing all along?

A laugh burst forth. He couldn't help it. He was being foolish. This was nothing more than Sean being there for the family like he always was. Sean was the one who'd helped him reconcile with Vanessa after they'd decided to try to make things work. Sean had been the one to sit them both down and walk through the steps it would take to get their lives together. He'd been there for Liam more times than he could count. Why wouldn't he do the same for Vanessa? Of course he would. Sean was the patriarch of the family, the leader who everyone else followed without question. And in this instance, Sean was the shoulder Vanessa could lean on when she needed to talk. After the fight they'd just had, he was certain she'd have plenty to say.

Liam pulled off the road and parked on the street adjacent to his brother's house. He watched as Vanessa drove into Sean's driveway, climbed out of her car, and ran up the front steps to the door. She rang the bell and then looked around while she waited, but there was no way she'd be able to see him. He was hidden behind a set of hedges from one of the neighbors' houses and within the shadow of the streetlights that were popping to life.

The front door opened, and Sean appeared. He and Vanessa exchanged words Liam couldn't hear, and then Sean reached out and gently brushed back a lock of hair that had fallen across her face, tucking it behind her ear. She let him do it, and when he was done, she reached up and placed her hands on his chest, lightly pushing him inside. The door closed behind them.

Liam stepped out of the car. He wasn't exactly sure what he'd just seen. What was going on? The way they'd looked at each other. The way they'd touched. There was something there. He couldn't interpret it as anything else. Vanessa had looked at him like that once. And now . . .

He stopped when he got to the edge of Sean's driveway and bent down behind a cluster of pine trees. He tried to see inside from where he was, but the house was perched on an incline, and he couldn't make out anything past the front end of the porch. Moving without knowing exactly where he was going, Liam ran up the front yard and over to the side of the house. He peered through each of the windows. There was nothing to see. All of the shades had been drawn. He pressed his head against the glass to see if he could hear anything, but there was only silence.

What are you doing?

He ran around to the front of the house and carefully climbed the wooden steps onto the porch. He bent down to look through the window next to the front door. There was no curtain, but the hallway inside was empty. Where were they?

"Liam?"

Liam jumped and spun around, almost falling over the railing on the opposite side of the porch. Sean was standing down below on the gravel path that led to the garage, looking at him.

"Jesus! You scared me."

Sean walked up the front steps. "What are you doing here?"

"Vanessa and I had this huge fight."

"Yeah, I know. She's inside."

"I followed her here."

"You followed her?"

Liam shrugged. "I left, and then I saw her leave, and I wanted to know where she was going."

"She wanted to talk," Sean replied. "She comes to me every once in a while when things are a little shaky with you two."

"She told me."

"Come inside. We can all talk about this together."

Liam shook his head. "No way. I don't want her knowing I was following her. I feel like an ass as it is."

Sean walked across the porch and gently grabbed his brother by the arm. "Come inside, and we can talk this all out."

"No. I'm serious. I can't."

"Get in the house, Liam. You both need this."

Liam yanked his arm away and pushed past Sean. "I said no. You go talk to her and be everyone's hero like always. I don't want to be part of your therapy session. Not today."

"Is this about what I said yesterday? Look, I'm sorry. I was drinking, and I acted like an idiot."

Liam hurried down the driveway and into the street. "You tell her I was here, and you'll regret it. You got that?"

"Come back," Sean pleaded. "We can talk. All of us."

Without another word, Liam turned and ran from the house. Fear, anger, anxiety, and confusion balled in his stomach to the point he thought he might be sick. He got back into his car and drove away.

39

The bar was off the Walt Whitman Bridge on the outskirts of South Philadelphia. Liam didn't know the name of it and didn't much care. He sat in the corner next to a pool table that looked like it hadn't been used in more than a decade. The felt was ripped, the pool sticks were missing, and only half the balls were scattered across the top. The rest of the place was in the same condition. A cluster of patrons sat around a dirty bar, and another small group of friends huddled around a table near the restrooms, which had curtains instead of doors. The wallpaper above the mounted television in the center of the dining area was torn and fell across half the screen. It was the perfect place to disappear and think. He had to think.

He'd left Sean's house and driven down 295 with thoughts crashing in on themselves, one after the other. By the time he'd focused on where he was, he realized he'd driven halfway over the bridge into the city. He'd turned onto the first street he came upon after crossing into Philadelphia and had seen the half-lit sign for the bar he now sat in. Instead of turning back around to head home, he'd pulled into the bar's parking lot and shut off the engine. The rest of the night had been spent looking down at the bottom of his mug.

Tomorrow. Tomorrow he'd talk with Vanessa and then with Sean, and he'd try to set things straight again. That was the best he could do at this point. Perhaps he should've gone inside when his brother asked him to, but that ship had sailed. He'd missed his opportunity and could now only wait until tomorrow to start anew.

"I knooow you."

Liam looked up to find a short, pudgy man swaying back and forth as he stood over his table, a drink in his fat hand, a stupid grin on his face. He looked vaguely familiar, but he couldn't place him.

"I said I knooow you."

"I heard you the first time."

"You're one of those cops from my hotel who came to clean up the girl from B11."

Now Liam recognized him. It was the hotel owner. Guzio something or something Guzio. Aside from being more than a bit tipsy, the man looked about the same as when he'd seen him that night at the Tiger. Liam wondered if he slept in his clothes.

"I get my place back tomorrow," Guzio slurred. "Get you friggin' cops out of there so I can reopen. I got money to make. People in this city are relying on me. They need my hotel to open. They need me."

"I'm sure they do."

"You find the killer yet?"

"We're working on it."

"Sick bastard." Every time Guzio spoke, he bumped into Liam's table and splashed some of his drink onto the floor. "You see the way she was all carved up like that? Crazy."

Liam pushed his mug to the side and leaned back in his chair. "I really can't talk about an open investigation. You have yourself a nice night."

"Hanging up there like a rag doll. Blood all over the place. You know, it cost me a pretty penny to scrub that blood off the carpet. Rug guy says I should replace the whole room, but screw that! Saved a ton of dough getting my boys to scrub it. Left a little stain, but no one would know what it is. We all have our secrets, right?"

Liam closed his eyes, and all he could see was the scene from the hotel again. Kerri, the blood, the paper flowers.

"Cops and detectives been back and forth a bunch of times. In and out. Always asking the same questions. I just want my place back. I gotta make some money! Been closed too long. Just 'cause that bitch gets cut up and hanged don't mean I can keep losing money."

Liam shot up from his seat and stood over the short, sweaty man. They were inches apart. "I told you I can't talk about an open investigation," he sneered. "I think it's time for you to go away."

Guzio's face contorted and twisted as if he'd just sucked on a lemon. "You trying to get rid of me?"

"Yes."

"Do you know who I am?"

"Yes. Go away."

Guzio backed up a step, and more of his drink splashed onto the floor. "You don't tell me what to do. Cop or no cop, you don't tell me what to do."

Liam matched his step. He tried to keep his voice at a hushed whisper, but he could see the others in the bar starting to turn to see what was going on. "You're either going to sit back at that bar, or you're going to leave. I don't care which. Just get away from me. Now."

"Screw you!"

"Go."

Guzio threw his glass down as hard as he could. Liam didn't follow it, but heard it smash onto the floor; the sound of tiny shards bouncing across the stained black-and-white tiles filled the place. Vanessa had done the same thing to him in their kitchen only hours earlier.

"Hey!" the bartender cried. He was an older man with a thick white beard. "Both of you get out, or I'm calling the cops!"

"The cops are already here!" Guzio shouted, laughing. "This pig right here is threatening me."

"I don't care who's saying what. Get going, or you'll have to tell your stories to the responding officers."

Liam stared at the little man as the rest of the place went quiet. He wanted nothing more than to throttle him so he'd never get up, but he couldn't risk the repercussions from either the police that would be called or the other patrons who would undoubtedly take the side of the insignificant blue-collar hotel owner over a cop. He stepped to the side to make his way out of the bar.

"No need to call anyone," he said calmly. "I'm leaving."

As Liam passed Guzio, the pudgy man grabbed him by the arm and pulled him closer. "Maybe instead of getting drunk at a dive bar, you and your boys should be out looking for the guy who made corned beef hash out of that pretty young thing."

And that was what it took. Without any further thoughts of reason or consequence, Liam punched Guzio as hard as he could. He felt his knuckles crush the little man's nose and heard the crunching of bone and cartilage echo throughout the bar.

Guzio fell back, unconscious before he landed on top of the table Liam had been sitting at, then onto the floor. Within seconds, two sets of strong hands grabbed Liam and threw him onto the ground. He couldn't see who had him but couldn't mistake the sound of a cocked shotgun. The voice of the bartender was loud and clear.

"Cops are on their way," he said. "You stay put until they get here."

40

When Guzio opened his eyes, the first thing he noticed was how dark it was. Night had taken over, and he couldn't see. The second thing he noticed was the pain. His entire head pounded. He pushed himself up from his couch and stretched into a sitting position, using what little strength he had to wipe the drool from his cheek that had seeped onto one of the cushions. When the room stopped spinning, he gently touched his nose and winced as he felt the pain course through his entire body. It'd be a while before that healed.

By the time he'd fully regained consciousness at the bar, the police were already on scene, and they had the other cop in the back of one of their cars. Guzio had given his statement and wanted to press charges, but he knew how pigs covered for one another, and there was no way these guys were going to allow that. In the end, the EMTs had patched him up, given him a handful of painkillers, and called a cab to take him home. When he'd arrived at his house, he'd popped a few pills, crashed on the couch, and passed out.

Guzio stood on shaky legs and walked into the hall where the keypad to his alarm system waited. The numbers were fuzzy, his eyesight coming in and out of focus. He stabbed at them with a fat finger and set the code to activate.

Beep . . . beep . . . beep . . .

"One more day," he said aloud to the empty room. "Tomorrow I'm back in business. Enough with those cops. Tomorrow night the Tiger reopens, and it's gonna be huge."

He rushed toward the landing before the ground floor sensors came on, and when he reached the top of the stairs, he heard the alarm sound off to indicate the device was now live. He had door alarms on both the front and back doors, window sensors on each ground floor window, and motion sensors in his living room, kitchen, and hall. There was nothing on the second floor. A full system was too expensive. If someone were to break in, they'd use the bottom floor. If they bothered to climb a gutter or scale one of the large oaks in his backyard or drop in from the roof, they could take whatever they wanted. At that point, they would've earned it.

Guzio stumbled into the bathroom and started the shower. He turned on the radio that sat on the side of the sink and could feel the beating of his heart in his head. A few minutes in the hot shower before turning in would surely make him feel better. Then it was back to business tomorrow. Back to life.

The water was hot, just the way he liked it. He took off his clothes and kicked them into a pile under the sink. He stepped into the tub and allowed the slow burn to run over his head and down his body. He lay down in the tub and let the shower massage him. The heat felt good. He placed a washcloth over his eyes and winced as it hit the bandage on his nose. The sound of the radio began to carry him to a different place. Tiny dots of light starred the black canvas of sightlessness and randomly popped different colors as his thoughts began to run into one another, eventually trailing off into nothing. He fell back to sleep in a matter of minutes.

———

Again, Guzio opened his eyes, and again he momentarily lost his center, forgetting where he was. The darkness. The pain. His sight line was partially obstructed by the water splashing onto his chest. He moved to sit up. The washcloth that had been on his face fell into the tub.

A noise had woken him, but in his dreamy state, he couldn't place it. It was beeping. Something was beeping. He knew the sound. He'd heard it before. In the fogginess of near sleep he tried to make the connection.

Beep . . . beep . . . beep . . .

It was so familiar.

Beep . . . beep . . . beep . . .

What was it?

Beep . . . beep . . . beep . . .

His alarm.

Guzio scrambled to his feet as both fear and anger caught him off guard. His head whirled when he straightened up, the bathroom tilting slightly to the left, then the right, then back to center. The pain tried to overtake him, but he fought through it. He turned off the shower and listened.

Beep . . . beep . . . beep . . .

Footsteps now. He could hear them bending the wood of the stair treads, climbing to the second floor. The alarm counted down the final seconds before it would activate the siren and automatically notify the police. In the background, behind the footsteps and the alarm, the radio played on.

Beep . . . beep . . . beep . . .

"Who's there!" He stepped from the tub and bent to grab his towel from the floor. He wrapped it around his belly and walked to the edge of the bathroom. "Who the hell is that? You better turn around and leave before you get an ass kicking! I'm not fooling around!"

The footsteps continued. Almost to the top now. The alarm and eventuality of the siren did not cause the intruder to move any faster. The slow, methodical footsteps carried on.

Beep . . . beep . . . beep . . .

Guzio poked his head out into the hallway in time to see the shadowy figure reach the top landing and turn toward him. "Get out of here!" he cried, but his voice cracked and gave away the fear he tried to keep hidden. He backed into the bathroom and frantically looked for something to defend himself with. If only he hadn't been asleep when the alarm was initially tripped, he would've had time to get to the bedroom, where his .38 sat in the top drawer of his nightstand. He had nothing where he was now. The figure kept coming.

Beep . . . beep . . . beep . . .

Guzio stopped when he saw the person standing before him. He was confused. What was happening?

Then he saw the gun.

The siren began to sound, screaming through the house.

The visitor held up one gloved finger. "First thing we need to do is shut off that alarm. After that, the police are going to call. You're going to tell them you didn't make it to the code panel on time and that everything's fine. They're going to ask for your password, and you'll give it to them. You got that?"

Guzio nodded.

"Let's go."

Guzio and his visitor made it back to the first floor, siren blaring. Shaking hands fumbled with the keypad, fat fingers punching the numbers until the house was silent again.

The phone rang.

"Showtime," the visitor said. "Password and an excuse. Then we need to talk."

41

Sean and Don sat in front of what remained of a bucket of wings and a handful of beers. The Hard Rock was packed. Every table was taken, and the bar itself was two rows deep. The Sixers were playing the Cavs, and it seemed tonight was as good a night as any to catch LeBron in action.

"You take the last one," Sean said, pointing to the remaining wing among the bones of its brethren.

Don shook his head. "That's all right. I've had enough. It's all you."

Sean grabbed the wing and drowned it in blue cheese. Don watched him as he ate, his thoughts elsewhere as the night drifted on. There was a part of him that wanted to come clean about having made that second copy of Kerri's computer files and the fact that Rocco was hacking into them, but it seemed secrets and distrust was the way things were playing out lately, so he swallowed his guilt and put on his best poker face. If there was information to share after Rocco broke into the files, it would be easier to apologize then.

"So you ready?" Sean asked, the corners of his mouth a combination of dressing and hot sauce. "Back on the big board tomorrow."

"Never stopped being ready. Had to wait for your trigger-happy ass."

Sean laughed. "Yeah, this one's definitely on me."

"You think you can still keep on top of things with Liam when we'll have our own caseload to handle?"

"I have no doubt. Being on the inside is much easier than poking my way around when I'm not on duty. I'll keep an eye on things, and

I won't let our load slip either. I figure Heckle and Keenan have about two or three more dead ends to follow up on in the next week before they can file the case away unsolved. That's all I want. Let's get this thing filed away, and then we can get to the bottom of what really happened. If Liam is being framed, I'll find the son of a bitch that's doing it. But if my brother really did have something to do with Kerri's homicide, I'll get him the help he needs."

"Have you even had a chance to mourn Kerri?" Don asked. "I mean, she was your friend and a huge part of Liam's life, and it seems like all you're doing is trying to make her go away. Have you even stopped for a second to mourn her?"

"I think I have," Sean replied. "In my own way."

Don fell back against his seat. "It's tough even being out here drinking and eating with all this mess going on."

"This isn't a celebration. This is camouflage. We have to look like everything's normal. Like it's all mundane, okay? We start sulking around and acting nervous, people will start asking questions. And the more questions they ask, the more risk we take of this getting out in the open. We play it cool, let Heckle and Keenan put Kerri's case to bed, and then we find the truth. You with me?"

Don nodded and held up his beer. "Always. You know that. You don't even have to ask."

42

Deep within the peacefulness of a sleep that was heavy and uncompromising, Liam began to hear a faint buzzing sound that was neither loud nor soft but simply there. He opened his eyes and was instantly blinded by light peering down at him from a sun that was rising over the Delaware River. He sat up slowly, suddenly aware of the ache in his head.

The storage containers were piled three high in rows that seemed to stretch on for miles. They were different colors, each one having come in from the Atlantic for distribution throughout the eastern half of the United States. He looked down at himself and could see his clothes were dirty and stained with oil. The ground under him was dusty and dry. He could hear seagulls squawking as they circled the sky offshore. He was at the shipyard.

His phone began to ring, and he recognized the sound from when he was asleep. He leaned against one of the containers as he climbed to his feet.

"Hello?"

"What in God's name are you doing?"

It was Sean. Liam rubbed his head and looked up at the sky again. "What are you talking about?"

"Where are you?"

"At the shipyard."

"Why?"

"I . . . I don't know."

As reality began to seep into his clouded mind, Liam looked up and down the rows of containers. He appeared to be alone. What was he doing in the shipyard?

"It was almost over," Sean barked from the other end of the phone. "Heckle and Keenan were going to put the case away, and that would've given us the time we needed to figure out what to do next, but you had to go back for more. What's wrong with you?"

"I don't know what you're talking about," Liam replied. Little flashes of memory began to burst in his mind's eye. The bar. Police. His house. Had he been home last night? He couldn't recall any of it with certainty.

"The hotel owner from the Tiger was drowned in his tub last night. A neighbor called it in after they found his front door open and went to make sure he was okay. His hands were tied behind his back. Sound familiar?"

"Wait. What?"

"Jane found a set of partials on the outside of the tub that didn't belong to the victim. Where were you last night?"

"After I left your place, I went to a bar in South Philly. I don't know the name of it. Sean, I had a fight with the hotel owner last night at that bar. It's on record. The cops came. That's all I can remember. I just woke up in the shipyard."

"Yeah, I know about the fight at the bar. You wanna know how I know? Jane tried your cell when they got the call. You never answered. If you'd picked up, they could've given you the prints to run, and you could've made them go away like you did with Kerri. We could've ended this and gotten you the help you needed. But you weren't around, so she ran them herself. The prints are yours."

Liam fell to his knees as his vision blurred with tears. "Sean, I just woke up in the shipyard, and I don't know how I got here."

"You're sitting there feeding me lies about being framed. I tried to help you. I don't understand. Why? I told you to come inside my house and talk with Vanessa. I begged you. We could've worked it all out. Why didn't you call me after the cops came to the bar you were at? I could've come and picked you up. I was already in the city at the Hard Rock with Don."

"I don't know what's happening."

"After your prints hit as a match, the fight at the bar came up as a cross-referenced incident. So did Guzio's name. Internal Affairs went into your files and found the match report from Kerri's scene. They checked all your records and found out about what happened with Mom. It all comes back to you. They know everything. They got a warrant for your house and pulled hair samples. They're running them now. Liam, there's an APB out on you."

"I got rid of the match report and all that stuff."

"They went through the FBI's back door in the database program. They found it all."

"Jesus," Liam whispered. He banged the back of his head against the steel container, trying to loosen the cobwebs so he could think clearly. "I'm going to turn myself in. I have to. Before anyone else gets hurt."

"No," Sean replied. "You're going to run and hide until I figure out what to do. If you turn yourself in now, they'll nail you with everything they've got. You'll go away for life. You know what happens to cops behind bars. Let me see what I can work out on my end with IA and the DA, and we'll go from there. Maybe we can make a deal or something."

"If I run, I'll look even more guilty."

"You are guilty! This isn't about guilt or innocence anymore. This isn't about you being framed and finding some shadowy culprit pulling the strings from behind a curtain. This isn't about Don or me or Vanessa or whoever else you had on your list of suspects. We're beyond all that. This is about avoiding the death penalty. Let me do what I have to do. I need you to stay hidden until I call. Don't answer your phone unless it's me. Don't even answer it for Vanessa. The cops are over at your place."

Vanessa. Liam couldn't imagine how this news could be impacting her. "I can't believe this."

"Stay hidden, and I'll be in touch. Promise me."

"I promise."

"I'll call you when I know more."

"Help me, Sean."

"I'm trying."

The connection was terminated. Liam dropped the phone into his pocket and fell farther to the dusty ground, the sunlight warm on his skin.

"Hey! You can't be here!"

A small group of dockworkers was rushing toward him, pointing and yelling. They were dressed in identical blue overalls and yellow hard hats. Two men from the group broke from the pack and started to run.

"This area is restricted! Get over here!"

Liam scrambled to his feet and ran as fast as his aching legs could carry him. He was dizzy, his head a mass of pain. His boots slipped on loose gravel, and he crashed into the side of one of the containers. The men were coming. He could hear them approaching like horses galloping. He got to his feet and sprinted toward the river, weaving in and out of the container rows.

"I think he went this way!" one of the men shouted.

Liam ducked behind a stack of old railroad ties and scurried along the bank of the river. The men were only a few feet away. He thought about what Sean had said.

This is about avoiding the death penalty.

He kept running.

The half circle of a storm drain peeked from the base of the river about twenty yards away. Liam scurried to the edge of the water and stopped, his heart beating in his chest so hard he thought it might explode. The tide lapped lazily against the shore, lulling him into a false sense of calm. It looked so unassuming, but he knew that death was just beneath its surface.

The men were closing in. He could hear them. Closer.

Liam swallowed the lump in his throat and waded into the water until he was waist-deep inside the mouth of the storm drain. Each step was agony. He felt as if he might slip and could feel the current reaching for him, trying to drag him out to sea. The men's boots crushed the gravel beneath them as they came closer. He eased himself forward, pushing ahead until he was hidden in the darkness. No one would be able to see him without coming into the water. He was safe for now.

The footsteps carried past the drain, and Liam let out the breath he didn't realize he was holding. He would remain in the drain until half the day had passed, trying to figure out his next move, a fugitive from the law. A murderer.

43

Sean hung up his phone and then turned it off completely. He stared at the note that was written on a piece of copy paper, scribbled quickly and taped to his computer monitor. *LT wants you.* As he walked through the floor, the others stared at him from the safety of their own desks. They'd said little to him since word of Liam's crime had spread through the department. What could they say? His brother was wanted for a double homicide.

The lieutenant was talking on the phone when Sean knocked. Phillips motioned for him to come in. "I understand, sir," Phillips said. "Yes, I'll look into it. We'll get some units on it right away, and I'll call you back in an hour with a progress report. Yes, sir. Thank you. Goodbye." He hung up and collapsed into his seat. "Too much," he said. He looked outside his office. "I need traffic cam footage from the Guzio house!"

"On it!" a voice replied.

Phillips turned his attention back to his detective. "Sean, talk to me. What's happening? Where did this come from with Liam?"

Sean held out his hands in surrender. "I don't know."

The lieutenant leaned forward in his seat, his eyes focused, cold. "Tell me the truth. I have no time or patience for anything else. I need to hear it straight from you. One time, between you and me. Did you know her? The victim? This Kerri Miller?"

"Never saw her in my life."

"You're sure?"

"You're hearing it straight."

"I better be."

"You are."

There was a beat of silence before Phillips rubbed his eyes and let out a tired sigh. "We got all our men on it. It won't be long before we find him."

"I'd like to be there when you bring him in. If that's okay."

"Yeah, I'll talk to the captain and IA. I'm sure that'll be fine."

"No perp walk. We bring him in through the back, and I'm there with his PBA rep."

"I know how it works."

Sean rocked back in his seat. "I'm glad to hear that," he said. "Because this is a first for me."

Phillips shook his head and started playing with a rubber band that was on his desk. "Known that boy for as long as I can remember. Was in Don's wedding party. Part of my sister's wedding. How can this be?"

"I was his brother and had no idea. We were all in the dark on this one."

"And you never saw a violent side of him?"

"Never."

"And you didn't know the victim?"

"I told you, no. I'm as surprised about all this as you are."

"They're going to make an example out of him. This case is a gift as far as the press is concerned. Serial killer is a cop. There'll be too much pressure on the DA. She'll be forced to go full-on with everything. Death penalty. Life with no parole. Something like that."

There was silence for a moment, and then Sean spoke. "So what happens now?"

Phillips pulled his middle drawer open and came away with a yellow legal pad. "You write down everything you know about what's happened up to this point. This is going to be your official statement. When you're done, you can go back to the control room and help the team track your brother down."

"And we bring him in like I said."

"Just like you said. I don't want fanfare, either. I'm trying to keep this professional. As professional as I can, anyway."

Sean pulled at the shield that hung around his neck and slid the pad closer to him. He unclipped a pen from the inside of his jacket pocket and started writing. This would be the most important statement he'd ever make if he was going to stay on the outside to help bring Liam in. Any missteps and IA would find it. His story needed to be airtight. Don's too.

"Never thought I'd be doing this," Sean said.

Phillips rose from his seat and walked around his small office. "Never thought I'd see it. The whole thing just stinks. I knew this kid. I looked into his eyes. We've shared meals together. I never would've thought he could be capable of something like this. Never."

"You know what happened with my mom when we were kids, right?"

"Yeah."

"That's all I can think of. Maybe crazy is passed on. In a gene or something. Like blond hair or diabetes. Maybe he got Mom's gene, and one day he snapped."

Phillips stared out onto his Homicide Division. "Maybe. But God help me, I thought he was a good man. I thought he was one of us."

"Me too," Sean replied as he finished writing his first sentence. "Me too."

44

Dr. Cain's reception area was empty but for the nurse working behind her desk. Liam held his head in his hands, waiting for Gerri to arrive back from a meeting. His pants were soaked from hiding in the storm drain and dripped onto the carpet. He was cold. The nurse at the desk kept staring at him, and he suddenly became aware of how vulnerable he was. He scanned the floor and took note of the exits at both the stairs and elevators, something he'd never thought he'd ever have to do. But he was on the run now, and he couldn't wait for Sean to call. He had nowhere else to go.

"Am I ever on time?"

Liam looked up and saw the doctor approaching. He forced a smile and stood on legs that were still weak. "Not that I've ever seen. Thanks for seeing me last minute."

"Why are you all wet?"

"I'll explain inside."

"Okay, come on in." Gerri turned to the nurse. "Dorothy, hold my calls."

Dorothy nodded and went back to whatever it was she was doing at her computer.

Gerri walked into her office and shut the door. When they were alone, she dropped her bags and hurried toward the windows, shutting the blinds, one at a time. "What are you doing here?" she whispered. "Christ, Liam, you're wanted for murder."

"You know about that?"

"It's all over the news. Why are you here?"

Liam fell onto the couch and rubbed his eyes. He was exhausted and wanted so badly to sleep. He could feel his mind wandering. "I need help. The truth is I can't remember anything about last night, and I couldn't remember anything about the night Kerri was killed." He paused for a moment, trying to find the words. "I was the father of that baby, and I was having an affair with her. The night she died is all a blank. Like that suppression you were telling me about."

Gerri grabbed a towel from her closet and tossed it to him. "You were talking about *you* the other day?"

"Yeah."

"Liam . . . I . . . I don't know what to say. Do you really think you could be capable of doing those things we saw in the pictures you showed me?"

"I didn't, but that doesn't seem to matter now. Two murders point to me, and I can't remember where I was for either of them. It's gotta be me, as much as I can't believe it. I must've had one of those psychotic breaks. That's the only explanation at this point."

Gerri pulled a file that was sitting on her desk and opened it. "I did some digging after you left. This girl who was murdered, Kerri Miller. You said her head was shaved?"

"That's right."

"Have you found the hair?"

"No."

"Interesting." Gerri walked over to where Liam was sitting. "Look, it's absolutely possible you committed these crimes and don't have any recollection of them, but something's not clicking."

"What do you mean?"

"When it comes to the human mind, all bets are off, and there have been plenty of cases documenting people who've committed vicious acts with no recollection of committing them, but the head shaving changes things. The way I see it, the guy who killed Kerri Miller revels in the fact he can cause so much fear and intimidation in his victim. When we spoke last, I explained how cutting the girl's hair and hanging her was a power trip. He *wants* to remember the process. He wants to remember all the details. He's not going to let himself forget. The killing is what he gets off on. He took the hair as a trophy because he didn't want to forget. This isn't the act of a killer so traumatized that his mind suppresses the events. It doesn't make sense."

"Nothing makes sense. Her head was shaved because that's what my mother did to her hair the day she tried to kill me and my brother."

"Then you being innocent makes all the more sense. If you killed the girl and the trauma forced you to suppress the memory, I doubt your subconscious would want to keep the hair. The two forces of the brain don't work in conjunction like that."

"If I am being framed, I can't prove it. Everything points back to me."

Gerri pulled another sheet of paper from her folder. "Have you ever been to Lakewood, New Jersey, with Kerri?"

"Lakewood? That's by the shore. Near Point Pleasant, right?"

"Yeah."

Liam thought for a moment, then shook his head. "No, I've never been there."

"You remember my theory about bruising or past scars or something that would show us a history of violence?"

"Yeah. We looked at the body and couldn't find anything."

Gerri sat down on the couch. "I ran her name and social through the system, and it turns out last year Kerri was brought into Kimball Medical Center in Lakewood with a facial contusion and sprained wrist. She filed a police report with the Lakewood PD while she was in the ER. I bet if you find out who's named as her assailant in that report, you find her killer."

Liam took the paper and studied it. He was tired and cold. His hands shook as he read through the report. "I remember that. She told me she hurt her wrist falling on wet tiles and hit her cheek on the bathroom door."

"You don't file a police report after you slip on wet tiles."

"I have to get to Lakewood."

Gerri got up from the couch and rushed over to her desk. She pulled a second file from her drawer and opened it. "I also got a copy of your blood work back," she said. "They automatically send me a copy since I'm the department liaison. The other one went to you at the office."

"What did you find?"

"Clean. No traces of anything."

"That doesn't help me."

The intercom on Gerri's desk beeped once, breaking the silence in the room. "Dr. Cain, please pick up." It was Dorothy, the nurse at the reception desk. Gerri picked up her phone and stood quietly, listening. After a few moments, she hung up.

"I need you to stay calm," she said.

"What?"

"Don't do anything rash."

"Come on, Gerri. What?"

"Dorothy recognized you from the news reports this morning and called the police. They're on their way."

Liam jumped from the couch. "Dammit!" he screamed. "I came here for help!"

"This is the time to surrender, Liam. As your friend, I'm telling you this is the time to give yourself up, and we'll give them the information they need to track down what happened in Lakewood. I don't think you're guilty, but you can't keep running. We'll tell them what we know and let them handle it. We don't want anyone else getting hurt."

Liam ran to the door and cracked it open. The reception area looked clear. He could see Dorothy standing at her post, looking his way.

"You're only going to make things worse," Gerri cried.

"I'm sorry, but I can't turn myself in yet. I will, but not yet. My brother's working things out on his end, and I have to get to Lakewood. No one's going to listen to me about theories of a frame job once I'm in custody. I have to find out what happened before I get caught. It's the only way right now."

Liam threw the door open and ran toward the stairs next to the elevators. He slid quietly into the stairwell and listened for approaching footsteps. He could hear someone coming from down below, but no one was talking. He turned and made his way up toward the next floor, determined to find a way to escape the hospital.

The next floor was the Medical Surgical Unit. He walked into the busy corridor and quickly stepped in line with the other foot traffic, passing the main desk without being noticed. As he passed the rooms, he peeked inside and saw mostly elderly people lying in beds, semiconscious, tubes protruding from various parts of their bodies. It looked as if they were in suspended reality, stuck between life and death.

"Clear the way! Coming through!"

A small team of three officers at the far end of the hall came running in his direction. The sea of people clogging the corridor parted ways as they ran by, guns at the ready. Liam ducked down and slid into the closest room he could find, shutting the door behind him and hiding against the nearest wall. He waited until he heard them pass. When they were gone, he turned to find an old man lying in the bed, asleep with the television on above him.

The patient's locker was at the far end of the room. Liam ran over and opened it. Inside were street clothes the old man had worn when he came in. There was a pair of tan slacks, a black golf shirt, a brown leather jacket, and a Phillies cap. Judging from the man's frame, it appeared they would fit well enough to disguise him and get him out of the hospital. He grabbed the clothes and began changing, stripping out of his wet pants and throwing those into the locker. He pulled the golf shirt over his head, and then put on the pants, jacket, and hat.

When he was done, he stuffed his pockets with the cash and contents from his own pants. It was time to run.

"Hey, what are you doing?" The old man was trying to sit up, pointing at Liam, who stood frozen for a moment. "Those are my clothes!"

"As soon as I'm done with them, I'll give them back. Promise."

The old man pressed the red call button on the side of his bed. "Nurse!"

Liam scurried out of the room and back into the hall. He passed the nurse who was walking toward the room he'd just left. It wouldn't be long before she'd sound an alarm and alert the police. He had to get out onto the street where he could blend in better.

The elevator doors opened as he approached. He pulled the cap a little lower and stepped on, only then noticing two young officers who were already inside. The doors closed before he could react one way or the other. He kept his head down and waited.

The ride to the first floor took forever. He watched the light come on for each floor as it crawled along. The officers were talking behind him.

"All units, be aware suspect is still in the building and has changed clothes."

Liam bit the inside of his lip to keep from screaming as he listened to the report coming over the officer's radio. They were passing the second floor now. He was almost there.

"Suspect is now wearing a black shirt, tan pants, and a brown leather jacket."

The elevator stopped at the first floor. Liam could feel his knees buckling, struggling to hold his weight. The officers behind him stopped talking. He dared not turn around.

"Suspect last seen on the fifth floor. Also wearing a red Phillies hat."

Liam was off the elevator before the doors had a chance to open completely. In a matter of seconds he was swallowed by the crowd in the main lobby.

"Excuse me, sir!"

He could hear one of the officers calling after him, but he continued on. The exit was fifty yards away, clogged by police personnel.

"Sir! Stop! You in the brown jacket!"

Walking faster. Turning down the first hall he came upon. A sign reading **GARAGE** pointed him straight ahead and to the left. When he was free from the crowd and somewhat out of sight, Liam ran as fast as he could.

"Liam Dwyer! Stop! Police!"

The officers began their chase. He looked back and saw them both in pursuit, running hard as they shouted into their radios. He threw himself through the double doors leading to the garage and picked up speed. His legs were heavy as he pressed ahead, hoping he wouldn't trip or fall down. Arch Street was on the other side of a first-level concrete wall. If he could get onto Arch, he could get to the subway. In the background, he could hear the army of police sirens coming for him. They were getting closer, trying to block off any exits and pin him in the garage.

"Hold it right there!"

Liam slid under an orange mesh fence that was a corner perimeter of a construction area and was suddenly on Arch Street. A few people who were walking by backed away and watched him as he climbed to his feet and ran to the end of the block, where sawhorses had been erected to block the rest of the roadway. Heavy machinery was parked behind the barrier. He knew people were watching, so he hopped over the horses and ran around a dump trunk, then in between a front-end loader and a backhoe. The voices behind him were gaining.

"He went in there!"

Liam doubled back and slipped into the oversized bucket of the front-end loader. It was piled with crumpled drywall and chunks of broken concrete, so he did his best to burrow under the debris to hide, but there was no way he could get deep enough. If one of the pursuing officers happened to look inside the loader, he'd be caught, but he was counting on the men running at full speed, with their focus up in front of them. If the eyewitnesses on the street told them he'd run through the site, all the better.

It wasn't long before the galloping footsteps of what seemed like a dozen officers came up to the front-end loader. Liam held his breath and buried his face farther into the debris. The officers ran by without slowing. He waited until he no longer heard anything and then poked his head out just a bit to ensure he was alone.

The gaping mouth of the subway entrance waited on the opposite side of the street. Liam climbed out of the bucket and ran as fast as he could into the subway.

The police would be retracing their steps at any second and setting up a net around the adjacent blocks. His lungs burned as he jumped down the steps, hurdled the toll slots, and threw himself onto a train that was pulling away toward West Philadelphia. He looked through the windows to see if anyone was following, but it was clear. He would have to get off at the next station and get himself back aboveground where he could hide. It was the only way.

45

The control room was bustling with activity. Three men were set up to handle all computer traffic while two others were on special dispatch to the patrols on the street. Liam's blown-up photograph from his department ID hung on one half of a whiteboard with his statistics written all around it. A few pictures of Kerri at the Tiger Hotel and Guzio in his tub had been taped next to Liam's picture. Everyone was talking or moving about. Sean stood at the edge of the chaos, watching.

Don walked over to Sean. "They froze his credit and debit cards, and we have units at the bridges, airport, and train stations. It shouldn't be long before they bring him in."

Sean rubbed his eyes. "I just wanted this to go away, you know?" He pointed to the crime scene photo from the Tiger. "I wanted to find out if Liam really did do that to Kerri, and if he did, I wanted to get him help behind the scenes without anyone else knowing about it. Why did he have to go and kill the hotel owner? It doesn't make sense."

"I have no idea," Don replied. "I'm thinking this might be for the best. Bring him in now, and end this before someone else gets hurt. Do you have any idea where he might be?"

"None."

"You think it's time to tell them about what we found at Kerri's apartment?"

Sean shook his head. "I just told the lieutenant I'd never seen Kerri before. Ever. I suggest you do the same until we can find Liam and bring him in the right way. Let's get him in, and then we can figure out what to do next. If I can't buy him time, I can at least bring him in on my terms."

Heckle and Keenan burst through the doors of the control room. "You got some balls interfering with our investigation," Keenan cried.

A few of the men turned to see what was going on.

"What are you talking about?" Sean replied.

Keenan's face was red. His anger made him seem even larger than he already was. "You show up at our homicide with some excuse about maybe you knew the victim, and it turns out you're running your own investigation behind our backs to protect your brother." He held up a small business card. "Went back to the Miller girl's friends to see if they recognized Liam's picture, and they show me Don's business card and tell me he was around their house a couple of days ago asking questions. What the hell is that?"

Before Don could respond, Sean took Keenan by the arm. "Let's go."

The group of men walked down the hall and into one of the empty interrogation rooms. Sean went next door to the observation room behind the one-way glass and turned off the microphone. When he returned, he shut the door and stood against it.

"You gonna confess something?" Heckle asked. "Maybe we should be recording this."

"Shut up," Sean snapped. "I'm going to level with you guys, but I need this to stay here. Cop to cop. This is between us. Deal?"

Keenan dropped Don's card on the table. "Go."

"I knew about my brother's affair with the victim. That's why he called me to the Tiger that night. He's my brother. I needed to find out what was going on before I turned him in. I had Don check on a few things for me while I tried to figure out what was happening. At first we thought Liam was being framed. I couldn't tell you because I was hoping either you would find the perp, or this would get filed unsolved and I could figure things out on my own. And if it was Liam, I could get him some help without anyone knowing. I was trying to protect him."

The room was quiet for a moment.

"Jesus Christ," Heckle muttered. "This is obstruction in the worst way, Sean. Guzio's death is a direct result of you tampering with a homicide investigation."

"I know, but he's my brother. What am I supposed to do? And he's a cop. We stick together when it comes to our own. I don't have to tell you guys that. I had no idea he'd go after the hotel owner. I just needed to figure out if Liam killed Kerri or if he was being framed by someone else. That's the story. All my cards are on the table."

"Why would he kill the hotel owner now?" Keenan asked.

Sean shrugged. "Tying up loose ends, maybe? Might've thought the owner would recognize him? I'm not sure."

"Or maybe he just snapped."

"Could be."

"Do you know where he is?" Heckle asked.

Sean shook his head. "I don't. And that's the truth."

"How do we know you're not lying again?"

"What's there left to lie about? Everyone knows my brother killed Kerri Miller and the hotel owner. At this point, I want to bring him in and get him help. No more lies when it comes to the four of us. But this stays between the four of us. I just got out of a meeting convincing Phillips I didn't know Kerri and was unaware of Liam's affair. Phillips made me write and sign a statement. I gotta be on the inside to bring him in the right way. If he knows I knew her, he'll bump me from tracking Liam. Don't dime me out now."

Keenan hopped off the table and rubbed his hands together. He took a deep breath. "Okay," he whispered. "We're good. This stays here. But we know what you know from now on. Got it?"

"Agreed."

"I'm serious. If we find out we're out of the loop, we go to IA with everything you just told us, and you can share a cell with your brother."

"Okay."

Someone knocked on the door, and Sean opened it. It was a uniformed officer.

"They traced Liam's GPS on his cell phone. He's near Boathouse Row. They're rolling units now."

Heckle and Keenan filed out of the interrogation room. Before Don could follow, Sean grabbed him and pulled him back inside.

"What?" Don asked.

"You went to the friend's house?"

"Yeah. When you guys started investigating me, I thought it was only prudent to clear my name. I took a ride to the friend's house and asked some questions. I needed to hear what happened that night from their lips instead of reading it in a file. I needed to see the expressions on their faces."

"You never mentioned that to me."

"I know the feeling."

"Anything else I should know? Anywhere else you've been without telling me?"

"No."

"You sure?"

"Positive."

The two men stared at each other, neither saying a word. Sean finally turned and walked out into the hall. The rules of the game were changing by the minute. He had to roll with it and make his adjustments if things were going to work out in the end. He needed to bend without breaking. There was still time.

46

Liam walked among the throngs of people who meandered along the path of Kelly Drive, hidden within the crowds. He was still wearing the outfit he'd stolen from the hospital, but he'd gotten rid of the red hat. It was too noticeable. The jacket was tied around his waist. He approached the cluster of storage houses that made up Boathouse Row, on the edge of the Schuylkill River, and was relieved to see several members of a crew team working.

He approached the team with Kerri's photo in hand from the pictures he'd taken from Kiki and his grandfather at the dock. While he had been hiding in one of the subway tunnels in North Philadelphia, he'd studied the picture, and something had struck him odd about it. Now he needed confirmation.

"Excuse me," he called as he jogged from the safety of the crowd toward one of the kids who was lining oars next to his shell. "I was hoping you could help me."

The kid was tall with long blond hair, athletic and already tan despite just coming off a cold winter. He stood as Liam approached. "What's up?"

Liam held out the picture.

"Don't know her. Never seen her. Sorry."

"That's not what I'm asking." Again, he held the picture out. "Take a look and tell me if that's a crew team rowing behind the girl? Over her left shoulder."

The kid took the photo and held it close. "Yeah, that's crew. Not sure of the team, but it's definitely crew. You can see the coxswain with the megaphone right there."

"Does anyone around here practice on the Delaware River? By the Ben Franklin Bridge?"

A chuckle. "Are you kidding me? You'd get run over by the ships, and the current's way too strong. Around here you crew the Schuylkill, or you don't crew."

"You're sure."

"Positive."

"I was told this picture was taken at the docks by Penn's Landing."

The kid took another look. "Nah, this picture was taken about a half mile up the road. Right there you can see the orange signs on the other side of the bank where the old Washington Walk Bridge was closed. I don't know who told you it was the Delaware, but they don't know what they're talking about."

"Thanks. You've been a big help."

"No problem."

Liam left the kid and made his way back into the crowd. He was walking, but his mind was a million miles away. He knew he was being framed, but now that he was a fugitive and a suspect in two murders, it would be hard to convince anyone else. He had to get to Sean.

The cell phone in his pocket rang, and Liam looked at the caller ID. It was Sean.

"Hey, I'm glad you called. We need to talk. I found—"

"Shut up and listen. They're tracking you through your phone's GPS. They know you're at Boathouse Row, and they're coming. Shut it off and run."

"But I—"

"Run!"

The line disconnected. Liam powered off his phone and stuffed it back in his pocket. He looked around and saw a few police officers walking with the crowd. They didn't appear to be searching for anything, but he couldn't be sure. Another officer on mounted patrol took his horse through Fairmount Park, where he and his brother had met only a few days ago. Sean had asked him that day if he'd killed Kerri, and he'd said no. Today he was surer of that answer than ever.

The first set of steps leading up to the museum was only about a hundred yards away. Liam turned around and began to walk back up the street. He went quickly, his head down, the people around him his only cover. The crowd was thick and slow-moving, filled with tourists stopping to take pictures or study maps as they made their way toward International Boulevard. He moved around them as best he could, weaving in and out, jumping into the street, then back onto the sidewalk. When he was at a small clearing, he glanced over his shoulder. One of the two officers was staring right at him. He quickly looked away and kept moving, but there was no doubt. He'd been spotted.

Liam jogged to the stairs and began to hop up, two at a time. He could see in the reflection of a mirrored sculpture on the first landing that both officers were in a calm pursuit, one of them talking into his radio. They were closing in.

When he reached the top of the stairs, a small group of college kids clapped and cheered as they pointed at him and sang the Rocky song. He spun around and saw more officers below, cutting into the crowd and spreading out, covering the perimeter of the museum. He surveyed his surroundings, trying to find an escape route. Inside the museum itself would be his only real chance.

The line of people in front of the entrance moved even slower than those walking on the streets outside. Liam pushed his way through and ran down the hall to the right, then took a large set of stairs to the second floor. He knew police procedures. One team would cover all the entrances and exits while a larger team would each take a floor to begin an extensive yet quiet search. More officers would be placed outside. They would cast a net over the entire property. His opportunity to escape was closing with each passing second.

The gift shop was at the top of the stairs. Liam ran inside, breathing heavily. He was sweating and dizzy from having eaten nothing since the previous day. He grabbed a white souvenir T-shirt, paid cash, and ran into the bathroom. Inside the bathroom, he threw away the jacket and black golf shirt he was wearing and put on the souvenir shirt. He drank gulps of water from the sink until his stomach couldn't take any more and stared at himself in the mirror. Perhaps this new outfit would buy him some time.

There was a small window next to the urinals. He went to see if he could spot any more activity outside, but when he looked, his view was obstructed by the scaffolding that had been erected across the entire back of the building. He remembered seeing it when he and Sean were walking through Fairmount Park. The idea came instantly.

Several officers were already on the second floor, searching. Liam cracked the door and watched as they spread out, two men down each hallway. He slipped from the bathroom and quietly took a set of side stairs to the third floor. A custodian was mopping up a spilled soft drink next to a soda machine.

"Excuse me," Liam said as he held up his police ID. "Philly PD. I need access to the roof. We're conducting a search of the premises, and I need a bird's-eye view. Can you take me there?"

The custodian looked at the ID and nodded. "Nice shirt."

"Trying to blend in as a tourist. The guy we're looking for might see the guys in uniform, but he won't see me."

"Yeah, I saw all those other cops when they came in. Come on. Roof access is this way."

Liam followed the custodian through a door marked EMPLOYEES ONLY and up a small set of hidden stairs. At the top, the man unlocked another door and pushed through. They ascended an iron ladder sticking up from the floor, and he unhinged the access door in the ceiling. Liam took three more steps, and he was on the roof.

He ran to the edge and saw the perimeter the police had set up. If he could get down the scaffolding without being noticed, he could go south through Fairmount Park and come back out at Boathouse Row.

"Thanks. That's all I need. You can go."

The custodian shook his head. "Can't leave you up here alone."

"Well, then, I better head down."

Liam ran to the opposite end of the building and jumped from the roof onto the top level of the scaffold. He didn't bother to look up to see if the custodian was tracking him. He was too busy climbing through the rungs on the side, trying to stay hidden and alive at the same time. His palms were sweating, and his hands slipped, almost sending him crashing to his death. When he reached the ground, he ran toward the entrance of the park, through the budding brush, and onto the other side near Boathouse Row. He was safe. For now.

He crossed the street and jogged back up Fairmount Avenue, away from the activity around the art museum. As he ran, he looked for a way out of the area.

Suddenly, a patrol car turned off 27th Street and headed right toward him. He was the only person on the sidewalk and knew he wouldn't have much time before the officers inside the car got close enough to recognize him. The new clothes could only do so much. He ducked into a deli.

"Can I help you?" a man behind the counter asked.

Liam watched out the window as the cruiser passed by. "No, I'm good."

"What are you looking for?"

"Nothing, really."

"Well, if you ain't gonna buy anything, I gotta ask you to leave."

"Yeah, okay. Sorry."

He stepped back outside as the patrol car turned the corner. The Philadelphian was across the street. He made his move.

The Philadelphian was a high-rise built exclusively for wealthy seniors. Among retirees, it was a much sought-after place to live. Liam scurried across a small one-way road and up the exit ramp to the front of the building. As he approached, the private charter bus that ran residents around the city was pulling up. He waited among the small gathering of residents and boarded the bus in a single file.

"Who're you?" the driver asked when he saw Liam. "Gotta have ID to ride this bus. Residents and employees only."

Again, Liam pulled out his police ID, obscuring part of his name with his thumb in case the driver recognized it from the news reports. "Need to hitch a ride to Penn's Landing. It's a police matter. My partner is meeting me there."

The driver looked at the ID. "Yes, sir, Officer. Welcome aboard."

It worked. He climbed in and sat.

As the bus pulled out of the Philadelphian and onto the street, Liam could see the small army of uniformed officers beginning to canvass the area. No one would have noticed how many there were at ground level, but sitting atop the hill the building was perched upon, he could see them spreading out in the crowd. The windows of the bus were tinted. No one would be able to see him escape. He was on his way.

He needed to find the truth.

47

The dock was busy. The warm afternoon brought as many people to Penn's Landing as the art museum and, again, Liam blended in with them, working his way closer to Kiki and Grandpa. They were both at their spot under the tattered awning in front of the café. Kiki was shouting at those who passed by while his grandfather snapped picture after picture, aiming his camera at as many people as possible. Some folks exchanged money with the boy, but most passed by without so much as a glance.

Liam approached them and, as he got closer, noticed the grandfather pull his eye away from the viewfinder. The old man looked at him and then called to his grandson in his native language. The boy ran back, and they both watched as he split the current of bodies walking back and forth from the water.

"Hi, Mr. Liam!" Kiki shouted, waving. "You want Grandpa to take your picture? One picture, one dollar."

"No," Liam replied. He held up Kerri's photograph.

"You already paid us for that one. Big tip. Nice man."

"Yes, I know. You told me you took this picture here, but I know you didn't. Tell me who gave you this picture to sell me."

The boy's demeanor changed. He smiled again, but this time it seemed forced. "Grandpa take that picture. We sell to you."

"No," Liam said. "This was taken on the other side of the city. That's the Schuylkill River in the background, not the Delaware." He moved in closer so they could both see. "Who gave you this picture?"

Kiki shrugged. "We don't remember."

"What?"

"We don't remember. Sorry."

Liam showed the picture to the old man. "Ask Grandpa."

"He don't remember, either."

"You haven't asked him."

The boy leaned over and said something in Cantonese. The old man responded in kind.

"No," Kiki replied. His eyes were darting in both directions now, nervous, uneasy. "He don't remember. Sorry."

The boy tried to leave. He went to push past Liam as he began calling for other possible customers, but Liam put a hand to Kiki's chest and gently pushed him back toward his grandfather. "I'm going to ask you one last time. It's important. Someone got hurt, and I need your help. You won't be in trouble, but it's important you tell me who gave you this picture to give to me."

The boy looked at the photograph and then began shaking his head furiously. "I don't know picture! I told you! Leave us alone! Go!"

The boy's shouts began to draw the attention of others in their vicinity. Liam put Kerri's photo away. He left without saying another word, making his way into the tackle shop, where Bud was waiting on three customers.

"Hey!" Bud cried. "Back again?"

Liam ignored him and pushed through the swinging door at the end of the counter. "I need to borrow something," he said. "Just for a sec."

Bud stopped what he was doing with his customer. "You can't come back here," he said. "What do you want?"

Liam reached up on the third shelf.

"Hey, man! What're you doing?"

He pulled a flare gun down and held it in his hand. The imperfections of the weapon were as plain as day, but it looked real enough, and he doubted the boy would know the difference. "I'll give it right back."

"Hey!"

The screams that carried through the air as he walked back across the dock, gun in hand, were piercing, but he was so focused on Kiki and Grandpa it didn't register that the tourists and others on the dock were screaming and running from him. For a moment, the boy looked as if he was going to flee, but as Liam approached, he simply fell back against the old man, both of them watching him.

"I'm going to ask you one final time," Liam said calmly. He held the flare gun up against the boy's skinny chest. "I'm not fooling around anymore. I like you, Kiki. I don't want to hurt you, but I will if I have to because people *I* care about have been hurt. Badly hurt. And I have to find out what happened. This isn't a game. I want to know who gave you that photo of the girl, or I pull this trigger. Do you understand? If you don't tell me, you're going to die right here, today."

Grandpa began waving his hands frantically. "Okay! Okay!" He started talking in Cantonese as he rifled through his box of pictures.

Liam could hear more screams behind him and now realized what was happening. "Hurry up."

The old man came away with a picture and gave it to the boy. The boy quickly looked at it and handed it over. "We don't know who he is. He came up to us and gave us the picture to give to you. He pay us two hundred dollars to do it and keep it secret. We didn't know anyone would get hurt. Please don't shoot me. I don't want to get arrested. You go away now. Please. I won't ask for picture from you anymore. I leave you alone."

Liam took the photo and studied it. The figure appeared to be a man. He was dressed in a gray pullover sweatshirt and black sweatpants. The hood on the sweatshirt was up over his head, and his face was covered with a scarf. The figure had been in the process of turning away when Grandpa had taken his picture. Who was this man?

"You don't know who this is?"

"No."

"Did you see his face?"

"No," Kiki replied. "He come to us like that. That's all we see."

Liam stuffed the picture in his pocket and ran down to the edge of the dock. He stopped and looked back toward the street. The police would be approaching from both directions, and SWAT would be dispatched. There was only one place to go, although his legs refused to take him any farther.

"Come on," he urged himself.

Sirens. Louder now.

Liam carefully walked onto the slip that held Sean's boat. The platform rocked up and down as he inched his way forward, whimpering, willing himself to move faster. He stepped onto the back of the boat and climbed aboard, quickly running around, unsnapping the cover and throwing it into the water. He knew Sean kept a spare set of keys in a locked cubby above the steering wheel. He couldn't afford to get caught. Not now. This was the only way.

It took three shots with the butt of the flare gun to crack the plastic covering over the cubby. He grabbed the keys, pushed them into the ignition, and turned it on. The motor was out of the water. He pressed the button he'd watched Sean press so many times before and waited for the motor to lower itself down. His breathing was heavy and short. The boat rocked as the deck had done, lifted by his shifting weight and the swells in the current.

Four police cruisers pulled up onto the dock as people continued to scurry for cover. The officers spilled from each unit, weapons drawn, aimed at their suspect.

"Stop right there, and turn off the engine," a voice boomed from one of the patrol car's loudspeakers. "Place your hands above your head, and interlock your fingers. Do it!"

The blades of the rotor were just touching the surface of the water. Liam slipped on the life jacket that was next to the steering wheel and looked behind him. Two of the officers were making their way toward the slip. There was no time left. He started the engine and pushed the throttle forward, launching the boat, full speed, into the Delaware River as the side cleats popped under the thrust of the vessel that was still tied to the dock. He turned around and saw the officers running back toward their cars. They would call this in, and the police would launch their own marine unit along with a Coast Guard backup. He needed to use every second he could to his advantage.

His grip on the boat's chrome wheel slipped as he turned the boat east toward New Jersey. He was actually out on the water, the one place that frightened him the most. His knees would not hold him for long, as he was growing weaker with each passing moment.

The flashing lights from the dock grew smaller with distance. There was movement in his periphery, and Liam turned to see what it was. A helicopter, still nothing more than a dot in the sky, was heading straight for him. The boat bounced in and out of the water as he pushed the throttle even harder, slamming against the choppy surface. The helicopter was gaining on him. He could hear the rotor blades thumping as it closed in on its target. He weaved his way around other vessels as best he could. The other boats were moving both with and against him in the channel. The echo of their air horns momentarily drowned out the helicopter that was in pursuit.

"Come on!" Liam shouted aloud. He could feel his heart thumping in his chest.

He pulled the boat slightly north and could see a massive barge heading toward him, just under the Ben Franklin Bridge. The helicopter was very close now, almost on top of him. Without thinking through what he was doing, Liam pushed the throttle the rest of the way forward and steered the boat toward the barge.

"You can do this. You can do this."

The barge was about three hundred yards away. He aimed the bow toward the side of it. The coastline of New Jersey was right next to him now as he tightened his angle and pulled back on the throttle. He eased the boat as close to the barge as he could, then pointed it north.

"You can do this. You can do this."

The helicopter was practically on top of him. If he could make it to the bridge, it would have to peel back, fly over the bridge, and pick him back up on the other side. That was what he was counting on. This was it. Now or never.

As the shadow of the Ben Franklin caught the front end of the boat, Liam passed the massive barge. He let go of the steering wheel, stepped to the edge, and stared into the black water, knowing what he had to do to survive but unable to get his body moving. His bottom lip began to tremble as he held his breath and jumped. The river finally had him.

The water was ice on his skin. He broke the surface and for a moment could see Sean's boat bumping up against the side of the barge as the two vessels passed each other. It was still heading north, this time without him. Suddenly, he was sucked back under, but he bounced up again with the help of his life jacket. His body turned numb almost instantly, the current sweeping him south with a ferocity he hadn't been expecting.

"Oh my God! Oh my God!" he panted, panic overtaking him.

Arms that felt like logs began to slap at the surface as the survival instinct took over. The water was so cold. He started to gain control of himself as the current continued to try to take him out to sea. He fought with every ounce of energy he had as he began swimming closer toward the shore. Although the cover of the bridge still protected him, the current would sweep him out in a matter of seconds. He swallowed the cold black water as he tried to swim. Part of him wanted to stop paddling, take off the life jacket, and allow himself to sink. His mind began to fog over, and he wondered if hypothermia was already setting in. He heard his mother's voice.

We're going to visit your father. One happy family.

Liam's foot got tangled in a fallen tree that stretched out from the bank of the river. This stopped his momentum and spun him around, allowing him something solid to grab on to. He struggled with all the strength he had and climbed atop the trunk, first throwing one foot over, then hoisting himself up around the rest of it. He cried out in both pain and fear until he was finally out of the water and on the tree. His body shivered uncontrollably. Across the way and south from where he now sat, he could see emergency lights flickering at the dock. He could hear the helicopter but could no longer see it from where he was under the bridge. The boat that had saved him grew smaller as it continued north in a current that pushed it around. There was no time to rest. It wouldn't be long before either the helicopter or the marine units figured out the boat was empty. In situations such as these, it would be protocol to send the helicopter back around to retrace where he was last seen, which would be at the base of the bridge. Some of the men might board the barge to see if he had stowed away, but most would track him from the area he now sat at, catching breaths that came in harsh, raspy waves. They'd track both on foot and from overhead. They'd use dogs. He had to keep moving. He had to get to Lakewood.

48

The control room was a mass of confusion. Sean stayed out on the perimeter, watching everyone run this way and that, searching for his brother, who they were convinced was a murderer. The photo of Liam that had been up on the whiteboard was now replaced by a map of Philadelphia and Camden, New Jersey, which was also enlarged on a digital screen at the front of the room. There was a red dot on Penn's Landing where Sean's boat had been moored and a dashed line that showed the route the boat had taken, which ended in a second red dot upriver that represented the place where the boat had crashed onto the shore. Smaller green dots pocked the screen on the New Jersey side, representing all the possible ways Liam could've escaped into the woods and, farther on, into the neighboring cities. No one had any answers. Their suspect had slipped away with the precision of a real convict, which bought Sean the time he needed to get things back on track.

Keenan slammed down the phone. "The news chopper lost him after the barge passed. I can't believe this!"

"We have our own bird in the sky," Phillips called over his shoulder as he studied a computer screen in front of him. "Camden PD has scrambled their SWAT units, and the BOLO is going out to every department in the county."

"What about news coverage?" Heckle asked.

Phillips nodded. "Five and six o'clock. Lead story. Top of the hour. They'll get his face out there."

Keenan walked from behind the desk he was at and looked up at the display screen. "How could the chopper lose him? They were following him the whole time."

Don pulled a sheet of paper from the printer and scanned it. "News choppers are for car accidents and fires," he said. "Stable things. This isn't LA, where you film a high-speed chase every other day. They didn't have the expertise. They followed the moving object, which was the boat. By the time they realized the boat was empty, Liam was in the woods, and the brush cover camouflaged him from the sky. Not the pilot's fault."

Phillips stood up and put his hands on his hips. "Okay, people, no more bitching. I don't want to hear it, and it doesn't get us any closer to bringing Liam in. Camden PD is on it, and our bird is in the air with their permission. Let's keep working with what we have to try and figure all this out. And where is my traffic cam footage from the Guzio house?" He pointed to Heckle and Keenan. "You two get over to the command post in Camden. I want you on the ground if he's spotted. This is our guy, and we bring him in our way."

The two detectives headed toward the exits. As Sean watched them go, he saw Jane in the hallway, motioning for him to come to her. He pushed off the wall he was leaning against and followed her outside.

"What's up?" he asked.

Jane was nervous. She kept looking around to make sure they were alone. "I need to talk to you."

"Shoot."

"Back in the beginning of the investigation, Liam had me run an off-line search through NCIC. That's how we found the second victim. We started with loading the criteria from our victim at the Tiger and spinning our search outward from Philadelphia in ten-mile increments."

"Okay."

"We found more."

Sean nodded and took her gently by the shoulder, guiding her up the hallway and through one of the exit doors that led into the parking lot. The sun was setting, but he could still feel it on his face when he walked outside. "What do you mean you found more?"

Jane held out a file she'd been holding. "They aren't as comprehensive as the Delaware victim, but there are enough pieces here to fit the MO of both the Miller vic and the prostitute in Wilmington."

Sean took the file and opened it. Inside, there were pictures and PDF copies of police homicide reports from all over the Northeast. Boston, Mamaroneck, Nantucket, Bridgeport, Baltimore.

"NCIC picked them up because they were all prostitutes, abducted from remote locations like the train tracks or the harbor. Each victim was found the next day. It started with Boston. Vic was found behind a set of dumpsters in the back of a Starbucks. Strangled, hair cut off. Second vic was Mamaroneck, New York. Also strangled, but this time hung from a tree in a local park. Abducted in Yonkers. Hair cut as well."

Sean kept reading the reports while Jane explained. He scrolled through each one, reading every line.

"He goes back to Massachusetts for the third vic," Jane continued. "Found in a motel in New Bedford. Strangled but left on the bed. Hair shaved more than cut this time."

"He was building up to it," Sean said. "Liam was using these girls as models to build up to what he did to Kerri."

Jane nodded. "I was thinking the same thing because Bridgeport and Baltimore were almost identical. Vics were found hanged in a hotel, one from the clothes rack in the closet and one from the shower-curtain rod that was bolted in the wall. Heads shaved. By the time he got to our girl in Wilmington, he was almost perfect. The only thing missing was the laceration across the stomach. None of the practice victims were cut. I think our vic from the Tiger was what he'd been building up to." She paused for a moment. "Wilmington PD also got back to me on their bone analysis of the exhumed prostitute. They found traces of ketamine hydrochloride. This is all Liam."

Sean closed the file and handed it back to Jane. He put his hands up to his face and sighed deeply. "I can't believe this is happening."

"My only question is, Why would he suggest an NCIC search if he knew there was a chance we'd find his other victims?"

"I don't know. Maybe he wanted to get caught."

"Then why is he running now?"

"I don't know. Who else knows about this? These other vics?"

"Obviously I gotta bring it to Phillips and Heckle and Keenan. I just wanted you to know first. I thought that was the right thing to do. You didn't ask for this, so I figured I'd give you a heads-up that this was about to go down."

Sean dropped his hands away from his face and put on the best smile he could. "I appreciate the heads-up. Go tell Phillips. I'll be in, in a minute. I really don't want to see his face when you tell him."

"Understood."

Jane walked back inside, leaving Sean alone in the parking lot. He pulled his phone out of his pocket and dialed. Across the lot, a rat scurried from under a car with a half-eaten burrito in its mouth. It was gone in a matter of seconds, slipping through the opening of the sewer drain and disappearing into the darkness.

"It's me," Sean said as he walked farther from the door. "Update. They found out about the other girls."

49

The Lakewood police station was empty but for a lone officer working the front desk. Liam walked in and quickly checked his surroundings, trying not to act suspicious in the process. He marked each entrance and exit. There weren't many. He took note of how the front desk stretched to each end of the wall. The only way into the belly of the station was through a black metal door around the corner from where the officer now sat. He'd have time to run if he needed it.

There was no way to know if the BOLO back in Philadelphian reached as far as Lakewood, so Liam positioned himself halfway between the front desk and the door leading to the parking lot in case he was recognized. He'd found a change of clothes in a Goodwill bin behind a grocery store in Camden, so any description of what he was wearing would be different now. A taxi had taken him straight across the state to Lakewood without stopping. The cash he had was running low, and he knew his credit cards had probably been shut down, which would've been normal procedure. He was on his own, determined to find the truth.

There was a local radio station streaming through two speakers in the ceiling. Beyond that, the crackle of the police dispatch radio echoed in the foyer. The officer behind the desk looked up from a paper he was reading. "Can I help you?"

Liam cleared his throat, trying to project as much confidence as he could. This was risky but really the only way. "Hi. I'm Liam Dwyer.

Forensics with the Philadelphia PD. We're working a homicide and tracked a past police report filed from this department. I need a copy."

The officer stared at Liam. "You got ID?"

"Sure."

The officer took the ID, looked at it for a moment, and then shrugged. "No one called about any old records," he said.

"Really? They were supposed to call this morning so it would be waiting when I got here."

"Don't know what to tell you. No one called."

Liam took Gerri's hospital report from his pocket, unfolded it, and handed it to the officer. It was wet from the river, but legible. "Can you get it for me now then? I'll wait. The girl's name and social are on this hospital report. Your records will match the date on the form. Same incident."

Whatever the officer was reading was clearly more important or entertaining than pulling an old file. He glanced at the hospital report and then pushed it away. "I can't get it for you now. I'm the only one here, and someone has to work the desk. Come back tomorrow around noon, and we'll have it for you."

"Sorry, but I need it now. We're closing in on a suspect, and I need to be back in Philly with this report tonight. The victim is the woman named on this hospital record. You think you could do me a solid?"

"I'm working solo here. Can't leave the desk. I don't know what you want me to do."

"Where do you keep the files?"

"In boxes downstairs. We're getting a new computer system next month, and we hired some kid to scan all the files so they're electronic. Everything's downstairs waiting for the software to be delivered. I wish I could help, but you gotta come back tomorrow. If you want, you can sign the release form now, and we'll fax you the report, but it's going to be tomorrow either way."

The more time he spent at the station was more time he allowed those who pursued him to send word. He had to get in and out as quickly as possible. "I can go through them," he suggested. "I need this report, or my boss'll have my ass. Let me find it. I'll make a copy, and I'm outta here. Don't even need to sign a release, so no one needs to know you did me a favor. The faster I get down there, the faster I'm gone."

The officer thought about the proposition. He flipped through his paper, then finally looked up. "Your boss a prick?" he asked with a smirk.

Liam smiled in return. "Aren't they all?"

A buzzer sounded, unlocking the door from the foyer to the inside of the station. "First door on your left at the bottom of the stairs. Hurry up."

Liam rushed through the door, down the small corridor, and through a second door that led him downstairs. It was dark in the basement, and his fingers fumbled for a light switch.

The file room was nothing more than an oversized closet. Metal storage shelves were screwed against the wall with cardboard boxes filling each one. The boxes appeared to be in chronological order, which was helpful because all Liam had was the date from the hospital visit. He had no idea which officer originally took the report.

He worked quickly, pulling down anything that marked the date of Kerri's hospital visit. He was locked inside a police station, one floor down from the nearest exit. The BOLO had to have been spreading across the state. Each passing minute made him more vulnerable. All the Lakewood police needed was an email bulletin alerting them of the situation, and it was over. His hands moved as fast as they could.

The third box he checked that matched his month was marked "Snyder." He flipped through until he found the date he was looking for and slowed down. Officer Snyder had been busy that day, but what was in the file was not unmanageable. Drunk and disorderly, disturbing the peace, backup on a parking ticket argument, bar fight, another bar fight. All typical calls during the summer season at the shore. He stopped when he saw the report from Kimball Medical Center and pulled it from the box.

It was a domestic violence offense. According to Kerri's account, she had been at a local motel with her boyfriend when they'd gotten into an argument. The argument had intensified until other guests began calling the front desk to complain. When the manager had knocked on Kerri's hotel door, she'd opened it and begun screaming for help, stating the boyfriend had attacked her and punched her in the face and hurt her wrist. She said he was trying to kill her. The manager took Kerri to his office, and they called the police. Officer Snyder had taken the boyfriend into custody, and an ambulance had taken Kerri to the hospital. Liam scanned the document to see the named assailant.

Sean Dwyer.

How many people know about you and Kerri and what happened with Mom?

There was a note stapled to the report, handwritten by someone. He guessed Officer Snyder. *Charges dropped. Assailant released (on the job).*

It appeared Kerri had dropped the charges as soon as she was discharged from the hospital. Perhaps she'd panicked when she'd said he was trying to kill her, but with the witnesses and the call to 911, the police had to follow through. In the privacy of her own thoughts, when things calmed down, she must have decided to drop everything, and they'd both hidden what had happened that night. But why was she at the shore with him in the first place? She'd never mentioned it. Neither had Sean. How was Sean involved in all of this?

Liam took Kiki's photograph out of his pocket and studied it. The hooded man could've been Sean. The figure was the right height and build, but it also could've been a lot of people. Sean was average in height and weight, but seeing this new evidence of the arrest made the picture a little clearer.

He copied the record and made his way back up to the main floor, listening to see if he could hear anyone. The officer behind the desk hardly looked up from what he was reading to wave goodbye. When Liam got outside, he walked without knowing exactly where he was going. He just had to keep moving. Thoughts and emotions overcame him like a tidal wave.

He stopped when he saw the cell phone store across the street. An idea occurred to him. He jogged through the intersection and walked inside. Like the police station, it was empty but for one salesman behind the counter.

"Hey there. What can I do for you?"

Liam dug into his pocket and came away with Kerri's phone. "Yeah, my wife dropped this in the toilet. Any way you can bring it back to life for me?"

The salesman took the phone, opened the back, examined it, and then nodded. "No problem. You just need a new battery. Everything else seems okay. They make these things pretty watertight these days. I got a battery right here."

"You mind if I plug it in real quick when you're done? I have to make a call. It's important."

The salesman replaced the battery and handed over a spare charger. "That'll be seven dollars, ninety-five cents."

Liam handed him the cash.

"Got an outlet by the door if you want some privacy."

"Thanks."

Liam took his change and made his way over to the front door. He plugged one end of the charger into the phone and the other into the outlet. He had no idea if anyone had thought to shut off Kerri's phone, but he knew he couldn't use his. He watched as it came to life.

"You got Wi-Fi in here?"

The salesman nodded. "Wouldn't be much of a cell shop without it."

"Okay," Liam whispered to himself. "Let's see what we can see."

50

The department was in chaos as they hunted for Liam. Don stepped on the gas and listened to the engine of his new Mustang respond accordingly. His peripheral world passed by in a blur. He gripped the leather steering wheel and concentrated on the road ahead. Kelly Drive opened up to two lanes coming into the city, and with most of the traffic heading in the opposite direction, he tested the car to see how fast it could go. The road bent and twisted, following the path of the Schuylkill River. He wove in and out of each lane, increasing pressure on the accelerator, feeling the tires hug the pavement. His body shifted in the bucket seat. Sometimes driving helped to put things in perspective.

Don had purchased the car at the auction house the summer before. It was a midnight-blue GT with white racing stripes running from hood to trunk. A failed investment banker had it repossessed by the city after he'd gotten laid off, and Don had called in a favor with the dealer, paying what the banker owed in cash before it had a chance to see the auction floor. It was his. All his. Sure, it was a midlife crisis purchase, and of course Joyce teased him about being a cliché, but he didn't care. He loved it. This was his toy, and when he took it out, he liked to play.

The latest trip to Doylestown had been another unexpected visit. Just after the helicopter had lost Liam on the banks of the Delaware River, he'd gotten a call from his mother. She was feeling ill, complaining of dizziness and nausea. Adena had already gone home for the day and wasn't due back until eight the following morning. She didn't want to be alone and refused to call the evening nurse because they didn't have the same relationship that she had with Adena. Don had pleaded with her to call the front desk, but she had stood her ground. When she'd begun to cry, he knew he had to go. What else could he do? So he'd told her he'd clear it with his team and come up. The relief in her voice came immediately, and that made him feel a little better.

When he arrived at her condo, he helped her do her stretches, fixed her pain medication, and gave her some tea to chase it with. When the symptoms subsided, he fixed a plate of eggs for dinner, and they talked about nothing in particular. After she ate, he helped check her blood and gave her the two white pills for her diabetes. It wasn't long before she was feeling like herself again, and he was able to leave with a kiss and a promise to visit over the weekend.

The Mustang sped around the bend. He could see the tip of the museum on the other side of the hill. There was no music playing on the stereo. Only the roar of the engine and the whining of the tires. He thought about Liam and the investigation as he drove into the city. Something wasn't sitting right with him. How could a person whose profession it was to uncover crime scene evidence leave his own fingerprints at two separate crime scenes? How could he be so reckless? Sean had theorized that perhaps it was Liam's way of crying out for help, but if that was the case, why would Liam order an NCIC search, knowing there were other victims out there to find? At the beginning of all this, Liam had been certain he was being framed. Don was beginning to think that perhaps he was right.

The road turned again, bringing him past Boathouse Row, closer to the museum. He could see the back of it now, the classic architecture, the pillars, the stone stairs leading up the rear, the scaffolding Liam had escaped down earlier that morning. His phone rang, and he hit the Bluetooth button on his steering wheel.

"Carpenter."

"Hey, Detective, it's Rocco. I'm done with the encryption. All solved."

"Excellent. That was pretty fast."

"I'm pretty good."

"Is this the part where you show off by explaining all the ways you got into the system, purposely using words and phrases you know I won't understand in order to make yourself look smarter?"

"Nope. Found the back door to the system. Got in. Done."

"I love it."

"If you bring the flash drive back, I'll load everything onto it so you have one source with everything you need."

Don pulled onto Benjamin Franklin Parkway. "I'll be there in a few."

"Cool."

The phone disconnected, and he looked out his window as the Philadelphia skyline swallowed him. Despite all the chaos surrounding the department, there was a thread of truth somewhere. He just had to find it, follow it, and let it lead him to the big picture. All cases were solved in this manner. Liam's case would be no different.

51

Don was pretty sure Rocco was still wearing the same clothes from yesterday. As before, he followed the hacker inside the cramped space and stood by the rows of mainframes and towers, next to the laptops that lined his desk.

Rocco sat down in front of the desk. "You got the drive?"

Don fished the flash drive out of his pocket and handed it over. "Be honest with me—did you look at the content after you bypassed the encryption?"

"I told you I would. I'm a hacker, Detective. That's what I do. That's all I do. My sole purpose in life is to break into systems that are thought to be impenetrable. Within the confines of whatever it is I break into, there is information being held that is supposed to be kept from the general population. This is my pot of gold at the end of every rainbow."

"So you looked at everything?"

"Of course I looked at everything."

Rocco plugged the flash drive into the laptop and started typing. The computer screen flashed once and then changed. Don leaned in so he could see better. Kerri had saved PDF copies of almost fifty photographs. Some looked as if they'd been taken out in public but from a distance. The others looked as if they'd been taken while she was hiding. He could see the corners of the buildings she'd hidden behind and the branches of trees and shrubs she'd taken pictures from. The subjects—a man and a woman—were kissing, holding hands, smiling, caught in an embrace. They were the same two people in all of the pictures.

Sean and Vanessa.

On the bottom of each photograph, Kerri had written in dates, times, and locations.

"She'd been tracking them for over a year," Don mumbled.

"Yup. Who's the girl? Who's your partner touching that he shouldn't be touching?"

"None of your business."

"Ah, so you *do* know who she is. Nice."

"Shut up."

Rocco minimized the file with the photos and clicked on the second file that had been encrypted. Six different screenshots appeared, each one showing a black-and-green map of the Northeast. A red line followed a path to a harbor. Each red line originated from Penn's Landing.

"These are maritime GPS mapping trips," Rocco explained. "That red line there is the path a boat took to and from the destination."

"Yeah, I see. Can you tell specifically which boat it is?"

"Only the slip it launched from. Looks like it was Penn's Landing Marina, slip 28."

Slip 28 was where Sean's boat was kept.

Don fell back against the mainframe towers. Sean and Vanessa had been having an affair, and Kerri knew. Now Kerri was dead.

"Hey, you okay?" Rocco asked. "You don't look too good. Is this worse than you thought?"

"I'm fine," Don replied. He cleared his throat and straightened himself. "Give me the drive and erase your copy. Trust me, this is for your own good. You know how to erase something permanently from the system. I suggest you do it. I'm not fooling around."

"Yeah, sure. No problem."

"You don't talk about this to anyone."

"Okay."

"Anyone."

"I won't. I swear."

The small apartment was suddenly stifling. Don took the drive and left quickly. Rocco said something to him as he was leaving, but he didn't hear it. His mind was elsewhere.

Sean and Vanessa.

When he was back out on the street, Don walked half a block to his car. He climbed in, started it, and pulled out into traffic, heading toward Old City. He had no idea someone had been parked three spots away and had been watching him the entire time.

52

It was pushing nine o'clock, and Jane was still in the lab loading data into a computer when Don walked in.

"You got a sec?" he asked.

Jane turned away from her screen. "Of course. What's up?"

He dropped a small sandwich bag onto the table. "I need this analyzed against the material found in Kerri Miller's fingernails."

"Is that what I think it is?"

"I was hoping you could tell me."

"Where did you get it?"

"I can't say. Not yet." Don closed the door so no one could hear them. "And for the time being, I need this kept between us. There's a good chance I'm wrong, and I don't want things blowing up before I get the results back."

Jane nodded. "Understood. I can have them back to you first thing tomorrow morning. It's not hard to analyze."

Don saw a file sitting on the edge of Jane's desk marked "Miller Case: Other Victims." "What's that?" he asked.

"You'd already left when I briefed the lieutenant and the others. We found additional victims through an off-line NCIC search. I'm just uploading the info into the database so we all have the same information."

"More vics?"

Jane handed him the file. "Yup. Caught one down in Wilmington that matched the Miller girl, so we spun out the search radius and found more in Boston, Mamaroneck, Nantucket, Bridgeport, and Baltimore. Pretty much the same MO."

Don read through each report, his mind churning as he went. The women were abducted, then found the next day. Strangled. Hair cut off. But the cities. They were the same cities from Kerri's file.

"Theory is Liam was building up to the Miller girl. Another possible theory is these killings are of a serial nature."

"Liam's no serial killer."

"I wish I had your conviction, but after these past few days, I don't know what to believe anymore."

"Whose idea was the NCIC?" Don asked.

"Liam's," Jane replied. "And yes, it is strange that he would order a search if he knew there was a chance we'd come across these girls. I've been struggling with that all day."

"Can I borrow this file for a second? I'll bring it right back."

"Knock yourself out."

Don hurried from Jane's office and ran down the hall. He hopped down one flight of stairs and burst through the door to the Homicide Division. Most of the unit was deserted, with the extra manpower either on the street looking for Liam or in the control room doing the same. He walked to his desk and sat down in front of his computer. The laptop came to life, and he plugged in the flash drive Rocco had given him. As the file was downloading onto the screen, Don opened Jane's file. One by one, he matched the discoveries of the other victims with the maritime GPS coordinates Kerri had tracked. Wilmington, Boston, Mamaroneck, Nantucket, Bridgeport, Baltimore. Every trip Sean took on his boat was a direct match to a victim.

"This can't be."

It was all right there. The ruse. The betrayal. The lies. It was Sean. Kerri had been killed because she'd discovered too much about Sean, Vanessa, and the other women he'd killed. Sean was the killer. It all fell into place now. Liam wouldn't be foolish enough to leave his own prints behind a murder scene. But if Sean was framing his brother, the prints would be the evidence they'd need for a conviction. Sean was making Liam run because he was controlling how these crimes were unfolding. Sean was a killer, and Kerri had discovered his secret. For that, she'd paid with her life in a most gruesome way.

In the solitude of the Homicide Division, Don rose from his seat, took Jane's file over to the scanner, and began copying everything she had into a PDF. Nothing was what it seemed anymore. Everything had suddenly changed.

53

The pounding on the door resonated through the tiny apartment. He could hear footsteps approaching. "I'm coming!" a voice shouted from inside. "Damn, man, hang on a sec." The deadbolt turned, the chain lock unfastened, and the door opened. "Oh, hey," Rocco said, his voice catching in his throat just a bit. "What's up?"

"I need to talk to you."

"Dude, it's late."

"It's important."

"Okay."

"Can I come in?"

"I guess so. But you gotta make it quick. I'm bingeing on *American Horror Story*. Been watching nonstop since yesterday. Completely addicted."

Sean stepped inside and closed the door behind him. He'd been in Rocco's apartment several times before. Rocco flopped down in the chair by his desk. His computers were still running. It was only a question of what they were running, and Sean really didn't care.

"How can I help you?"

"Don and I are working on a case, and I know he dropped off something for you to take a look at. You get that done for him?"

Rocco spun around in his chair so his back was to Sean. He was quiet for a moment. "Sorry to inform you, but Detective Carpenter didn't come by here."

"He did. It's okay. I know he did. He told me. Said he needed you to take a look at something for us, but he forgot to tell me exactly what it was that needed your expertise. I was in the neighborhood, so I figured I'd stop by to see what you found. We're working the case together."

"I'm telling you, he wasn't here."

Sean leaned over and turned the chair back around. "Rocco, I'm not screwing around. I need whatever he gave you, and I need to know what you found."

Rocco swallowed once, his eyes locked on Sean's. "I'm not screwing with you," he said slowly, carefully, as if each word needed to be formed before it could come out of his mouth. "Detective Carpenter didn't come by here. I don't have a drive."

"Ah, so it was a drive."

In a flash of movement, Sean grabbed his gun and pressed it against Rocco's head. He pulled the hammer back and leaned in. Rocco was about to scream, but before he could, Sean pushed his hand against his mouth so all that came out was a muffled sound, too low for the neighbors to hear.

"No more lies," Sean said. He was panting and shaking as his adrenaline kicked in. "I get it that you want to keep a secret my partner asked you to keep, but this is bigger than you, and I need answers."

Rocco nodded over and over.

"I'm going to take my hand away from your mouth. You scream, and I end you."

Again, Rocco nodded emphatically.

Sean let go of his mouth, and Rocco immediately fell forward in panic, tears streaming down his face.

"Tell me what he gave you."

"I don't have anything! Don came here and asked me to decrypt a file. I already gave it back to him. I swear I don't have it. I swear!"

"Did you see what was on it?"

Rocco took a deep breath. "Come on, man! Don't make me do this."

Sean pressed the gun harder against Rocco's temple. "Did you see what was on it?!"

"Pictures! Pictures of you and some chick. I don't know her. Never seen her before."

"Did you make a copy?"

"No!"

"What else?"

"GPS coordinates taken from a boat. It showed the route some boat took to like five or six destinations."

"Whose boat?"

"I don't know. It didn't say."

"Whose boat?"

"I swear, I don't know whose boat it was. You gotta believe me. Penn's Landing Marina. That's all I know. Detective Carpenter has the flash drive. That's all I know!"

Sean finally took the gun away and straightened up. "I believe you," he said. "But I can't have any loose ends. This has already gotten way too out of control."

"What do you mean? What are you talking about?"

"I need to set things straight."

"No! No! I won't say anything. I won't!"

Sean shook his head as he grabbed a pair of scissors from the desk. "I'm sorry."

54

As the sun rose over the horizon, Liam stood by the locked gate that closed off visitors from the amusement rides. From this vantage point, he could see everyone who came onto the boardwalk, and should the police close in, he had a route that would help him escape unseen through the small alleyway that led back out to the streets. The boardwalk at Point Pleasant was deserted. It was still early, and the air coming off the Atlantic was cold. A mist hid most of the beach, but he could still hear the waves crashing onto the sand, one after the other.

Don approached slowly, his head on a swivel. His hands were in the pockets of his trench coat, the oversized collar turned up to protect him from the wind. He walked up the ramp that led from the road and stopped.

Liam waited a few minutes to ensure he was alone and then stepped out so Don could see him. "Over here."

Don made his way toward him, and they walked into a dark alley. The sounds of the ocean were muted here, the wind only a simple breeze.

"You alone?" Liam asked.

"That's what you said in the text, right?" Don pulled out his phone and started reading. "Need to talk. I'm innocent. Meet me at Point Pleasant boardwalk. Come alone. No Sean. Life or death. Liam." He looked up at his fugitive. "It was dangerous contacting me like that."

"I'm still not totally sure I can trust you."

"I get it. If I were in your shoes, I'd feel the same way. What you're doing shows a lot of faith, considering I could take you down right now and be everyone's hero."

"I'm wondering why you don't."

"Because I know you didn't kill Kerri. Or the girl in Delaware. Or the others."

"What others?"

"Exactly."

Liam searched Don's face for any sign of doubt but saw nothing. "What makes you so sure I'm innocent?"

"I've learned a few things." Don held up a small white envelope. He opened it and pinched a piece of yellow foam between his index finger and thumb.

"What is that?"

"It's the answer to a question I wished I never had to ask. It's another missing piece of the puzzle. Could be part of your get-out-of-jail-free card." Don searched behind him for a moment and then turned back. "I couldn't wrap my head around the fact that you could be guilty of what I saw in the crime scene photos at the Tiger, but when you suspected that *I* could've killed her, I got scared. I don't know why, really. I think it was the fact that someone I'd trusted so completely could think I could do something like that. I thought I might have to clear my name, so I started my own investigation. Just me. I didn't know if I could trust Sean. I figured he'd always side with you over me, and if you had me as a suspect, I needed to preemptively clear my name."

"Did you find what you were looking for?"

"I made two copies of Kerri's computer on two separate flash dives. Sean only knew about the one he destroyed. I found some things on the copy I kept."

Liam was silent.

"I have an extra key to your brother's house and his truck. Always have. Yesterday I found myself snooping around, trying to find something that might make sense of what was going on. I waited until Sean was out and looked through the house, but I couldn't find anything. When he was at the station, I took a peek inside his truck. All of it was just a cop's hunch. But that's the thing about cop's hunches. There's usually something there."

"What'd you find?"

"Did you know there was a rip in his seat, passenger's side by the door?"

"No."

"This is foam stuffing. I asked Jane to run it against the material that was under Kerri's nails. It was a match."

Liam's world dimmed into a blackness that engulfed everything else. The noise of the waves lapping against the shore disappeared. The seagulls above. The sun hanging in the sky. His breath would not come. He felt as if he were suffocating. As if he were drowning in his mother's tub all over again.

"It was Sean," Liam said.

Sean knew about him and Kerri. Sean knew about the paper flowers their mother had left for them the day she'd tried to kill them. Sean knew how to make the paper flowers and knew their mother had cut her hair. He knew about it all. Everything. His brother's words echoed in his mind.

Those flowers scare me. Somebody knows something.

Don placed the foam back in the envelope. "Kerri found out about things your brother was trying very hard to hide. It's tough to say this. Sean was having an affair with Vanessa."

Liam fell against the wall, stunned. Everything he knew about his life was crumbling before him. "Are you sure?"

"Yes. For over a year."

Liam said nothing.

"I don't know how, but Kerri found out about the affair and spent a good deal of time following them. I found the pictures she'd taken of them on the flash drive I copied from her hard drive. I also think that while she was following them, she came across another secret Sean was hiding. He was killing other women. She'd tracked his coordinates on his boat, and they match the vics we found. Up and down the coast, Sean was abducting prostitutes and killing them. Kerri had the GPS coordinates with the pictures. Your brother killed Kerri, the girl you guys found in Wilmington, and five others. For whatever reason, he's pinning it on you. That call you got from Kerri the night of her murder could've been her wanting to tell you everything. Show you the pictures she'd taken. Tell you about the boat trips your brother was taking."

"But I still don't remember anything about that night."

"I don't know what to tell you about that. Drugged maybe?"

"My blood came back clean."

"I don't know."

Liam's voice was barely more than a whisper. "I came here to convince you I was innocent. I guess this'll be easier than I thought." He showed Don the copy of the police report he'd taken from Lakewood and explained how Gerri Cain had found Kerri's old medical record that led him there. He also explained what happened during his encounter with Kiki and Grandpa.

Don lowered his voice as a small group of joggers ran by on the boardwalk next to them. "There's even more," he said. "I read through Keenan's case file again to see what else was uncovered and get up-to-date on things. Since Guzio, everyone's attention has been focused on bringing you in. No one's even talking about Kerri."

"Why would they? I'm the target. I'm the conviction. I know how it works. You bring me in, perp walk me, and the media rests. Until then, I'm the lead on every broadcast. The mayor needs this to go away ASAP."

The wind cut through the alley. Don pulled his jacket tight. "It turns out Teddy went down to the navy yard a few days ago and showed some of the guys pictures of the knots we found in the extension cord at the Tiger. One is called a Prusik knot, which secured the cord around the pipe that Kerri was hanged from, and the other was a slipknot tied in a figure eight. According to the navy guys, these are technical knots mostly used in mountain climbing and boating. Something Sean would need to know to get his boating license."

Liam blew into his hands. It was getting colder by the second. "How do you know I didn't take the boat those nights? Or borrow Sean's truck the night Kerri was killed?"

"I've seen you near water. You're terrified."

"Could've been faking it."

"You can't fake that kind of fear. Besides, we saw the video stream from the chopper that was following you when you took his boat. You clearly had no idea what you were doing. The trips Sean took to kill these other girls took hours and were in the dark. They needed precision maritime navigation, even with the GPS. It's not you."

"Are you going to turn all this evidence in to IA? Talk to Phillips?"

"Yes, but not yet. Not until I have this thing airtight."

"What more do you need?"

"Something concrete. The foam from the seat is a match, but it's also likely to be the same foam used in thousands of other cars. Your picture of Kerri at Boathouse Row wouldn't do us any good in court, and the medical records and police report would only do so much. The information I obtained from Kerri's computer about the GPS tracking was taken without a warrant, and I'm not even assigned to this case. The photos she took prove an affair, but that's not against the law. We have a lot of evidence, but most of it is either circumstantial or inadmissible. I want to dig deeper into these other murders. If we take him down, it's gotta be flawless."

"I don't think we have time for flawless," Liam said. "This needs to be exposed now."

"That's why I'm here. I have an idea. They found hairs at your house when they were doing their sweep. They were Kerri's. There were traces of oil on the hairs, and Jane matched it to Olin gun oil. Sean uses Olin."

"So do I," Liam replied. "So does half the department."

"I'm guessing he's keeping the hair he took when he shaved her head, and the heads of the other vics, in his gun-cleaning kit or close enough to get the oil on them. If you had enough time to search his house, you might be able to find something."

"He cleans his gun in the basement. I know where he keeps the kit. You get him out of the house, and I'll go in and see what I can find."

"Exactly."

A few more people made their way onto the boardwalk and walked toward the ocean. Don watched them as they passed.

"This ends now," Liam whispered.

Don began to make his way out of the alley. "Come on, I'll give you a ride back into Philly, and we'll figure out our next steps. Where can you hide?"

Liam thought for a moment. "South Street Mission. Father Brennan will help. I just saw him the other day."

"Good. You hide there until I contact you. When I get Sean out of his house, you go in."

"How was all this happening without us knowing?" Liam asked. His eyelids were heavy. He was so tired. "He killed those girls, and we never suspected a thing."

Don kept walking, head down, fighting the wind coming off the ocean. "He's always had the charisma of a leader. With that comes a trust you put in him. We're all victims of his manipulation. None of us saw this."

"But he's my brother. He's the only family I ever really knew."

"He's not the man you thought he was. He's not the man any of us thought he was."

55

As morning turned to afternoon, then on to dusk, Don sat alone in his bedroom, sipping a cup of coffee and staring at the white envelope on his nightstand. Everything he'd thought he'd known was crumbling in his fingers, creating a new reality he wasn't sure he was ready to acknowledge. So many signs had been right in front of him for so long, yet he'd been blind. Now things needed to be fixed. There was no other way.

He'd dropped Liam off at the South Street Mission and then headed home. Joyce was downstairs, preparing dinner. She had no idea what he was dealing with.

The ringing of his phone snapped him from his thoughts. He answered before it could ring again.

"Hello?"

"Ah, so you are alive. I've been calling you all day. Glad to hear you're still breathing."

Don's stomach tightened at the sound of Sean's voice. He'd been avoiding him as he tried to figure out his next move. Hearing him now brought everything to the present and reminded him he could not run from this issue no matter how desperately he wanted to.

"Hello?" Sean said. "You still there?"

"I'm here," Don replied. "I thought Joyce was calling me." He tried to lighten his tone. "I checked in at the station house this morning and then took a quick run back up to my mom's to make sure she was still okay."

"Is she?"

"Yeah, she's fine. And how about you, partner? How you doing?"

"I'm fine. Still nothing on Liam. All of Camden County has the BOLO by now."

"Any idea where he might be? Is there somewhere in Jersey you think he'd go?"

"I can't think of anything specific."

"You talk to Vanessa? She hear anything?"

"Yeah, I spoke to her, but Liam hasn't called. I told him to turn off his phone. I guess he listened."

Don rose from the bed and began pacing the room. "So you calling to make me feel guilty about not calling you?"

Sean chuckled on the other end. "No. I need a favor."

"Name it."

"We need to find Liam. You and me. I know I'm supposed to stay away in light of the other victims, but this is my brother. I was hoping you could pick me up, and we could head over to Jersey and start poking around. I can't keep sitting here on my hands waiting for something to happen. We have to find him. I gotta bring him in myself."

"I don't think that's such a great idea. Phillips told you he wanted you to keep your distance on this for now."

"I know, but I need to do something. Anything. Sitting around here is killing me. You watch my back; I watch yours. That's the way it goes. Do me this favor. He's my brother, and he's like family to you too. Please."

Don fell back onto the bed. What could he say? He had to keep his discovery to himself and act as natural as possible. If he was with his partner, he could at least control the situation, which would allow Liam access to Sean's house to look for the proof they needed. And if he refused to go, Sean could suspect something. He had no choice. "Yeah, okay. I'm in."

"I appreciate it, man. I owe you."

"What time do you want me to come get you?"

Papers rustling. "Pick me up at my place at ten."

"Go it. Ten o'clock."

"You'll be home by midnight. Promise."

"That's what you said about Sullivan's the other night, and I didn't get home until two."

"I'll see you later." There was a slight pause. "I know I don't have to say this out loud, but this is between us. No one knows about this. Corporate could bust your ass for helping me, and I could get thrown into a hole for disobeying an order from Phillips."

"You're right; you didn't need to tell me that."

"Bring the sedan. I don't want to draw any attention with the Mustang."

"Okay."

Sean hung up. Don listened to the void of silence on the other end until a recorded message came on instructing him to disconnect. "Joyce!" he called. "Come up here a second!"

What could he do? He had to go so he wouldn't raise suspicions. His gut told him this was a bad idea, but he could find no other alternative that would keep his secret under his own control for the time being.

"Yes?"

Joyce was standing in the doorway. She was so gorgeous with her mesmerizing eyes, her flawless dark skin, and her hair in braids falling to her toned shoulders. She was wearing an orange nightgown that accentuated her plump breasts. He suddenly wanted to make love to her but knew there was no time. "My African queen."

Joyce smiled. "My king."

"Did you speak to Vanessa today?"

"Yes. Poor thing. She's beside herself. I just wanna hug her and tell her it'll be all right, but what can I say that I would actually mean? Her husband is wanted for murder. I don't think she's fully grasped that yet. Hell, I don't think I've fully grasped that yet."

He grabbed the white envelope from the nightstand, licked the glue, and sealed it. "I need to talk to you a minute," he said. "It's important. Come sit."

56

Liam was sitting at the kitchen table, slumped over a bowl of cereal, absently running his spoon around the edge of the bowl as the small television propped on the counter next to the stove replayed highlights from the previous night's Phillies game.

"It's your first day of high school. You better get your head out of your ass and finish that cereal before you faint from hunger during second period."

Liam dropped his spoon and turned. A smile instantly appeared on his face, and his eyes lit up. "Sean! What're you doing here? You have class."

Sean closed the front door behind him, walked through the foyer and into the kitchen. He hugged his little brother as he ruffled his hair, then sat next to him at the table.

"Don't worry about my classes," he said. "It's my brother's first day of high school. That's a big deal. No chance I would miss it."

A sense of relief came over Liam. His shoulders loosened, and his brow relaxed. He took a spoonful of his cereal and then another.

"How you doing?" Sean asked.

"It's weird here without you. Even after two years. It's just weird."

"You know I'm always a phone call away, and Temple is just on the north end of the city. Not that far."

"I know. It's just empty when you're away."

Sean nodded and looked around the kitchen. Dirty dishes filled the sink. "How's Grandma and Grandpa?"

"Good. Grandma's still sleeping. She wasn't feeling great last night. Grandpa went to the barber. I'll tell them you came by."

"Yeah, you do that." Sean got up from his seat and made his way to the sink. He turned on the water, grabbed a sponge, and started washing. "So you nervous about today?"

"Duh."

"I could tell. What're you nervous about? The same kids you went to middle school with will be in your classes. Same kids from the neighborhood will be in the halls. No biggie."

Liam brought his bowl over to the sink. "That's easy for you to say. You were popular. You had a ton of friends."

"You do too."

"I have a handful of friends, and I'm not popular. People don't know me like they know you. And if they do know me, it's because of you."

"That still doesn't answer my question why you're nervous."

Liam leaned against the counter. "It's just . . . high school. What if I can't find my locker? Or get it open? What if I can't find my class, or I'm late because I get lost? What if I walk into the wrong class? That would be devastating."

Sean couldn't help but laugh. He loaded the clean dishes into a plastic drainer on the counter and wiped down the inside of the sink. "Look, I can't lie. Some of those things might happen, but what I can tell you with one hundred percent certainty is all the other freshmen are having the same concerns. You'll be fine. And who cares if you get lost or can't open your locker? By this time next week, you'll be a pro."

"I hope you're right."

"I lived it for four years myself. I'm definitely right. Trust me."

Liam walked around the kitchen table and grabbed his backpack. He stopped when he reached the hallway. "You wouldn't want to walk me to school, would you?" he asked. "I mean, just to keep me company."

Sean folded the towel and hung it over the side of the sink. "Why do you think I'm here?"

"Seriously?"

"Seriously."

Without another word, the two brothers walked out of their grandparents' home and onto the street, big brother leading little brother, a hand on Liam's shoulder for added support. His rock. His everything.

———

The night stretched on. Sean sat on the edge of his bed, waiting for Don to pick him up. It was almost time. His body was numb as the memories of his brother and their childhood infiltrated a mind that was beginning to have doubts. He wondered if things had already gone past the point of no return. Perhaps it wasn't too late to change the course of his actions. He could turn himself in, save his brother, and end all of this madness. But just as quickly as the optimism came, he batted it away with the reality of this being what it had to be. This was *always* how it had to be. There was no turning back now. And tonight would put things back in order.

Vanessa was lying in the bed next to him, her body a tangle of skin and sheets. Perspiration still glistened on her face and chest. She seemed satisfied. At peace. His hands shook as he reached for a bottle of Xanax next to the phone on his nightstand.

"I can do this," he whispered to himself, popping two pills into his mouth, chasing them with a glass of water. "I can do this."

It was a strange sensation. Sean could feel his overworked and tired mind beginning to collapse in on itself. He knew things were spinning out of control, but he didn't know how to stop it. The prostitutes. Kerri. Rocco. And now . . .

"I can do this."

Vanessa was sleeping. For a moment, there was no death or murder or future plans to worry about. There were only the two of them in that tiny bedroom.

Outside, a car horn sounded off. Sean rose from the bed and walked over to the window.

"Who's that?" Vanessa asked as she opened her eyes and rolled over.

"It's Don. We're going out for a bit to look for Liam."

"At this hour?"

"I've got to do something. Sitting around all day isn't helping anything."

"Be careful."

"I will."

Sean turned away from the window. "Go out the back way. I can't afford anyone seeing you going out the front."

"I know."

He left the bedroom and turned out the light, hiding his most precious secret in the darkness. It was time to go.

57

It seemed as if the world had turned in for the night. The streets of Camden, New Jersey, were empty. Storefronts were dark, metal shades were drawn, alarms were activated, and inventory was locked away. Houses and apartments no longer held a window's dotted light of life inside. Most everyone had gone to bed.

Sean and Don drove aimlessly through the streets, looking down alleyways, pulling into parking lots, checking bus terminals, and driving through the aquarium campus, searching for Liam. They each sipped a cup of coffee but said little on the ride over the bridge. The few pedestrians who were out this late hurried along the cracked and buckling sidewalks, heads down, hoods pulled up, making it difficult to identify them. Finding Liam in such a city was virtually impossible. But both men already knew Liam wasn't anywhere near Camden. This was all a ruse.

Don turned another corner and drove slowly down another dark street. "I thought you said I'd be home by midnight."

"Yeah, this is taking longer than I figured it would. Sorry."

"We shouldn't be out here. This isn't our jurisdiction."

"We're not here as cops. We're here as family. There is no jurisdiction for family."

Don placed his coffee in the cupholder and flipped through the radio, looking for a sports talk show. He wasn't sure how much time Liam would need to search Sean's house and wanted to get himself out of this situation as quickly as possible. They'd agreed that Liam would text him when he was out so Don could take Sean back home. He felt vulnerable here. Exposed. "Where do you think he could be?" he asked.

"Not sure."

"Maybe we should try again tomorrow when it's light out."

"He'll be hiding in the day. That's when the rest of the force is looking for him. If we have any chance at spotting him, it'll be at night."

Don found a talk show and sat back in his seat. "You try calling him?"

"All day, every day. He hasn't turned his phone back on. Rolls straight to voice mail. Left him a bunch of messages. Nothing." He turned to his partner. "Look, I know how crazy this is, thinking we can find him by just driving around. I get it. But this is more about me keeping busy than anything else. I need to do something, you know? I can't sit around and wait for them to call me to tell me they caught him. I'm his brother. I won't stand down, regardless of what Phillips says."

Don nodded and kept driving. He checked the clock on the dashboard. Liam had to have made it to Sean's house by now. It was just a matter of how long it would take him to find the evidence he was looking for, if it was there at all. So far no text had come through.

"I appreciate you doing this," Sean said.

"No worries. I understand."

"Let's do one more circle around Nineteenth Street, and then we'll head into Farnham Park. We can split after that. I've had you out too late as it is. Joyce is gonna be pissed."

"You got it."

The DJs on the radio were arguing about the upcoming draft and who they thought the Eagles would pick. Don listened to the chatter until the arguing grew to be too much, and he leaned forward to cut it off. "Can't take all that yelling."

Sean pointed. "Pull up here, and then take a right."

Don drove up 19th Street and noticed that most of the streetlights were out. This was heavy gang territory, and the gangs were known to knock out the lights to keep their activities as hidden as possible. On these streets, survival was the number-one priority. Kill or be killed. There was no other way. He thought about that as he drove in the dark next to a serial killer. Liam had to be done soon. Where was his text?

"In here."

Don pulled the sedan into Farnham Park. With the trees hovering overhead and blocking out the moon, it was even darker than it had been in the neighborhoods. He followed the twisting road as they drove up a hill into the main field area next to the Cooper River. What had once been jogging paths and picnic areas were now cracked blacktop with tree roots protruding and dilapidated barbeque pits used more for drug transactions than family fun. This had been a beautiful place once, and the beauty was still there, just below the surface. Don had come to this park many times growing up. It was a way for his parents to escape Philadelphia without having to go too far. Perhaps one day that beauty would return. Right now, all he could see was the blight.

"Stop!" Sean suddenly cried. "There!"

Don pulled over and craned his neck to see. "What?"

"No . . . nothing. Forget it."

"Was it him?"

"No."

Sean turned from the window and faced his partner. He was pale, the expression on his face blank. The only indication that he was even breathing came in the form of his bottom lip quivering ever so slightly. "Look," he said. "We need to talk."

"About what?" Don asked.

"I know."

"Okay. What do you know?"

"More than you think, and I want to get you out of it, but you need to trust me, and you need to do what I say."

Don instinctively pushed himself against the driver's side door. "Sean, what the hell are you talking about?" He tried to make his voice firm but thought he heard weakness in it.

"I know you dropped Liam off at Father Brennan's mission after you guys met. Father Brennan called me. I thought Liam might try and hide there when he first started to run, so I'd stopped by and asked him to keep a lookout."

"Well, I—"

"I also know about the extra copy you made of Kerri's files. The copies you made of Jane's file with the other girls. You got your hands on so many secrets, and I didn't want you involved in all that. I just wanted you to go to Kerri's house, take the evidence that linked her to Liam, and go on with the rest of your life. Why did you have to go snooping?"

Don could only stare at his partner, the man he'd known longer than anyone else. Longer than Vanessa. Longer than Phillips. Longer than Joyce. Sean had been like a son to him, but now, sitting in the darkness, staring at the man he'd known for so many years, there were no words.

"I know you know I killed Kerri. We don't have to pretend anymore. The other day I followed you to Rocco's place. Been following you around a lot, actually. After you left, I went back and had a talk with Rocco. He told me what he found in Kerri's files. Said he made a copy on a flash drive and gave it to you. That's what I need. You give me the flash drive, and I'm out of your life. I'll leave tomorrow, and you'll never hear from me again. I'll be in Mexico or Canada or Argentina or whatever, but you won't have to ever see me again, and you won't have to worry about me getting caught. You give me the drive, I let you haul ass out of here, and I'm in the wind. How does that sound?"

Don took a breath and placed his hands on the wheel. "I don't have a flash drive," he said slowly. "What Rocco told you was wrong."

"Don't play with me."

"I'm not playing with you. He couldn't crack the encryption, so we scrapped the idea. What you saw was me coming out of Rocco's place empty-handed. There is no flash drive."

Sean shook his head and began to cry. His sobs were loud against the otherwise silent backdrop of the night in the park. "Don't lie to me, Don! This is too much as it is. Give me the drive!"

"I don't have it."

Sean reached into his jacket and came away with his Beretta. He pointed it at his partner. "I don't want to hurt you. I'm serious. I just want the drive, and we can go our separate ways."

Don chuckled. "You really think that's going to happen? You think I'm going to let you go after all this? You're done, Sean. You're going down. Now get that gun out of my face before I shove it up your ass. Who do you think you are, pointing that at me? Lower the gun. Now."

Sean was crying harder now, the Beretta trembling in his hand. "I don't want to hurt you."

"Put the gun down!"

"Give me the drive!"

"You son of a—"

In a flash of movement, Don reached for the Beretta. Sean pulled away, back toward the passenger's side door, and squeezed the trigger. The shot exploded in the tight confines of the car, burying a bullet in Don's sternum. Don cried out in pain and fear. The pain was more intense than he could've imagined. Blood streamed from the wound and pooled onto his lap, then onto the seat.

"I don't want to do this!" Sean screamed. "Why did you make me do this?" Don could hardly hear what Sean was saying. His head fell back as the pain intensified. He was certain he was going to pass out. He couldn't breathe, the bullet undoubtedly having collapsed a lung. The blood was rushing from his wound. He couldn't stop it. "You killed her because she found out about you and Vanessa," he mumbled. "You son of a bitch. She found out about the others too, and you killed her for it."

"Tell me where the drive is! Please!"

"That . . . poor . . . girl."

Don was losing consciousness. The car smelled of sweat and gunpowder. It smelled like a crime scene. Like death.

Sean grabbed him by the back of the head and pulled him into a tight embrace. "I'm sorry. I'm so sorry. I didn't want this. Please, you have to believe me. I didn't want this. I love you."

Sean let go, and Don fell back against his seat. He opened his eyes to face his partner. The pain was fading, which meant he'd be dead soon. Of that, he had no doubt.

"Please, Don. Where is the drive?"

"I . . . love . . . you."

"Where is the drive?"

Don closed his eyes.

"Don! Tell me! Please!"

Silence.

———

Sean screamed as loud as he could. It was a sound that was a combination of fear, sadness, and rage. His body shook violently as he took out a cloth and wiped down whatever he'd touched, then used the cloth to open the door. He climbed out into the cool night air and stumbled around to the driver's side of the car. He checked his clothes to make sure there was no blood on them. There wasn't.

"I'm so sorry," he mumbled as another set of tears broke free. "Forgive me."

And with those final words, Sean emptied the Beretta's clip into his partner from outside the car to make it look like a gang hit. When the clip was empty and the hammer clicked without firing, Sean stuffed the gun into his waistband, turned, and made his way to the SEPTA station, where he would hop on a train and get back to Philadelphia. In the dead of night, he hurried toward the station, but in truth, there was really no need to. No police were coming. The neighbors weren't calling anything in.

The sound of gunfire was nothing new here.

58

An hour had passed since Don picked up Sean. Liam stared from across the street, fiddling with the change in his pocket until he was certain no one was around. Sean's house was dark. There was no movement anywhere. He crossed the road without taking his eyes from the front door. An empty paper cup blew down the street with the help of a brisk wind that accompanied the night. He could hear the sound of an approaching car but figured it was still too far away to be a concern. He kept his legs moving.

He looked from door to window, first floor to second, confirming there was no one home. Don was with Sean—he knew that—yet he couldn't stop shaking from the surging adrenaline.

The five steps that led to the porch gave without creaking as he climbed toward the entrance. He scanned the area for a final time, then walked to the edge of the porch and took the spare key from under a large potted plant. He opened the front door and slipped inside.

The house seemed much more spacious on the inside when it was dark and empty. Liam stood in the hallway and, with the help of his flashlight, surveyed the living and dining rooms to his left. He rushed toward the kitchen at the end of the hall and turned toward the basement.

Sean kept his gun-cleaning kit in an old file cabinet next to his workbench, adjacent to his tools and extra scraps of wood from past projects. The musty aroma of damp dirt and mold consumed Liam as he made his descent.

The workbench and cabinet sat on the opposite side of the room. Liam walked over and pulled the plastic case that sat atop a pile of junk in the file cabinet's second drawer. As he took it out, he recalled all the times he'd cleaned his own pistol with his brother at the very bench he now used to lay the case upon. He turned on a light that hung directly overhead and, with his heart racing, popped the two metal locks.

The smell of gun oil hit him immediately as he leaned in closer to see what he'd been searching for. The evidence was there in all of its horrific glory.

A used can of Olin oil sat capped but overflowing. The rod, brush, and cleaning pads were stained and hardened with dried residue. The interior of the case was slippery, the foam padding crushed and torn. In the midst of spilled oil and soiled instruments were several bags full of hair. Black, blonde, brown. Hair from all the victims. Kerri's had to have been in there too.

Liam closed the case and backed away from the workbench. He now knew the absolute truth. Sean had killed Kerri and the other women they'd found. There was no more doubt. His breath came in shallow waves, and he suddenly felt as if he'd run a marathon. He couldn't steady himself, the room swaying from side to side, the floor buckling underneath his feet. He closed his eyes and leaned on the workbench, waiting for his dizziness to pass and his breathing to return to normal. He had known what he would find down there, yet seeing it, seeing the absolute truth, was too much for him. His older brother, the man who had been like a father to him, the man who had looked out for his well-being through all aspects of his life, the man who had literally saved his life, was a murderer and was framing him for the killings. Why?

Lights filtered through the windows on the other end of the basement. Headlights from a car. Someone had pulled into Sean's driveway.

Liam put the case back in the cabinet and pulled the chain on the bulb above. He tried to see who had come, but the windows were at ground level, and he couldn't get the right angle.

Footsteps thumped above on the first floor.

He froze in place, shut off his flashlight, and stood completely still. The footsteps were slow, deliberate. The floor above creaked as each step was taken. Whoever was in the house was in the hallway. Liam scurried toward the back of the basement and fell against the wall, waiting. The footsteps carried themselves into the kitchen and stopped. He held his breath, his eyes searching for another way out. Something was shuffling above him. He looked in the darkness for a place to hide or escape. There was a brief moment of silence above.

Then the footsteps began to come down the stairs, into the basement.

Liam moved quickly, feeling his way deeper into the blackness that had swallowed him. He couldn't see where he was going. The footsteps were halfway down.

He came upon a set of stairs that led up to hurricane doors and out into the yard. He climbed up, unlatched the lock as quietly as he could, and pushed the doors open.

The fresh air hit his face and felt colder than before. With his peripheral vision, he could see a red flashing light. As soon as he hopped from the basement, he heard the footsteps running across the basement, up the stairs, and through the hurricane doors he'd just emerged from. He was tackled from behind and slammed violently to the ground, his face pushed into the grass, almost smothering him. He tried to fight back, but whoever was on top of him had more leverage. A strong hand kept his head from poking up from the ground. For a brief moment, he was six years old in his bathroom, his mother on top of him, pinning him down.

We're going to visit your father.

"Stay still, you son of a bitch," Lieutenant Phillips commanded. "You're under arrest."

Liam quickly pulled his arms underneath him and spun around, knocking Phillips off of him so he could climb to his feet. As soon as he was up, Phillips was on him, tackling him at the waist and thrusting him back to the ground. Liam hit with a thud that knocked the wind out of him, and he ducked away from a flying right hand. He countered with a jab as hard as he could to the lieutenant's stomach, knocking him backward. Liam leapt on top of Phillips and pinned his arms down with his knees, panting and wheezing, his hands working frantically until he found what he was looking for and came away with the lieutenant's gun. He got back to his feet and stood over him.

"Take out your cuffs," he commanded.

Phillips remained on the ground. "Liam, it's over. No matter what you do to me, they're going to catch you. You're making things so much worse for yourself. Let me take you in. I'll do it the right way. I'll take care of you."

"Take out your cuffs!"

Phillips reached behind him and came away with his pair of hand-cuffs. The chrome glistened in the moonlight.

"Go cuff yourself to the handle of the basement doors."

"Liam—"

"Do it!"

Phillips crawled back toward the hurricane doors they had both just come up through. He laced one cuff through one of the steel handles and the other cuff around his wrist. When he was secure, the lieutenant raised his free hand to show he was done.

"Take out your phone and your radio and your keys. Toss them over."

Phillips did as he was instructed. Liam picked up the items and threw them farther across the yard.

"Lieutenant, I know you don't believe me, but I didn't do anything, and I didn't kill anyone. Sean did."

"What are you talking about?"

"I need a head start, so I have to leave you cuffed for now. But when you get free, all the evidence you need is in that basement. Sean is the killer. I can't believe I'm saying that out loud. He's trying to frame me."

"Why would he be framing you?"

"He's having an affair with Vanessa. All I can guess is he wants me out of the picture so he can have her to himself. He's killed other women too."

Phillips struggled in the cuffs. "How do I know you didn't plant whatever's down there and you're framing Sean? That this affair isn't just a lie to throw us off?"

"Because Don will tell you the truth. He found more evidence than I could. Don knows Sean's the killer."

Phillips was silent. Liam could see his mind processing all of this new information.

"I'm going to Don's now," Liam continued. "I'll call you later, and you can bring me in, and we'll tell you everything we know, but I want Don with me. He's my insurance. In the meantime, I suggest you get a BOLO out for my brother. I have a feeling this could get worse."

Phillips raised his hand that was fastened to the door. "I can't do anything like this!"

"Like I said, I need a head start. Give it some time, and then start calling out for help. Someone will come. Your phone and radio are by the bushes there. Keys too. I'll call you later. We'll tell you everything."

Phillips said something else, but Liam didn't hear. He ran from his brother's house toward the subway station that would bring him back to South Philadelphia and then on to Don's house. This would end tonight. It no longer mattered if they had enough evidence for a conviction. If he and Don let things go any longer, more lives would be lost. It was time to end this. One way or another.

He took Kerri's phone out of his pocket and dialed Vanessa's number.

"Hello?"

"Hey, it's me."

"Liam!"

"Don't talk. Just listen. I know about you and Sean, and I don't care right now. I'm heading to Don's house, and then he and I are going into the station. I need to tell you what's been going on." He rubbed a hand through his hair and kept running as he barked into the phone. "It's about Sean. He's not who you think he is."

59

Joyce placed her hand over her heart as she stepped back from the door. A look of concern washed over her immediately. "Sean," she said. "It's late. Where's Don? Is everything okay?"

It took every ounce of strength Sean had to force a smile. He nodded slowly, ensuring every action was one of confidence and normalcy. It felt as though he were in a dream, detached from himself. The scenes and people he interacted with no longer felt real. His entire world had become a fantasy, but at the same time, he was aware that every moment of it was real. His head throbbed, and his eyes floated in and out of focus.

"Sean?" Joyce said again. The urgency in her voice was palpable. "Talk to me."

Sean quickly refocused. "Sorry. No, everything's fine. I know it's late to come knocking like this. Don's back at the station. He called me when I was out getting us coffee and asked me to swing by to pick up a disk he had for Liam's case. We think we might have a lead on where he is."

Joyce exhaled a sigh of relief and ushered him in, closing the door behind them both. "I've been following the news," she said. "Oh, that footage of Liam driving your boat up the river was too much. I hope you find him soon. That boy needs help. Running ain't gonna solve anything. We need to get him in and get him help. I spoke to Vanessa this morning. She's in pieces."

Sean made his way down the corridor toward the kitchen. He stuffed his hands in his pockets so Joyce wouldn't see them shaking. His eyes burned from crying, his throat raw. "I know. I talked to her too. We think we're close."

"I pray you're right. Pray every day." Joyce walked into the kitchen and grabbed a teapot from the sink. She turned the water on and began to wash it out.

Sean came up behind her and leaned against the refrigerator, watching in silence. He noticed a picture of Don holding a supersized flounder on one of the doors and plucked it from its magnet. "I remember this day," he said. "I took this picture."

"I know."

"We booked a charter off Point Pleasant. It was a birthday gift. I didn't think we'd catch anything. Spent most of the day drinking, but nothing was biting. Not even a nibble. Captain was just about to turn around and head in when Don gets this thing on his line. Took us like a half hour to reel it in. Ends up catching a record breaker. It was unbelievable. That was a good day."

"Every day is a good day with my husband."

"You got that right."

Joyce put the pot on the stove. "You want some tea?"

"No. I'm just gonna grab what I need and get out of your hair. Let you get back to sleep."

"You sure you're okay? You don't look so hot."

Again, Sean forced a smile and choked down the scream that wanted to escape. "Yeah. Just this Liam stuff has me all messed up. I need to find him. And we all need to understand what happened."

"Yes, we do."

There were a few beats of silence before Sean held up the picture. "You mind if I keep this?"

"It's yours if you want it. Don has a blown-up version on his desk upstairs."

Sean folded the picture and slipped it into his back pocket. He took out his phone and found a stock image of a flash drive. "Speaking of Don's desk upstairs," he said. "Any chance you've seen something like this laying around?"

Joyce looked at the picture on the screen and shook her head. "No, I haven't seen anything like that, but then again, I haven't been looking. Don didn't tell you where to get it?"

"No. He just said it was at the house."

"Probably in his office. Why don't you call him?"

"He turned his phone off. He's conducting witness interviews for possible sightings, and we're not allowed to have our phones on in the interview rooms. How about I just poke around? Can't be too far, right?"

"Sure," Joyce replied. "Knock yourself out. You know where his office is, and you can check his work area in the basement too. Although I don't think he did much computer stuff down there. Used it more for storage and his tools, but you can look."

"Thanks. I'll be back in a sec."

Joyce turned back to her pot of water, which was starting to boil. Sean made his way upstairs and into Don's office. After a few seconds, the house was filled with the sound of drawers being opened and closed, papers being rustled, and items being moved around. The serenity of the late night had been disturbed, and there would be no turning back until morning.

Things had been set in motion that could no longer be undone.

For Sean, this was now or never.

60

Lieutenant Phillips stood on Sean's porch, looking down at the cluster of police cars and unmarked units. New Jersey State Police were there along with a few uniforms and a pair of detectives from the local Gloucester Township Police Department. His own car was still parked in the driveway from when he'd initially tracked Liam to the house. Heckle and Keenan were inside. They'd found everything Liam had promised.

They'd found the truth.

After Liam had disappeared, Phillips called out for help until a neighbor appeared with a flashlight and a shotgun. Phillips had identified himself and instructed the neighbor to call for assistance. Police units arrived shortly thereafter and unlocked the cuffs. They found what Liam had told him would be there. Along with the hair, they also discovered pictures of the victims taken in a surveillance-type setting and a box full of new orange extension cords, same make and model that had been used in the other murders. One of the cords had a Prusik knot on one end and a slipknot tied in a figure eight on the other. He'd been practicing.

A new BOLO had been issued with Sean's information on it now instead of Liam's. The street had been closed off in both directions, so the element of surprise was long gone. This hadn't hit the news outlets yet, but if Sean happened to be coming home, it wouldn't take him long to see the aura of emergency lights floating over his house. He could make a clean getaway before they even knew he was in the vicinity. With that in mind, Phillips had stationed officers beyond the perimeter in case Sean did, indeed, try to come home.

Keenan came out onto the porch. "We're all done in there," he said. "Bagging it up and taking it back to the station. We'll get Forensics on it right away. We also got a team at Sean's boat. We had it dry-docked after Liam took it. They'll process it again now that things have changed."

"Good. Keep me posted."

Keenan walked back into the house as one of the New Jersey State Troopers came up the steps to the porch. He was slim and looked young, but the stripes on his arm showed that he was a sergeant and the senior man on the scene.

"We have perimeters set up in a ten-mile radius. My men are aware of make and model of his truck, license number, and suspect description. If he tries to come home, we'll get him."

Phillips shook the trooper's hand. "Thank you."

"You have no idea where he might be?"

"No, but I'll check in and see if anyone has spotted him."

He took out his phone and dialed Don's cell phone, but it rolled to voice mail. He then tried the station house. Neither the dispatcher nor the desk sergeant had seen or heard from Sean or Don. He called the owner of Sullivan's and asked if Sean or Don had been in there for a drink. They hadn't. He tried Liam's cell, but that number had been disconnected. A call to Vanessa went unanswered. Finally, he tried Don's house again. He had to let him know what was going on.

Joyce picked up on the third ring. "Hello?"

"It's me," Phillips said. "I'm sorry if I woke you. I need to speak to Don."

"Don's at the station. They think they have a lead on Liam."

"Have you talked to him? Because I just called the station and they said they haven't seen him or Sean all night."

"Sean's here now," Joyce said. "He's the one who told me Don was at work."

Phillips froze in place and pressed the phone tighter to his ear. "Did you say Sean is there now?"

"Yes."

"Alone? Don's not with him?"

"He said Don was at the station. They're working on a new lead for Liam."

"Joyce," Phillips said. "I need you to stay calm and listen to me. Don't react to what I say. Just act natural, but listen."

"Okay."

"We've found evidence that points to Sean as the killer. Not Liam. You need to get out of the house. Now."

"What?"

Phillips walked down from the porch and motioned for the other officers while he spoke. "Liam is on his way over to the house now to talk to Don. I spoke to Liam tonight. He showed us evidence that links all of this to Sean. Sean's the one we've been looking for. You need to get out of there."

"No," Joyce whispered, her voice trailing off. "That can't be."

"You need to get out of the house. Now. Can you do that?"

"Yes."

"I'm sending units, and I'm on my way."

"I'm scared."

"Don't be. Just get out of the house."

Phillips hung up the phone and ran toward his car. He looked up and saw Heckle and Keenan running out after him.

"What's going on?" Heckle shouted.

Phillips pointed to his men. "Get some help over to Don's house. Sean's there alone with my sister."

"Where the hell is Don?"

"I don't know. Just go!" He climbed into his car and reversed out of the driveway, skidding across the street and almost hitting another unit that was parked to block traffic. Tires screeched as he pressed on the gas and headed back toward the city. His world was spinning out of control.

61

Sean stood in the doorway to the basement and watched Joyce hang up the phone and lean against the wall in the kitchen. "Who was that?" he asked.

She spun around and, for a moment, had a look of unadulterated fear in her eyes. "You scared me. You been down there for a while. Still nothing?"

"Nothing."

"You should call Don. Maybe he's out of that room and can talk now."

"Who was on the phone, Joyce?"

"No one." Joyce pushed herself off the wall. "Wrong number."

Sean let go of the basement doorknob he'd been holding on to and stepped into the kitchen. "Sounded like you were having a pretty extensive conversation for it to be a wrong number."

"Nope. Just a wrong number. Calling about ordering some car service. Told them it wasn't me."

"Pretty late to be calling."

"I guess it don't matter what time it is if you need a car service."

Sean walked the room clockwise, which caused Joyce to step back in the same circular pattern, pushing her farther from the doorway that would lead into the hall toward the front door. There was a strange silence between them that hadn't been there before. Sean was tired. His eyes were heavy, and his head hurt. He didn't want to do this anymore. He just wanted to sleep and wake up and have it all be over.

"I can't find that drive."

"Call Don. He'll tell you where it is. You want me to call him?"

"Why are you walking away from me?"

"I'm not."

"Yes, you are. Every step I take toward you, you take one back."

Joyce waved her hand to dismiss his comment but never stopped moving. She was almost all the way around the kitchen now. "You're running out of places to look for that drive thing. I don't know what else to tell you."

"Who was on the phone, Joyce?"

"I already said. Wrong—"

"Who was on the phone!"

The sudden rage in Sean's voice sounded unfamiliar, even to him. There was something inhuman about it. Animalistic. A plain unadulterated rage. Before he could say anything else, Joyce turned and grabbed a large carving knife from the counter behind her, holding it out as tears began to stream down her face.

"You don't scream in my house," she said. "Not after what you did. You wanna know who that was? Fine. That was my brother. That was *your* lieutenant. He was calling for Don to tell him they found evidence at your place showing that *you* killed those girls and Liam's innocent. He told me to get out of the house. The police are on the way. He's sending them. So you stand there, and I'll stand here, and we'll wait for them to come, and you'll go quietly because it's the right thing to do. I know there's still good in you. I know it. We'll just wait together, and this can be over."

Sean stood still for a moment. The house was quiet. There was no other sound. No approaching sirens, no cars hurtling down the street, no flashing lights. That meant there was still time. He needed that drive.

Joyce pushed a chair in between them and tried to get into the hallway. As she turned the corner, she lost her balance and slipped down against a small table Don had always thrown his keys on. By the time she got back to her feet, Sean was closing in, running through the dining room and cutting her off at the front door. He grabbed her arm and pulled her toward him just as she swung her knife around and plunged the blade into his shoulder. Sean screamed and instinctively punched her in the face. His grip loosened, and she pushed away, staggering back into the kitchen and down the basement stairs.

"Joyce!" he cried. The pain in his shoulder was spreading down his arm. "Joyce, this isn't what you think. Your brother is lying. I didn't do anything. The things they found at my house were Liam's. I was hiding them to protect him. The flash drive is full of more lies. I need it to prove my innocence. Please! You have to help me. Joyce!"

The basement was dark. Sean stopped at the top of the stairs and tried the light switch, but it just clicked without anything turning on below. He carefully walked down to the bottom landing and unholstered his gun, waiting for his eyes to adjust before he started moving any farther. His adrenaline had kicked in now, and he was no longer feeling remorse or fear or sadness. He just knew he had to get the drive and get Joyce before she could escape from the house. Too many loose ends.

He held his gun out in front of him as he slowly scanned the area. His other hand pressed on his shoulder as blood seeped between his fingers and dripped onto the floor.

"Joyce, please," he said. "I don't want to hurt you. I need you to help me. I need you to be my hostage for a little while so I can explain things before SWAT busts in here and ends it. I didn't do what's on that drive. My brother is framing me. They won't listen unless I make them. I need you to help me make them listen. Do you understand? Please. I don't want to hurt you."

Like many row homes that had been built in Philadelphia in the nineteenth century, this one had a secret door in the basement that led to a neighbor's house. During the Civil War, these passageways had been used to move money, weapons, and supplies through other underground doors and tunnels throughout the city. Today, most had been bricked over or locked, but Don had once mentioned that their neighbor, who had lived next door longer than they had, had paid them to store a few extra things he couldn't fit at his place. They kept the door accessible should he ever need to get in and out to retrieve something. Sean could see that the old rusted door handle was unlatched, and the door itself was pulled back on its disintegrating hinges. He made his way over to investigate. It was hard to see into the next room. He walked inside.

The neighbor's basement was just as dark as Don's. Sean took out his phone and turned on the flashlight. The small space was full of storage boxes, old clothes, piles of books and newspapers, and a single green kayak propped diagonally across it all. He shined the light in a sweeping pattern but couldn't see a place where she could be hiding.

"Joyce, please. I need your help."

There was a noise from behind him, coming from the other room. Sean scurried back in time to see Joyce leaping from behind the washing machine. His flashlight caught her face, and he saw it was bloodied and swollen from when he'd punched her. She scurried up the stairs, her feet thumping on each wooden step until she reached the kitchen.

"Joyce!"

"Somebody help me!"

"Joyce! Get back here!"

Sean flew up the stairs, two at a time, and lunged into the kitchen just as Joyce was turning the corner into the hallway that would bring her to the front door. He followed, sliding around the corner, stopping suddenly when he saw Joyce standing halfway between him and the door, frozen, unmoving. He raised his gun and aimed it at the man who'd just come in.

"What're you doing here?" Sean asked, his head cocked to one side, his breath heavy from running. "You . . . you shouldn't be here."

Liam took a single step forward and stopped. He raised the Glock he'd taken from Phillips and aimed it at his brother. "No, this is exactly where I should be."

62

Joyce slid against the wall and fell to her knees. Liam could see her out of the corner of his eye but concentrated on his brother. Phillips's gun felt heavy in his hand, and he struggled to keep it up and straight.

"Sean, I need you to put the gun down and let me help you."

Sean spat out a laugh and shook his head. "I don't think you can help me, little brother. I'm pretty sure we're way beyond that."

"We're not. I know everything. I know you killed those girls. I know what you did to Kerri. I know about you and Vanessa, and that's why you tried to frame me. But it's not too late. I can still help you. Despite all of this, I still want to help you."

"You don't know anything," Sean replied. "You think you know, but you have no idea."

The two brothers continued aiming their weapons at one another.

"I know I want to help you," Liam said. "I know you're my brother, and I know you've been there for me my whole life. For Christ's sake, Sean, you saved me when Mom tried to kill us. Now it's my turn. Your head's just all messed up right now, but I can help you make things right again. It doesn't have to end like this."

Sean looked up at the ceiling, his eyes welling with tears. "Why do you want to help me? I don't deserve it. What I did to you. I don't deserve it."

"I don't care about that. Put the gun down, and we'll call this in. I'll ride with you to the station, and we'll have Don meet us there. We'll all do this together. You won't be alone."

"Don's . . ."

Joyce lifted her head from her knees and looked up at Sean. "Don's what? Don's what, Sean?"

Sean began to cry. "I'm sorry."

Joyce climbed to her feet, a fresh set of tears forming in her eyes and falling down her cheeks. "Sorry about what? What did you do? Where's Don? Where's my husband? What did you do?"

"I'm sorry."

Joyce rushed over to Sean and grabbed him by the jacket, tugging him back and forth, no longer fearful of the gun in his hand. "What did you do!"

"Leave me alone!"

Sean pushed Joyce away, and she fell to the floor.

"Drop the gun!" Liam shouted.

"No!" Sean screamed. He swung the Beretta away from his brother and aimed it at Joyce, who was cowering and crying on the ground below him. "Enough of this! You drop the gun, or I kill Joyce right here. If you know everything, then you know I'm not bluffing. I'll kill her like I killed the rest of them. You can shoot me if you want, but I'll kill her first. Now drop it!"

"Sean, I—"

"Drop it or she dies!"

"Okay!"

Liam placed his gun on the floor.

"Slide it away from you."

He kicked it behind him and heard it hit the wall by the front door. Sirens began to fill the air but were still a good distance away. Liam raised his hands. "I want to help you. Please. I just want to help. We can get through this. Together. Like we've always done it."

Sean opened his mouth to speak, then stopped and looked past Liam. "Why are you here?" he muttered.

Liam turned around just as two shots exploded from behind him. Sean grabbed at his chest as he was thrown backward and to the floor, his gun skipping out of his grip and sliding away. He lay at the end of the hall, motionless. The immediate quiet of the house was in sharp contrast to the commotion and screaming that had been going on only moments before.

Vanessa was standing inside the doorway, the gun she was holding—Phillips's gun—still raised in a shooting position, her hands shaking violently, smoke rising from the barrel.

"Vanessa?"

She looked at her husband, then collapsed, unconscious.

Liam ran over to his wife as Joyce scurried past them both, pushing the front door open and falling out onto the porch as neighbors spilled from their homes to see what was going on. Outside, he could see the flashing red lights of emergency personnel turning onto the street accompanied by the beautiful sound of an intrusive and wailing siren.

63

The emergency room was already busy without the army of police personnel taking up most of the area. With all the extra bodies, it was almost impossible to move around. Uniforms stood post at the entrance to the ER as well as at the ambulance bay and stair exits. The press was kept outside in the parking lot, but more news vans were turning in and setting up their live feeds. It was going to be a long night.

Phillips walked into Vanessa's room with Heckle, Keenan, and the two Internal Affairs detectives, Farmer and Nix. He had his phone out, ready to record the conversation they were about to have. Vanessa was sitting up in her bed, physically unharmed but emotionally scarred. She'd been forced to shoot her brother-in-law in order to save Joyce and Liam. It was a heroic act but one that had consequences on the back end. Phillips knew her sleepless nights and debilitating nightmares were still to come.

"How's Joyce?" Vanessa asked.

"She'll be okay. Broken nose. Loose tooth. Bumps and bruises. She'll be fine."

"What about Don? Did you find him?"

"We found him," Phillips replied, then shook his head.

"Oh."

"How are you?"

"I'm okay, I guess."

Phillips slid a plastic chair across the room and sat next to the bed. The others stood in the corner. "I need to ask you a few questions."

"Okay."

"Let's start with what happened. Walk me through everything."

Vanessa took a breath. "I was at home, and a call came to my cell. I didn't recognize the number, but with everything going on, I figured I should answer. It was Liam. He was frantic. He told me he found evidence that pointed to Sean as the killer and that Sean was dangerous and I needed to stay away from him. He said he was going to Don's house to get him, and they were going to go to the station together. He said he found out about our affair, but he didn't care right then. He just wanted to make sure I knew Sean was the killer and to stay away from him. I hadn't seen Liam since everything went crazy, so I got in the car and drove to Don's. I wanted to see him and hear everything for myself. I couldn't believe what he was saying, but at the same time, I knew he was telling the truth. I just knew it."

Phillips nodded. "Why didn't you call 911? Or me?"

"I don't know. I wanted to see Liam, and I figured if Don was there it would be okay. I had no idea Sean was going to be there. When I got to Don's house, I heard all this yelling, so I snuck up to the porch to see what was going on. Sean was chasing Joyce. He had her cornered, but then Liam was there. Sean made Liam drop his gun, and it ended up right where I could get it. I knew I had to do something. In, like, a split second, I thought about what Sean did and how he was trying to blame it all on Liam. Instead of being scared, I got angry. I wanted him dead. I wanted all this to be over, so I crept inside the door, and before Sean knew what I was doing there, I shot him. Twice. He had to die for what he did to all of us. He had to."

Vanessa fell back on her pillows. Phillips waited a few beats before continuing.

"How long were you and Sean having an affair?"

"A little over a year. It just kind of . . . happened. He was so supportive of me and what I was going through after my mom died. He became like this security blanket for me, and at the same time, things between me and Liam started falling apart. I guess one thing led to another."

"And you had no idea about this other life he was leading?"

Vanessa looked at the lieutenant. "Of course not. Those other girls. The only thing I can think is maybe he wanted Liam out of the way so we could be together. Maybe he thought he could expose the affair Liam was having by killing Kerri? Maybe he was going to pin those other murders on Liam too. I have no idea. Or maybe no one was supposed to find out about those other killings."

"That's quite a theory."

"What else would make him do all those things? It's all such a mess. Maybe he knew I'd never leave Liam. We never talked about it, but he knew I wanted to work things out in our marriage. And we were getting better, Liam and me. I love my husband."

Phillips nodded and stopped recording. "We're going to have to match some dates and times with you to officially clear the investigation, but we can go over all that later. You need to get some rest."

"Okay."

"You did the right thing. My sister's alive because of you. You're a hero."

"I don't feel like a hero."

"I know. But you are. You saved lives tonight. You're my hero."

The door swung open, and Liam walked into the room. Vanessa sat up when she saw him, a smile appearing instantly on her face. "You made it."

"I made it."

Phillips rose from his seat and motioned toward the other detectives to leave. "We'll let you guys catch up. I need to get back over to Joyce's house. She needs me right now. Vanessa, they're going to discharge you first thing in the morning. They want you to stay here tonight so they can monitor that bump you took when you fainted. Better that way.

Let the media out there die down a bit. I'll come by in the morning, and we can talk more."

"Okay."

He looked at Liam. "You holding up?"

"Yeah. Considering."

The men filed out of the room, leaving husband and wife alone together. There was a silence between them that was thick and uncompromising.

"Liam, I'm sorry," Vanessa finally said.

"For what?"

"That you have to go through all this. Your brother. What he did to you. What I did to him. What I did to us. Everything."

"Thanks. You came at just the right time. I'm pretty sure he was going to kill me and Joyce. You saved us."

"I did what needed to be done."

Liam walked farther into the room. "I can't stay. I have to get back to the station and finish filing my statement. It's been a long few days."

Vanessa wiped a tear from her eye. "Can I have a hug?"

"I have to go."

"Just one."

Liam leaned over and hugged his wife. She whispered in his ear as she pulled him tighter.

"I'm not proud of what I did. I'm sorry."

"It doesn't matter," Liam whispered back. "It's over. Everything. We're finally over. I'll have my stuff out of the house in a few days."

"Why? Why would you say something like that?"

"Because whatever we once had isn't there anymore, and people died because of it. We both need to start fresh. There's no recovering from something like this."

"We can fix it."

Liam let go of his wife and made his way toward the door. "I'm sorry, but this is how it has to be. Otherwise, every time I look at you, all I'll see are the people who died for nothing. That wouldn't be fair to either of us."

"Please, Liam."

"I have to go check on Sean. I'm sorry."

Vanessa wiped another tear that slipped down to her chin. "Check on Sean? What do you mean?"

"He's still in surgery. They think he's going to make it."

"Sean's alive?"

"Yeah."

Before Vanessa could say anything further, Liam walked back out in the hall and shut the door, leaving her in the solitude of her own thoughts.

64

Don's house was empty and still. Word was beginning to spread about what had happened in Camden, but thus far no one had come by. A PBA representative and a priest were out on the back porch talking quietly. Soon, as the sun rose to usher in a new day, there would be a house full of officers, more lined around the block, waiting to pay their respects and offering support. Phillips would let them in, thank them, and then pass them on to Joyce, who would be on the couch, still numb and in shock. That's the way these things worked.

The shooting had been called in by a Camden PD unit that worked the area. The two uniforms had been patrolling the park and came upon the abandoned vehicle, prompting them to investigate. Phillips had still been at Don's house when the precinct phoned. The desk sergeant on duty told him Don had been shot and killed in Camden, and he'd had to pinch himself to make sure he wasn't dreaming. For the second time that night, he'd driven over the bridge and had been met at the scene by the investigating officers, a few responding units for backup, and a crime scene unit, all from Camden. They'd escorted him to the car, where he'd positively identified Don's body. He'd placed a call to the chief and the mayor. There hadn't been much left for him to do, so he'd driven back to Philadelphia and broken the news to his sister. She'd collapsed in his arms, and they'd cried together. He really couldn't remember much past that.

Phillips meandered through the living room, looking at the photos of Don and Joyce and the rest of their family. He picked up each one and examined it, rubbing the side of the frame as if rubbing a magic lantern, wishing his friend to return. Each picture showed a happy, playful couple. They had been, indeed. In one, Don had his nephew riding on his shoulders, both of them giving monster faces to the camera. In the background was a Ferris wheel of an amusement park he didn't recognize. In another, Don and Joyce were holding hands, looking into each other's eyes as the sun of the Caribbean set behind them. Each photograph stamped a place and time in their lives when joy was abundant and they were shielded from the wickedness of the world. Those feelings were gone now, blown away in an instant. It would return one day, the happiness, but it would never be the same as it was before. Sean had destroyed his sister's innocence.

Joyce was upstairs sleeping with the help of two Ambien the PBA rep had brought. Phillips tripped over the leg of a chair that had been pulled out from a corner desk and almost fell to the ground. He stopped himself at the last moment, regained his balance, and placed the chair back under the desk. His body was weak. He was tired and still in shock himself. He opened a few windows and felt the cool night air floating in from outside, then went into the kitchen to prepare a pot of coffee.

"What are you doing?"

Joyce was halfway down the stairs, dressed in Don's navy pajama pants and a white tank top. Her eyes were red and swollen, sunken. She stood on the stairs, swaying slightly from side to side.

"Making some coffee," Phillips replied.

"I'll make it."

"I don't mind."

Joyce took a few more steps toward the bottom landing. "Please. I'll make it. I need something to do."

He stepped away from the coffee maker and watched her wobble down to the landing. She stopped and sat. He walked over to her.

"What are you doing up?" he asked. "Those sleeping pills should've kept you down for a while. You need your rest."

"I can't sleep. Don't want to. Every time I sleep, I dream of him; then I wake up and have to feel the loss all over again like it's new. I never want to sleep again. Never."

"I know. But you need your rest. You have to try and gain your strength. Why don't you go back upstairs, and I'll hang out here? People from the department are going to start coming by."

Joyce looked at him, then closed her eyes and allowed her head to fall back against the wall. "I miss him," she whispered. "I can't believe he's gone. I just can't believe it."

Phillips sat beside his sister and rubbed her arm. "I'm so sorry. I don't know what else I can say. I love you. All I can do is be here for you as long as you need me. It's all I can give."

"I know," Joyce replied. She sighed and pushed tears away from her face, then offered a white envelope she was holding. "Last night Don called me up to the bedroom and gave me this envelope. He told me that if anything should ever happen to him, I should give this to you and only you. When Sean came by looking for that flash drive, I figured he might be looking for this, but I wasn't going to give it to him. Don said only you." She handed it over.

Phillips took the envelope, turning it over in his hand.

"I should've known something bad was going to happen when he started talking like that. He never talked like that before. I should've known. I should've stopped him from leaving the house."

Phillips stood from the landing and walked across the kitchen. He pulled his thumb across the envelope's lip and ripped it open, not really sure if he wanted to see what was inside. So much had already happened.

"He trusted you," Joyce said. "He loved you."

He tipped the envelope, and a single flash drive slid out into the palm of his hand. The cool breeze from the open windows in the living room caressed his bare arms, sending a shiver down his spine. Outside, where life continued unabated, the night moved on. Inside, lives kept changing.

65

Morning had come and the sun was beginning to rise in the city of Philadelphia. Liam pulled into his driveway and shut off the engine. It was still early, and everything was quiet. There was no traffic. No one was out walking a dog or taking a run. It was perfect.

He climbed out of the car, walked up the front stoop, and stopped when he saw a bouquet of paper flowers sitting on the doormat. Just like the ones his mother had left for him the day she tried to kill him. Just like the ones that were left at Kerri's feet. He bent down and picked them up, studying them, turning them over and over. The paper seemed fresh, crisp, dry. These were just made, untouched by the morning dew. He opened the door and walked inside.

"Vanessa," he called. He could hear his voice shaking just a bit. "I'm home."

There was movement somewhere in the house. Sniffling. Vanessa was there, and she was crying.

"Where are you?"

"Right here."

The living room was empty. The kitchen. She was in the kitchen.

Liam made his way through the house and stopped when he saw his wife sitting at the head of the dining room table. Her eyes were swollen and full of tears. Her skin was pale. Mascara had run down her face, making her look hauntingly ghoulish. A gun was sitting on the table in front of her.

"I didn't see your car out front."

"I parked it in the garage. Turns out there's room enough in there for one car."

"I thought you weren't getting discharged until morning."

"I discharged myself," she said. "I'm glad you're home."

"Where'd you get that?" Liam asked, pointing to the gun. From where he was standing, it looked to be a Glock, like the one he'd taken from Phillips, only this one was silver.

"Can't use the same gun twice," she replied. "They took Phillips's after I shot Sean with it. This is the one I had in my purse, but it turned out I didn't need it. Sean got me this from a runner he arrested a few months ago. Untraceable." Vanessa slowly wrapped her fingers around the grip, lifted it off the table, and aimed it at her husband. "I need you to sit down."

66

Lieutenant Phillips walked into his office and shut the door. The rest of the night and early morning had been agonizingly long. He tossed his keys on the desk and collapsed into his chair, too exhausted to even remove his coat.

Joyce had been exceptional, given the circumstances. His sister was so brave. The line to get in to see her had grown as the hours passed, and by dawn it had stretched outside the house, down to the sidewalk, and around the corner. He'd been by her side the entire time, thanking each person who came, ushering the people on so the next well-wisher could step up. Tray after tray of food had been delivered. Phillips had had to assign two uniforms to stack everything in the kitchen to keep the flow of people moving. The other wives had come by and made sure coffee was always on. They'd helped put out a buffet of food and fruit in the dining room. The house was quiet. Hardly anyone spoke, yet they all thought about how fragile life was on the job. This time, it was Don and Joyce. Next time, it could be one of them.

By the end of the first round of visitors, Joyce had directed the two uniforms to take the bulk of the food to Father Brennan to use for his mission. No sense wasting it all. It would take an army to eat what had been delivered before it went bad. The officers had loaded up a squad car and had taken off, leaving Phillips alone with his sister. He'd offered to stay, but she'd pushed him out. She was going to take a couple more pills and try, again, to get some sleep. In the afternoon, they would meet up and take a ride to the funeral home to make arrangements. On the way, he promised he would drop Don's dress blues at the dry cleaners for one last cleaning. He would be buried in the uniform he was most proud of.

His desk was full of papers, files, and several envelopes he hadn't opened yet. Phillips started grabbing things randomly, trying to prioritize what should be taken care of in the proper order. As he flipped through a small stack of internal briefings, he noticed the corner of a square black envelope protruding from beneath a PBA newsletter. He took it and slid his finger across the seam.

It was a DVD. On it, someone had written in marker "Francis Guzio Street Surveillance" along with the date of his murder.

"Traffic cam footage," Phillips said to himself. "Now it comes."

The footage had been taken from a camera mounted on the signal box on Guzio's street, installed, like the rest of them throughout the city, after 9/11 with funds from Homeland Security. All the major cities had them. Phillips flipped it around in his hand several times, then opened the disc drive in his computer, popped in the DVD, and sat back in his seat.

The footage was from the entire day. He wondered if anyone had already gone through it and how long it had been sitting on his desk.

It started in the morning. Sidewalks filled with people setting off to work as the general hustle and bustle of a new day began. He fast-forwarded and at midday saw a couple walk down the street with their dog and a homeless man begging for change as people strolled past. A car stopped to talk to the man for a moment and then sped away. Again, he pushed the tape forward to a little before the coroner's estimated time of death and watched.

It was dark now. A vehicle pulled around the corner and parked at the far end of the block, away from the streetlights. Phillips recognized the car instantly, and his stomach turned. He held his breath as he watched the driver climb out of the car and walk down the sidewalk toward Guzio's house. As the figure got closer, Phillips paused the footage and zoomed in. The driver filled the screen. Phillips could feel his heart beating in his chest.

It was Vanessa.

Sean had never been there because he had been with Don at the Hard Rock the night of Guzio's murder. He had the perfect alibi and the perfect accomplice. Vanessa Dwyer.

Phillips let the video roll, and he watched as she climbed the steps, picked the lock on Guzio's front door, and disappeared into his house. He forwarded until she came out again and scurried back down the sidewalk, the front door left open on purpose so Guzio's body would be discovered.

Phillips jumped out of his seat, ran around his desk, and threw his office door open to find Keenan sitting at his desk. "Has Liam Dwyer left yet? He was giving his statement."

Keenan nodded. "Yeah, left about an hour ago."

Phillips pulled his phone out of his pocket and dialed Liam's cell. It rolled to voice mail. He tried the Dwyer house, and that too rolled to voice mail. He hung up and dialed the hospital.

"Connect me to Three West."

There was a pause on the other end.

"Three West. Nurse Connolly."

"Vanessa Dwyer's room, please."

"Mrs. Dwyer was discharged earlier this morning."

"On whose authority?"

"She checked herself out. ADO."

"Dammit!" Phillips hung up the phone and ran out of his office. Vanessa killed Guzio. She'd been working with Sean all along, and now Liam was with her.

Another one of his men was in danger.

67

Liam sat at the table across from his wife, easing himself carefully into the seat. His eyes moved from Vanessa to the gun and back again. He knew he should be confused or shocked or overwhelmed by the situation, but seeing her like this somehow made sense.

"So this is the end of our story," Vanessa said, her voice calm and in control. "The end of everything."

Silence. It was if the house itself were waiting to see who would make the next move.

"What are you doing?" Liam finally asked.

"Making things right. This is how it has to be. This isn't how I envisioned it—I'll give you that. But there's really no other choice at this point." Vanessa sighed and let her shoulders sag. "I always knew this family had a past, but I never realized how many of us had *secrets*. I thought you and I loved one another. Even during the rough spots when my mom was dying and with us trying to get pregnant, I always thought that our foundation was one of real love that we could always build off of. I didn't need fairy tales and roses. I just needed to know you'd be there for me through the good and the bad."

"I was."

Vanessa looked at him for a moment. "Secrets. I found out about you and Kerri almost right away. A couple of my friends at the hospital saw you with her at dinner one night. Holding hands. Sneaking kisses. I can't tell you how embarrassed and hurt I was. How could you do that to me? How could you turn your back on us like that?" The gun remained aimed at him, her knuckles white around the smooth mahogany grip. "I couldn't believe how wrong I'd been about who we were. I was confused. I mean, I was supposed to take care of you. I was supposed to be the mother you never had. And I wanted to take care of you. But you cheated on me and ruined it all."

"It just happened."

"I followed you. I watched you put your hands around her waist. I watched you touching, kissing. I could see you falling in love with her. I could *see* it."

Liam slowly reached out his hand. "Vanessa, give me the gun."

"All I ever wanted was to be loved, and I thought I had that. I thought *we* had that. When my mom finally died, I needed you, and you turned your back on me."

"That's crap," Liam snapped. He scanned the room for something to use to defend himself with, but there was nothing. He was completely exposed at the table. "I was with you every step of the way. I tried to be there for you. I would've done anything. You pushed me away. You wanted your sorrow all to yourself, and you pushed me away. Into the arms of another woman."

"No," Vanessa replied. Her eyes were beginning to fill with tears. "That's not true. We were meant to be together. We were the only ones who knew what true hurt was. We were the only ones who knew what it was like to lose a parent as a child, and those experiences gave us a bond no one else could share. That's in us. Always. Then when I needed you, you weren't there for me. You were with that slut instead. You shut the door to our future and started a new one with Kerri Miller. You left me all alone."

"Give me the gun. Please."

Vanessa ignored him. "It took a little time. I had to go through some stages of grief, like they say in the books. Depression, denial, bargaining. But when I landed on anger, it stuck. I couldn't shake it. No matter what I did, I couldn't quell the anger that was boiling inside me. It was like a virus that just kept spreading until it consumed me, and all I could think about was taking that anger out on you and everyone around you. I wanted you to suffer. I wanted you to know what real pain felt like, and I had the perfect plan. I would kill your girlfriend, frame you for her murder, and watch you rot in jail for the rest of your life."

Liam leaned forward in his seat. "My God, Vanessa. What have you done?"

Vanessa shifted in her seat, but the gun remained steady, aimed. "Secrets. The first part of my plan was to seduce Sean, get him to fall in love with me, and show you what it felt like to be cheated on. This took some time, but that was okay. He was a very loyal brother. He loved you, and the thought of him having an affair with me was, initially, too much. But a woman's touch can be an intoxicating thing. After a while, that touch took precedence over his allegiance to you, and something real started to grow between us. Believe it or not, I actually ended up falling in love with him." Vanessa laughed. "Can you believe that? I was supposed to seduce him, and he seduced me."

Liam looked behind him to measure the distance between where he was sitting and the front door. It was too far to escape without being shot. They were sitting too close. He knew she'd never miss at this distance. He looked back at his captor and saw a woman he no longer recognized. The expression in her wild eyes reminded him of his mother's eyes the day she tried to kill him. That scared him the most.

"Secrets. One day, completely out of the blue, Kerri confronts *me* about *my* affair with Sean. She comes right up to me in the hospital parking lot after one of my shifts. I was stunned. That slut had the nerve to approach me? It took all I had not to throttle her right on the spot and strangle that perfect little neck, but she wasn't coming to chastise me or make a scene. She was coming as a friend. She was coming to *warn* me."

"Vanessa, please."

"I listened to what she had to say, and what she told me was stunning. First, she confessed to having an affair with you and told me

293

that she was pregnant with your child. Your child. I knew I would kill her right then and there, but I was calm, choking down the hate until I almost passed out. You gave her a child when I couldn't have one. There's nothing else you could've done that would've hurt me more."

"I—"

"Shut up." The house grew quiet again. "Kerri told me she didn't want to interfere with my life, but she needed me to know about Sean and his secret. She was afraid for my life. She told me Sean had been seeing her ever since the two of you broke things off. Another secret. Another betrayal. I don't know how, but Kerri found out about me and Sean and confronted him one weekend when they were in Lakewood together. She showed him pictures she'd taken of the two of us together and confessed to being pregnant with your baby. But she'd found something else while following him around, tracking his every move. She'd found his real secret. Of course, Sean flipped out. Totally lost his mind and beat her up, but she didn't press charges. I listened to her, swallowing the screams that wanted to burst out of me, and I'm glad I did because she told me what she found, and at that point, everything changed. I knew I could no longer love Sean the way I'd thought I could. In fact, I knew I couldn't love him at all."

The room was growing so hot. Liam could feel his face beginning to perspire. "Give me the gun," he said again. He could hear his own weakness in his voice.

"Your brother turned out to be an unanticipated gift. That's when I knew this was all meant to be. With Kerri's help, I came to find out that Sean is a creature all to his own. He can't be manipulated and molded to fit someone's bidding. Yes, he was charming and caring and handsome and confident, but at the same time, he's the most vile, destructive, and evil person you'll ever know. He is a master sociopath. The mask he wears was created over years of loss and pain and anger and suffering. He was the big brother tasked with taking care of his entire family, even while still in middle school, and who never had the opportunity to work through what had happened in his own life. Who puts that kind of burden on a child? He could never express how he really felt, and after a while, when a person bottles up so much of that toxicity, it has to come out one way or another. Your mother was crazy. Sean told me once that the police originally thought she'd cut the brakes to your father's car because he was threatening to leave her. Did he ever tell you that? They could never prove it, so no charges were filed, but they always suspected. Sean used to wonder if insanity could be passed down as a gene, like blond hair or blue eyes. Maybe."

Liam pounded his hand on the table. "Enough of this! Please!"

Vanessa smiled and remained calm. "Kerri told me that your brother is a killer of women, Liam. Those other bodies you all found. The prostitutes in the hotel rooms and by the dumpster and in the park? That was Sean. That was the secret Kerri found. He'd been killing for some time now, and his actions were escalating."

The news, delivered so matter-of-factly, stunned Liam even though he knew everything she said was true. He wanted to deny it, to rush across the table and scream to anyone who could hear him that his older brother wasn't capable of the things he'd seen in Delaware and inside room B11 at the Tiger Hotel, but he knew that would only be wishful thinking. Of course the other murders were Sean's. They were too similar to Kerri's, and the hair he'd found in Sean's gun-cleaning kit were from more than one head. He knew Vanessa was telling the truth.

"So there I was, furious, confused, and standing in front of the woman I wanted dead. Sean cheated on me with the same woman my husband cheated on me with, and she was pregnant with my husband's baby. I was a cliché. A goddamned *Lifetime* movie. Kerri wanted to go to the police about Sean, but I convinced her to wait. I told her I'd help her and look for more proof at Sean's house while pretending to still be with him. At first she was skeptical, wanting to get the police involved right away, but I explained how cops stick together and cover for each other and that no one would believe her without hard evidence. I told her I could get that evidence. She finally agreed, and that bought me time.

"The very first thing I did was confront Sean about everything. I needed to know if that bitch was telling me the truth or if she was scaring me away so she could have him all to herself. I talked to Sean, and instead of demanding apologies or ending our affair, I told him I understood. I played it cool. I wanted to know about his secret. I wanted to know everything. No judgment. Just the truth. When he was done, I told him my secret and my truth. I told him I wanted him to help me kill Kerri and frame you, and when that was over, I promised him our love would grow stronger and we'd be rid of all the bad in our lives. I made him see that Kerri knew too much. She was dangerous and had to die. And you had to suffer."

"I can't hear any more of this," Liam said. He wanted to put his head on the table and fade away. His mind screamed for him to get up and run, but he knew he couldn't. He was trapped.

"In truth, I had no intention of continuing my affair with your brother after what Kerri told me," Vanessa continued. "Once Kerri was dead and you were in jail, I was planning to collect your pension and life insurance, kill Sean, and then escape to parts unknown with a new identity and a new life to live. I took some ketamine hydrochloride from the hospital to knock you out so you'd have no memory of what had happened during the time of Kerri's murder. It would be untraceable in your bloodstream, so there'd be no proof you were drugged. Once you were unconscious, I extracted blood and microscopic flakes of skin from you and placed them under Kerri's fingernails. I even scratched you myself to make you think Kerri had done it during a struggle. It was all so perfect. Sean stole your phone and texted Kerri to meet him at the club. He wore your boots and clothes to the hotel so he could leave the proper boot print. You found your clothes in your trunk. He'd taken your fingerprints from a drinking glass I gave him, saved them on a slip of tape, and transported them to the crime scenes. Everything fell into place with such ease. It was important for Sean to convince you to keep your affair a secret. We needed you vulnerable, and if you thought Sean was working behind the scenes to find the real killer, he figured he could control you more. You needed to believe you were both in this together."

"Why would Sean do that?"

"Because he loved me. More than his own brother, it turns out. I knew his secret and accepted him. That was the real bond, stronger than blood or family. It was acceptance. I was ready to take care of him, or so he thought, and that was what he needed to hear. That's all it took."

Vanessa pushed her hair out of her face, the gun steady in her other hand. "I had to convince him to let me help with Kerri. I wasn't going to let him kill her alone. She took my life from me, so I was going to take hers. He drugged her at the club with the same ketamine hydrochloride, got her into the hotel room, strung her up, and tied that perfect knot of his. I wasn't strong enough for all that. We waited until she woke up. I wanted her to look me in the eyes so she would know I was responsible for what was happening to her. I was going to kill her and that baby."

"Vanessa, please put down the gun."

"Things were moving along as planned, but then you got into the fight with the hotel owner, and it was too good an opportunity to pass up. We had to move a little quicker than we were expecting. The responding officers called Sean after they learned who you were, and Sean convinced them to let you go. Professional courtesy. Knowing we had to act then and there, we put the rest of the plan into motion. Sean got to you at our house when you were coming home and injected you with the ketamine hydrochloride before you even knew what was happening. We needed to make sure you didn't accidentally establish an alibi, and if there was still a chance you thought you could be committing these murders, then all the better. Your confusion was our advantage. He dumped you at the shipyard and went out with Don. I killed that greasy man, and Sean had his alibi. We needed your brother safe so you'd be convinced he wasn't part of anything, and the people trying to find you would know he was in the clear. I transferred your print from the tape to the tub like Sean showed me, and we waited for your team to find it without you there. That evidence at the hotel owner's home launched everything."

"Who are you?" Liam asked. "You're completely insane. I've never seen this side of you before."

"This is what revenge looks like," Vanessa replied. "This is a woman's scorn."

Liam looked into his wife's eyes and could see a void that hadn't been present before. It was as if she were looking through him, like he was a ghost. "So what now?"

"Now," Vanessa whispered, "we die."

"What do you mean?"

"There's no longer any point in living. In any of this. The police found the truth. Sean's secret is exposed. Don found Kerri's evidence on that flash dive. I didn't even know about the flash drive. Sean kept that from me. I can't fix what's spun out of control. Things are too far gone. When I had that gun at Joyce's, I had to choose who I would kill and who I would stay with. I chose you, Liam. I chose you because, deep down, I knew I still loved you. I always will. I shot Sean because he'd become a liability. I thought with him dead, maybe we could start fresh and build on that foundation I know we once had. Funny, Sean was always talking about tying up loose ends. Ironic how he became one."

"You don't have to do this. Please."

"What I said to you at the hospital was the truth. I am sorry. I thought maybe we could both use this experience as a catalyst to grow closer and learn to love each other again. But Sean's alive. My bullet missed, and when he wakes up, he'll tell them everything. And I know you'll never love me again. I understand. What you said made sense. Too many people have died. We could never be fixed. There's nothing left between us. It's all gone. I ruined it. Everything. And I can't go to jail. I won't. So I'm going to kill you, and then I'm going to stick the barrel of this gun in my mouth and pull the trigger. The end. Suburban murder-suicide. Just like your mom tried. That will be my epitaph. My dedication to our family. No more secrets."

Liam tried to stand, but Vanessa was fast, moving right along with him and aiming the gun at him. He sat back down as beads of sweat began to run down his face. "We could've worked things out the right way. We were seeing a therapist. It was working. People didn't have to die."

Vanessa shook her head. "This is how it has to end. You couldn't have been clearer at the hospital. We're over. I get it now."

"Please, Vanessa. You don't have to do this."

"I'm sorry, Liam, but I do."

"Vanessa, I—"

The shot rang out in the quiet house. Liam felt the impact of the bullet rip into his chest, then found himself tumbling backward onto the floor. As soon as his head hit the coarse area rug at the edge of the dining room, he heard the front door burst open.

"Freeze! Drop your weapon!"

It was Phillips. He recognized his voice as clearly as when the lieutenant had tackled him in Sean's backyard. But before he could react, a second shot was fired, and Liam felt another bullet explode in his hip and lower stomach. As his consciousness began to fade, he heard more gunfire erupt, but that was all in the background, somewhere far from where he was, somewhere in a reality he was no longer a part of. He was caught in a dream now. Just before he closed his eyes, he saw Vanessa collapse next to him, her eyes open, staring at him, yet vacant. Blood seeped from the corner of her mouth. He tried to call out to her but couldn't speak. She remained next to him, unmoving.

Then blackness.

EPILOGUE

One Year Later

Liam sat on one side of the scratched and cracked Plexiglas window, waiting for his brother to be escorted in by one of the guards. He had the phone receiver in his hand, waiting to talk. He hadn't seen Sean since the trial, and his attempts to talk with him thus far had been met with refusals and silence. Letters had gone unanswered. Messages had gone unreturned. But Liam would not relent. Not now. Not after all that had taken place. Vanessa had been right about one thing. No one should have to be alone in prison. Liam would be there for his brother.

The security door buzzed. Liam straightened up in his seat and placed the phone receiver to his ear. A lone guard walked into the prisoner's side of the communication room and sat down where Sean should've been. He took the receiver from the wall.

"He won't come out."

Liam nodded. "You told him it was me?"

"Yeah. Doesn't want to see you. Just like all the other times."

"Has anyone else come to visit?"

"Nope."

Liam leaned in closer toward the scratched window. "Can you give him a message for me?"

"Always do."

"Tell him I'm not going to stop coming. I'm not giving up. It's my turn to be there for him. Tell him to deal with it. That's just the way it's gonna be. We're family, and I'm not going anywhere."

"Got it."

"Thanks."

The guard paused for a moment. "I gotta hand it to you," he said. "If my brother did all that to me, I'd let him rot in here."

"I know," Liam replied. "You wouldn't understand. What we've been through together is bigger than both of us. Besides, he's my brother. He needs me. I'll be here."

———

The sun was warm on his skin.

"Dwyer!"

The voice boomed around him, distant at first.

"Dwyer! Wake up!"

Sean looked up from his place on the picnic table at the far end of the prison yard. Exercise was over. The other inmates were getting in line to walk back inside. They were waiting on him. One of the guards, a large man in both height and girth, stood with the prisoners, screaming from across the yard, jarring him from his nap.

"Dwyer! Lift your head off the table, and get moving before I come over there with my pepper spray!"

It was late May at the federal correctional complex in Allenwood, Pennsylvania. Sean was three months into a triple life sentence for the murders he had committed. Vanessa was dead. He was the lone survivor of their crimes.

It had taken several weeks to recover after taking the two bullets, but he was eventually brought into custody and booked. After another two months of physical therapy, he had been strong enough to go before a jury and had stood trial. A guilty verdict came within thirty minutes of deliberation.

Sean pushed himself off the picnic table and happened to look up and out, past the first line of fencing, toward the acres of woods that surrounded the prison. He saw a figure standing at the fence, alone, looking at him, its head pressed against the mesh. He shielded his hands from the sun and tried to get a better look.

"Dwyer!" the guard called. "You got ten seconds to get your ass over here, or you're getting dragged into line, and it's gonna hurt."

Sean backed away from the table toward the others who waited but continued staring at the man who stared at him. A twinge of familiarity suddenly struck, and he knew.

"Liam."

The guard left the back of the line and started toward the prisoner who refused to cooperate.

Sean took a step toward the fence. "Liam?" he said, louder this time.

The figure continued to stare. Then he waved. Just once.

"Liam!"

Emotions overtook him, and Sean found himself running toward the fence as his brother waited, leaning on a cane, watching him come. He made it halfway across the yard, close enough to see his brother's face under the baseball cap he was wearing, before three guards tackled him.

"Liam!" he screamed. "Liam, I'm sorry. I'm so sorry!"

One of the guards twisted Sean's neck to roll him over onto his back and sprayed him with pepper spray until his entire face felt like it was on fire and he could no longer breathe. Sean turned his head, choking as the guard cuffed him and pulled him to his feet. Through watering eyes he could see the blurry image of his little brother dropping something to the ground, then turning and walking from the fence, limping back toward the woods and out of sight.

"I'm sorry!" He gagged. "Liam!"

"The next time I tell you to get in line, you get in the line!" the guard screamed as he dragged Sean toward the prison door.

At the fence they remained, blowing in the wind that had begun to pick up. They were the colors of the rainbow, perfect in shade and shape. They would remain there until someone from the maintenance crew came by to pick them up and discard them.

A bouquet of paper flowers.

ACKNOWLEDGMENTS

I've been waiting a very long time to write an official acknowledgments page in a book that I've published. Still feels like a dream. Here goes . . .

First, to my agent, Curtis Russell of PS Literary Agency. You took a chance on an unsolicited manuscript in your slush pile, and here we are. Thank you for taking a leap with me. I won't let you down.

To my editors, Megha Parekh and Don D'Auria. Megha, you went to bat for me and the book, and I will be forever grateful. You literally made my lifelong dream a reality. Here's to the road ahead for both of us. Don, you helped me shape and shift this story into a relentless piece of suspense that keeps pushing the reader forward, which is all I ever wanted. Your insight and suggestions made this story so much better. Thank you for your guidance.

To Sarah Shaw, Gabrielle Guarnero, and the rest of the Thomas & Mercer team. Your enthusiasm for the book makes working with you guys an experience better than I could've imagined. Thank you for being my advocate out in the marketplace.

To Jennifer Sawyer Fisher of JSF Editorial. You were my first editor before I even had an agent. You helped shape the story and cut away a lot of the fat so it read with the pace and suspense that would attract an agent and publishing house. It worked. I can't thank you enough.

To David Prockter, for opening the door to *Heavy Metal* magazine for me, and to David Boxenbaum, for allowing me to walk in.

To Vincenza Corcoran, licensed clinical social worker and professor at Fordham University. You helped me see the perspective of a serial killer and were instrumental in the dialogue Liam had with Dr. Cain about why killers might do the things they do. The fact that Dr. Cain sounds like she knows what she's talking about has nothing to do with me and everything to do with you. Thank you.

To Chief Inspector Christopher Calabrese, Westchester County Police. I've known you since I was a kid when you worked with my father, and you've always been willing to help. I appreciate the insight you gave around some of the police procedures I was struggling with. Police families are an extension of blood families, and you've always been a good example of that.

To Chris Iervolino, who helped me with the technical scenes surrounding computer hacking, rainbow tables, blunt force, and more. I still have no idea what any of it means and want to emphasize that if I misrepresented what these systems or techniques do, that's not Chris's fault. That's all me. Thanks, buddy.

To Martin Farrell (a.k.a. Dad), sergeant, retired, Pleasantville Police Department. Thank you for putting up with the random calls at all hours of the day and night to pick your brain about what a police officer would do or say in certain situations. You're always spot-on and have helped make the dialogue in the book stronger as a result. I also appreciate you hanging up right away before I lose my thought, ha ha. You're the best.

To my mother, Mary. There isn't enough space here or words to properly describe what a positive influence you've had on my writing. We all grew up in a house full of books, and that rubs off in so many fantastic ways. For me, it was writing, and your encouragement never wavered. You'd sit at a typewriter and type out stories I wrote by hand in the sixth and seventh grade, and you'd be my beta reader in the years to come as I honed my skills. You always pushed me forward and never once dismissed my dream as a fantasy. I love you.

To my family, Mandy, Mark, Michelle, Pedro, Marie, Angelo, Sabrina, Maria, Mark P., Ray, and all of my nieces, nephews, cousins, aunts, and uncles. Thank you for your continued support and love. It means a lot.

And most importantly, to my wife, Cathy, to whom this book is dedicated, and my two daughters, Mackenzie and Jillian. Throughout the years there have been countless nights, endless weekends, and too many vacations where I was sitting alone in a room, writing stories without an agent, without a publisher, and with only a dream. Never once, *not once*, did you suggest I give it up and move on with my life. Not many people would tolerate my excuses of "I have to go write" when there was nothing to write for except hope. Your unwavering support and encouragement have made this long process an easier one to bear. I love you more than I can properly describe. My heart and my life are complete with you in them. I'm proud to be your husband and your father.

So that's it. How'd I do? Good, I hope. The last thing I want to say is that any references to anything in the book that are not accurate are the fault of this writer and not the wonderful people who helped with their expertise. A final thank-you to all of my readers who took this journey with me into Philadelphia, Camden, Blackwood, and the surrounding areas. I hope you enjoyed the book and will be as eager to read the next one as I am to write it.

MF

ABOUT THE AUTHOR

Photo © 2017 Mima Photography

Matthew Farrell lives just outside of New York City in the Hudson Valley with his wife and two daughters. Follow him on Twitter @mfarrellwriter or like his page at Facebook.com/mfarrellwriter2 to get caught up on the progress of his next thriller along with his general musings.